Before he could tell himself not to, Griffin stopped her.

"Thanks," he said at last. "I'm glad Amanda apologized. You were right. She did take your watch."

Sunny half smiled. "And you didn't let her get away with it."

He shouldn't care that she sounded proud of him. He shouldn't be staring at that little uptilt at the corner of her mouth. "So what am I missing?" he asked, because nothing involving his daughter was simple these days. "Did she even sound sincere?"

"She...tried." Sunny hesitated. "But you didn't welcome my interference before, and I doubt you've changed your mind. I'm out of the advice-giving business."

Ouch. Forcing his gaze away from her, he noticed the growing darkness. The sun had slipped lower in the sky and the colors had bled into a deeper shade of almost burgundy. "I'm impressed, Counselor. Didn't imagine you'd give up that easily."

"I have my moments."

Dear Reader,

One of the things I like most about writing is motivation. Without it I'd spend my days staring out my office window (always a temptation!). Deadlines sure make good motivation for authors <grin>. But I'm talking here about characters and their histories.

In *Man of the Family*, something traumatic happened long ago to my heroine, Sunny Donovan, and she is now on a crusade to help other girls avoid the same fate. Griffin Lattimer, my hero, was quite young when he lost his dad, and that has made him responsible to a fault.

Now Griffin is trying to find his long-missing wife and protect his kids from further hurt. The last thing he needs is to fall for Sunny. Why would a driven New York attorney stay with Griffin, the manager of a Florida apartment complex?

But love has been missing from his and Sunny's lives for too long. Can they find true happiness with each other in a family of their own? Start reading to find out!

All the best,

Leigh

HEARTWARMING

Man of the Family

—

Leigh Riker

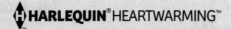

Recycling programs
for this product may
not exist in your area.

ISBN-13: 978-0-373-36732-0

Man of the Family

Copyright © 2015 by Leigh Riker

This edition published by arrangement with Harlequin Books S.A.

For questions and comments about the quality of this book, please contact us at CustomerService@Harlequin.com.

® and TM are trademarks of Harlequin Enterprises Limited or its corporate affiliates. Trademarks indicated with ® are registered in the United States Patent and Trademark Office, the Canadian Intellectual Property Office and in other countries.

Printed in U.S.A.

Leigh Riker, like many readers and writers, grew up with her nose in a book. To this day she can't imagine a better way to spend time than curling up with a good romance novel—unless it is to write one! When she's not in her home office on a small mountain in the Southeast, this Ohio native is probably traveling. For research purposes, of course. With added inspiration from her mischievous Maine coon cat, she is now at work on a new novel. You can find Leigh on Facebook at LeighRikerBooks and on Twitter, @lbrwriter.

Books by Leigh Riker

Harlequin Heartwarming

If I Loved You

Harlequin Intrigue

Double Take
Agent-in-Charge

Harlequin Next

Change of Life

Red Dress Ink

Strapless

Visit the Author Profile page
at Harlequin.com for more titles.

To the other members of CARA
(Chattanooga Area Romance Authors):
Kelle, Laurie, Nita, Cheryel and Carol.
Thanks for the friendship, the lunches and
the meetings filled with talk—yes,
about writing, too. What a great group!

CHAPTER ONE

SUNSHINE DONOVAN STILL trusted in the simple things—today's weather report, for example. She should have known better.

Sunny had just left the Jacksonville airport—with the car radio blaring a bright afternoon forecast—when the leaden skies opened up. A torrent of semitropical rain spilled over the windshield, reminding her again of a recent tabloid headline.

Sunny Clouds Up.

Oh, you'd better believe it. Only yesterday, in a Manhattan court, in front of her favorite judge, Sunny had blown up. She'd gotten a contempt citation for her momentary loss of control, but the jury's ruling really had been the last straw.

She was still as mad as blue blazes, even though she felt like a sun hat someone had left in the rain.

The disastrous trial verdict and a brand-new divorce decree weren't the end of the world, if she took the longer view. But her life right now could be summed up in another too-cute banner from the New York papers.

Defense Rains on Sunny's Parade.

If only the jury hadn't, too.

Pulling into her parents' suburban driveway a short while later, Sunny decided she deserved a rest. Coming back to Jacksonville was never easy, and this time, thanks to Nate's official exit from their marriage, she was alone.

Prosecutors lost cases all the time, she reminded herself, but she still couldn't believe the jury had bought the defense's claim that their client was crazy when he'd killed an innocent girl. She could still hear his threats. *Keep looking over your shoulder, Donovan. One day I'll be there.*

Sunny had heard such threats before. When she went back to New York, she'd no doubt hear them again, but she was determined to overcome this blot on her win/loss record. If she wanted to become DA, she'd have to.

And someday, she'd be able to think about the end of her marriage without wanting to cry. Even if, as Nate had always said, Sunny tended to wear her heart on her sleeve.

"Sunny?"

As soon as she stepped into the kitchen, her mother—a blur of flowered print shorts and top—swept her into a hug.

"We didn't expect you until tonight," she said, patting her hair back into place. It was even lighter than Sunny remembered, shot through with strands of silver. "Why didn't you call? Dad planned to meet you at the airport." She drew back to study Sunny from head to toe, and Sunny knew her mom wouldn't miss the limp hair that hadn't been combed all day, a rumpled suit and the laddered run in her pantyhose.

"Quite a mess, huh?" She forced a smile. "I caught an earlier plane. Staying in Manhattan for even a few more hours lacked—not to make a pun—appeal." All she'd wanted was to flee, as if she were the guilty one, rather than Wallace Day.

Her mother's blue gaze was probing. "Tell me everything."

Sunny drew a sharp breath. "Mom. I can't. Not yet."

As if to save her, the back door opened. Her dad saw her and broke into a grin. Smile lines radiated from the corners of his brown eyes. "Hey there, Sunshine."

He was still solid, tall and straight with

the same brown hair that showed barely any gray. Still her hero.

Without hesitation she launched herself into his arms. Enfolded, cherished, she was still his girl. She loved her mother, too, but things often grew complicated between them. With her dad she always knew where she stood. He'd taught her to throw a baseball and to swim. He'd hugged her tight when she lost her first boyfriend. She never doubted he would see her side about the trial and Nate.

"Welcome home. How long has it been this time?" he asked.

"Too long. Last Christmas," she said, "when you and Mom came to visit."

"And, as usual, hated every second—"

"—in what you always refer to as The City." On the verge of separation from Nate, Sunny had pretended everything was fine. "I think you were right years ago about me moving north," she said. "Life in the fast lane doesn't seem so exciting at the moment."

His hold tightened, but he didn't say *I warned you*.

"And can you believe that jury?" her mother said. "That dreadful man…"

Her dad shook his head. "If I were that poor girl's father—"

"You're not, thank goodness," Sunny said, then slipped from his embrace. "But I know how you feel. I can't stop thinking about Ana Ramirez's sweet face. At least Wallace Day will be confined to a facility in upper New York State to undergo treatment for his 'problem.'"

"Problem? He's a killer."

"That's why he'll stay there until—unless—a psychiatric review board decides he's no longer a threat to society."

Her father frowned. "He'll also be eating three meals a day, watching TV, lifting weights, and sleeping in a clean bed. That child's parents probably don't sleep at all. *She* has no life."

Sunny was glad he'd spoken out.

"What can I say? Wallace Day beat the system, even though an insanity defense usually doesn't play well with a jury." She frowned. "I still don't think Day is insane." And yet he had threatened her after his victory. How sane was that?

Maybe I didn't do my job well enough.

But her mother was done with that subject. "And when I think how we welcomed Nate with open arms," she tried again.

"Not now, Kate." Sunny's dad steered her

from the kitchen toward the stairs. On the way he scooped up her suitcase.

"Where are you going?" Her mother's brittle tone spoke volumes. "Have you forgotten? The upstairs is a disaster area. That hurricane a few weeks ago tore off part of our roof, Sunny—the part over your old room."

Sunny sighed. She'd been looking forward to a long nap there before dinner.

"The whole back part of the house is under tarps right now. It still leaks when it rains. And for who knows how long? It was the last straw for me," her mother murmured.

"I've called every contractor in town," her father said, his voice tight. "Sunny won't mind sleeping in my den. Will you, Sunshine?"

"Jack, that sofa bed is like sleeping on nails."

"I'll be fine, Mom." Sunny paused. "As long as I'm home, that's all I need."

Her mother was right about the lumpy sofa bed. Still, it beat staying another night in the apartment she'd shared with Nate— the apartment they'd soon have to sell. She wasn't ready to think about that either.

A moment later her father closed the door behind him, leaving Sunny alone in the den with her thoughts. No more quarrels with Nate. No more waiting for an unfair verdict. No courtroom overreaction. No more threats from Wallace Day. They were empty, she hoped, the result of his anger management problem, to put it mildly.

Sunny had never needed a hiding place more. Even in a house with only half a roof, her family was her foundation, her rock. Feeling boneless, she crawled into the lumpy bed. Her head nestled into the pillow, and with a heavy sigh she slept.

TEN MINUTES A DAY, that's all he asked. Wearing damp jeans, Griffin Lattimer padded across the gray carpet into his living room. He sported a temporary Batman tattoo, which he'd won after tonight's bath time water fight with his son. With both his children tucked into bed, Griffin checked his messages, steeling himself for trouble.

Beep.

This is Mrs. Moriarty, 27B. I called yesterday about those bathroom faucet washers, but you haven't replaced them. My water's dripping all over the place.

Beep.

Lattimer, my lease says I get painted every

three years. I'm not paying the rent until you redo my kitchen. That wet-behind-the-ears kid you sent over should be fired. He just slapped that paint on...looks like—

Griffin hit delete. The usual complaints. Nothing that couldn't wait until tomorrow. Besides, their words were already carved into his brain. His job as manager of the Palm Breeze Court Apartments complex could be a thankless one, but he'd made his choice. Boston, and his short stint as a TV news anchor, was a million miles away now. Like Rachel.

But Griffin wasn't going anywhere. He'd grown up without a father, and his kids wouldn't have to do the same.

In the nighttime silence, he thought back to that rainy afternoon. Ten years old and wearing his first black suit, standing at his father's graveside. His uncle stood beside him. His mother, on Griffin's other side, clutched his hand and wept into her handkerchief.

You're the man of the family now, she'd said. *Make Daddy proud.*

She was gone now, too. More than ever, it was all up to him.

Griffin headed for the refrigerator. With a cold bottle of water, he settled in front of the big-screen television he'd bought last Christmas, his second without Rachel.

The first year after she'd left, which seemed to be the way he measured time these days, he'd actually forgotten to put out milk and cookies for Santa.

"They're not homemade cookies anyway," his daughter had told her younger brother, not making Griffin feel better at all.

It was only September, but already he dreaded the season again. There would be no Christmas Eve with Rachel, the two of them installing batteries in toys or laying train tracks under the tree. Making memories together.

He sat and listened to the silence. The kids had stopped calling to each other across the hall. He didn't hear Amanda's stereo or Josh's small but noisy feet stomping to the bathroom for the tenth time. Each night Griffin anticipated this moment when their new home finally grew quiet, and he could stop worrying for a while about lost homework, stomachaches, neighborhood bullies, loose baby teeth and how the tooth fairy would come up with another five bucks.

Headlights arced across the windows, and his brother-in-law's truck drew up out front, a more than welcome sight. His smile usually lightened Griffin's mood.

Tonight, his eyebrows tucked low in a scowl, Chris Cabot stalked into the living room. He dropped onto the sofa. He still wore his khaki work clothes, and the pungent aroma of fish stung Griffin's nostrils. He fought a grin. The problem had to be Griffin's sister, who could drive a man to thoughts of mayhem.

"What's Bronwyn done now? Overloaded all the credit cards? Replaced the living room furniture? No," he answered himself, "she did that a few months ago. This is too soon, even for Bron."

Griffin sprawled on the sofa beside Chris. His hair—lightened from days spent on his charter boat—was tangled, and his blue eyes seemed darker than normal.

"I'm just fried," Chris said. "I spent all day out with a bunch of neurosurgeons from the Mayo clinic, and their catch was 'unacceptable.' They'll probably never come back. Ever since the hurricane that tore off Mom and Dad's roof, my business has been off." He paused. "Then I get home and no one's there. You seen Bron tonight?"

Griffin shook his head. "She probably met

up with one of her friends. You know, her life didn't start the day she met you."

Chris didn't respond. Griffin had never seen him like this, but since Rachel had disappeared he'd soothed Amanda's and Josh's feelings often enough. He peered into Chris's worried eyes.

"Yep," he said, "they look green to me. For no good reason."

Chris's mouth twitched. "Shut up. Let me miss my wife—and feel miserable." The smell of fish wafted through the air between them. "What would you know? It's not like you've been around anyone over the age of thirteen since—"

"Thanks." Pain coiled inside Griffin like a rattler. But Chris was right. Who was he to talk? In his experience, happiness didn't last, and he wasn't looking for another chance. All he cared about was finding Rachel. Protecting his kids.

Chris grimaced. "Hey, sorry. I didn't mean…"

"Look, save it. I've heard your speech a hundred times since last New Year's, and nothing's changed."

"Maybe that's the problem. It's more than time for you to—"

"Back off, Chris," he said, but it was Griffin who moved a foot away. "I'm not exactly free to socialize. I have two kids to raise."

"That doesn't mean you need to be a martyr. Don't you ever get lonely?"

Griffin didn't answer. For a long time after Rachel had left, he would have been able to say no. He hadn't felt a thing then. He didn't want to, even now.

Chris tried again. "My sister's home. You remember Sunny? She's feeling sort of unhinged, my mother says."

"Unhinged? And that's a recommendation?" Griffin remembered her from Chris and Bron's wedding. He'd been best man, and Sunny Donovan had been matron of honor. Tall, blond hair, gray-blue eyes…similar coloring to Rachel's. She wasn't his type now. No one was, really. "A hotshot lawyer, isn't she? Driven?" Which was about as far as possible from Griffin's present life.

Chris laughed. "I know she comes across that way sometimes, but Sunny's all right. She has a big heart. She's just having a rough time. Maybe the four of us could get together some night. No obligation. Just a fun evening out. With adults."

Griffin tried to switch topics as if he were

changing channels on the TV. "Your sister's married. So am I."

"After two years?" Chris wouldn't give up. "Rachel isn't coming back, Griff."

"Maybe not, but I have my standards."

"You don't even know where she is."

"I'm still looking," he said.

"Know what I think? You should file for divorce." He paused. "Sunny's already divorced. As of a few days ago, it's a done deal. Then, after that—"

"No, thanks."

Not quite to his relief, he heard Amanda in the hall. He and Chris turned as she came into the room, and Griffin's heart rolled over. He couldn't believe she was already a teenager, though barely.

"It's late," he said. "Why are you still up?"

"I'm hungry." Her shy smile blossomed, but not for him. "Hi, Uncle Chris."

"You knew I was here."

She nodded. Her dark blond hair hung to her waist and shimmered in the light. Her hazel eyes warmed.

"Josh knew, too. But he fell asleep while you and Daddy were fighting."

"We're not fighting," Griffin said quickly. "We were having a discussion."

"Did Aunt Bronwyn do something bad?"

Looking guilty, Chris closed the distance between them to hug her. "No, Mandi. She's good, and I love her. You, too." He tapped her nose with a forefinger that probably smelled like tuna, but she giggled. "Now be a good kid." He lightly spun her toward the kitchen. "Get your snack and go back to bed."

She would have given Griffin an argument, guaranteed. Josh at five was still manageable, despite his tendency to worry about everything; but with Mandi he no longer seemed able to connect.

"It'll be time for school before you know it," Chris added.

"I hate school."

That didn't bother Chris. "So did I. Par for the course." As she went into the kitchen he lowered his voice. "You think she was standing in the hall, listening?"

"Probably." He hoped not, especially the part about Rachel. Griffin said no more until Amanda came back with a banana and a glass of milk. He didn't look at her when she drifted down the hall, didn't want to ask himself why. The spray of freckles across her nose made him yearn for simpler times when she'd been the little girl who worshipped him. "Good night, baby."

"I'm not a baby," she said. "Night, Uncle Chris."

"Keep taking those Gorgeous pills." He grinned at Griffin. "Man, I don't envy you in another few years. Scrawny boys ringing your bell day and night. She's going to be a beauty, Griff."

"She already is." Like Rachel.

He walked Chris to the door, but his brother-in-law lingered without opening it. He gazed at Griffin's forearm and the smeary tattoo he hadn't seemed to notice before.

"That's a great look for you," he finally said, then let himself out into the night.

Shaking his head, Griffin locked up. He didn't envy his brother-in-law, having to make adjustments to his new marriage with Bronwyn. She'd been born strong-willed, bent on getting her way, but he'd never seen a happier couple the day they married—except for him and Rachel long ago.

He shut off the lights and went to his room. Never mind the talk about Sunshine Donovan. Divorced now, was she? Yet Chris's words stayed with him. Every night Griffin looked forward to his few moments of quiet time, to his solitary thoughts. And every night he ended up wishing he wasn't alone with them.

Maybe for the rest of his life.

CHAPTER TWO

As if it were her first day in court, Sunny gazed at her sister-in-law's classroom filled with middle school students. She'd only been home for a week. Why had she let Bronwyn talk her into taking part in Career Day?

Sunny had never been much of a speech maker. Funny, for a woman who earned her living by performing in front of a jury. But in a courtroom, before making a motion to the judge or examining a witness, she had plenty of time to prepare.

Now she shuffled her notes. And rubbed at the ache in her lower back. Her dad's sofa bed was living up to its reputation.

What could she tell these kids about her dedication to a legal process that had recently failed her? She still believed wholeheartedly in the law, but the Wallace Day verdict had shaken her confidence.

Bron's students had listened raptly to the minor league ball player now squeezed behind a desk in the front row, and to the bulky city police officer next to him. Would they listen to her?

As if in answer, a pair of spitballs sailed across the room, and all at once she knew how to begin.

"Good morning," she said. "It seems we have some future felons in our audience today." She leveled a look at two lanky boys in the rear who were obviously the culprits. "No more missiles, gentlemen," she said with a smile and a pointed glance at the police officer.

A few kids laughed. The boys turned red.

Sunny set her watch on the teacher's desk in front of her. She had twenty minutes to sway this jury, and the oversized timepiece with its thick band of multicolored glass beads would keep her on track. Sunny had bought it one weekend down in SoHo. She liked to wear it as a contrast to her usual prim business suits—today, a subtle navy blue pinstripe.

"So you want to be a lawyer," she said and heard a few snorts from the class. "I hope in the next few minutes you'll discover how exciting a career in law can be."

From the back of the room Bronwyn gave

her a thumbs-up, her bright hair turned to copper in the sun that flooded through the windows behind her.

Sunny took a deep breath. She surveyed the students, distracted by a girl with dark blond hair and what looked to be a permanent frown, then hit her stride. This was what she did best. By the end of her presentation, the knot in her stomach had loosened. She checked the watch.

"We have a bit more time. Any questions?"

The faces looked uniformly friendly now, except for that girl in the center row who slumped in her chair, and for an instant Sunny froze. That sweet, heart-shaped face reminded her of Ana Ramirez, lost forever because of Wallace Day. Yet this girl seemed familiar in another way, too. Wondering why, Sunny leaned against the desk and chose a towheaded boy, who posed the first question.

"How much money do you make?"

"Not nearly enough." The boy smiled, but the girl didn't. "Seriously, as a government employee, I don't get the big bucks like a defense lawyer, but I make a good living." She named a figure range typical of lawyers coming out of school to take their first jobs, then a larger span for established attorneys. "My advice would be to aim for *Law Review* if you want to command a higher starting salary."

"What's *Law Review*?"

Sunny explained the importance of third year and the prestige attached to the journal, especially at the top law schools. "I was editor at Harvard. Anyone else?"

The girl's hand shot up.

"Aren't all lawyers crooks—and liars?"

"A common misconception," Sunny answered to mild laughter from the other students. The classic joke ran through her mind. *What do you call a group of lawyers at the bottom of the ocean? A good start.* "I won't deny there are some bad apples out there, but for the most part, lawyers are decent people who happen to love debating fine points of the law." She smiled. "And winning." Although that sometimes meant going over the top when you lost.

The lunch bell rang, ending Career Day's morning session. Sunny thanked the kids for their interest, and a smattering of applause followed. Not bad for a woman who'd slept twelve hours a day for a week and refused to take any phone calls—including Nate's—except, finally, at her mother's insistence, Bronwyn's.

"You need to get back in the saddle," Bron had claimed. "Talk to my class. They're bound to be easier than that jury in New York. You can't sit in your parents' house waiting for the cuts to heal."

That had been enough to make her say yes. She couldn't continue to fret over Nate either, about what they'd once had, what might have been. She had to pull herself together some-time, and the classroom forum had made a simple start. Satisfied, she gathered her note cards, which she hadn't consulted as much as she'd expected to.

As the room emptied and the students filed past, a few kids even stopped to thank her until Bron ushered the last child from the room toward the cafeteria. The cop and the ball player had already left.

In the hallway Bronwyn linked her arm with Sunny's. "Fabulous. Thanks for com-ing."

"I enjoyed it myself." To her surprise, she had. Sunny stifled a yawn. "Guess I've had enough excitement for one day. Time for my afternoon nap."

Bron's amber-brown eyes softened. They didn't know each other well—they'd met after Bron and Chris became engaged when

Sunny had been living in New York—and Sunny looked forward to becoming better acquainted. So, apparently, did Bronwyn. "I'm happy you're home," she said. "Let's get together soon." Her smile turned sly. "I'm dying to know what kind of settlement you got from the evil Nate."

Without answering, Sunny said goodbye and continued down the hall to the front entrance before she remembered her watch. It was still on the desk in the classroom. Threading her way through the noisy students eager for lunch, she noticed the same girl from Bron's class. Her long hair swinging, she walked several feet behind the other students, then turned away to say something to a friend.

When they passed, she and Sunny bumped shoulders. Sunny glanced down and found herself staring at the girl's fine-boned wrist. She wore an outsized watch with a band of blue, cream and green glass beads. Sunny's watch.

For an instant they exchanged looks. Sunny could have sworn the girl smiled in triumph. Why would she take the watch? With a look at her own bare arm, Sunny stepped toward her, but the girl turned her back to hustle her friend around a corner and into the lunchroom.

Sunny had no qualms about confronting the girl; she did that every day in her job. When she faced a jury, no one ever saw her blink—not even Wallace Day. And if she didn't approach the girl, she might never see her watch again. On the other hand... Oh, no.

Sunny stopped in her tracks. No wonder the girl had looked so familiar. She was Bronwyn and Chris's niece. She'd been a junior bridesmaid at their wedding, her father the best man. She was Griffin Lattimer's daughter.

Did he or Bronwyn know she was a thief?

LATER THAT AFTERNOON, Sunny parked her father's Bronco in a visitor's space at the Palm Breeze Court Apartments. Bronwyn, incredulous about her niece, had warned her this wouldn't be easy.

"Let me handle it," she'd said. "Griffin can be prickly about his kids. There's no telling how he'll take your accusation."

"It's not an accusation. It's a fact, Bron," she'd replied.

Taking a deep breath, Sunny studied the complex. The low, stucco-sided buildings were arranged in horseshoe-shaped courts around broad streets lined with palm trees. The style, common to the area, didn't appeal to her. From the high-rise apartment she'd shared with Nate, she could see the East River but not her neighbors. Here, the wide windows of each unit virtually invited passersby to look inside.

The front entrance to number 17A was painted colonial blue with gleaming nickel hardware and a matching knocker below the security peephole. The flowerpots on the porch held drooping annuals, and another planter held wilted white geraniums.

Sunny knocked. Twice.

From within she heard the music of a string quartet. She didn't recognize the composer, but her taste ran more to classic rock. Sunny liked her music to make some noise.

"The kids are at the clubhouse," a male voice called out.

The voice, which Sunny remembered from the wedding, belonged to Griffin Lattimer. She felt a twinge of regret for bringing him bad news and knocked again.

Finally, he swung the door open, blinking at the rush of sunlight.

Sunny blinked, too. She'd remembered

that Griffin was an attractive man. He'd looked great in a tuxedo two years ago. Now he wore jeans with a black T-shirt, and his dark hair was longer. The style wasn't intentional, Sunny guessed; it seemed as if Griffin needed a cut but didn't have time to bother. He didn't appear to have time for her, either.

Upon finding that his visitor was an adult, he tensed. His gaze slid over her before the flare of interest—if that's what it was—quickly disappeared.

She held out a tentative hand. "Griffin, hi. Sunny Donovan."

His eyes—with their clear hazel irises rimmed by a deep brown—looked exactly as she remembered, but they seemed even more remote. He didn't shake her hand, and she wondered if she could manage this confrontation after all.

She forced a smile. "We met at Bronwyn's wedding to my brother, Chris."

"Hi," he said at last but didn't move from the doorway.

He'd seemed preoccupied at the wedding. He hadn't said five unnecessary words to her, and he wasn't any more sociable now.

Like Nate toward the end of their marriage.

She was surprised he kept calling her, though she still wasn't tempted to answer.

"May I come in?" She glanced behind her at the street. "I have something to tell you, but I'd rather say it in private. It's about your daughter."

Griffin looked toward the center of the complex, and Sunny could have bitten her tongue. She saw fear in his eyes and hastened to reassure him.

"Amanda is perfectly fine. But something happened today at school. I thought you should know." She didn't see how else to say it. "Amanda stole my watch."

Griffin stared at her for a long moment before he stepped back, motioning her inside. Feeling more uncomfortable with every second, she eased past him. In the small foyer, Sunny explained that morning's incident. "The watch was unusual, not expensive but different. Handmade." She described the beaded band. "When I finished my talk it was gone."

"Why would Mandi want a cheap watch?" His gaze skimmed her again in obvious disapproval. "I'd expect you to wear a gold Rolex."

Sunny flushed but refused to be derailed.

"During my talk Amanda glared at me the entire time. She later asked a question clearly meant to embarrass me." Sunny paused. "I didn't expect her to remember me from the wedding, and I didn't recognize her at first."

A muscle twitched in his jaw. At least she was getting some reaction now.

"You've got the wrong girl."

"No," she said, "I don't. Your daughter was seen wearing the watch."

"By whom?"

"Me."

He half smiled. "That's pretty circumstantial, isn't it, Counselor?"

Sunny stiffened. The one word seemed to draw a line between them. All she'd been trying to do was help. But if he wanted to see her as an opponent—a prosecutor interrogating him on the witness stand—rather than as a woman who simply wanted to keep his family from more heartbreak…then, okay. Fine. The gloves came off.

"No," she said. "It's eyewitness."

"Your word against hers."

His attitude made her see red. "Griffin, I could have taken this to the principal—for starters. But because you and I have met before and Amanda is my brother's niece, I decided to keep this in the family. I suggest we ask Amanda to explain."

"And I suggest you leave."

Sunny looked toward the clubhouse area. All right. Change of tactics.

"Not before I speak to Amanda."

He moved, faster than she'd thought possible, and tried to catch her arm, but Sunny evaded the contact.

Griffin's voice was cool but harsh. "Why don't you go back to ambulance chasing or whatever it is you people do, and leave us alone?"

Another wave of adrenaline surged through her. First, the Rolex comment and now, *you people*. She tilted her chin up to hold his gaze.

"Listen, *Mr.* Lattimer—if that's the way you want it. I'm well aware you've lost your wife and you have more than a full-time job raising two children on your own. That does not give Amanda an excuse to steal anyone's property."

"My daughter is not a thief."

"I've worked with lots of teenagers and young adults in court, and I know all the signs of trouble to watch for. Swift mood changes, uncharacteristic behavior, furtive-

ness, unwholesome friendships, depression…
any of that sound familiar?"

His darkened gaze faltered. "Mandi is not
unhappy."

"Maybe you aren't looking closely enough."

"Maybe you're butting in where you don't
belong. I asked you to leave." He took another
step toward her. "Now I'm not asking." Before Sunny could react, he had grasped her
upper arm. A light touch but still…

She tried not to panic. His fingers felt
hot through the layers of her suit jacket and
blouse sleeve, as if he were touching bare
skin. She jerked free.

Still bent upon getting her out of the apartment, he opened the door. "I'll talk to Mandi
about the watch, but I can tell you right now,
she had nothing to do with it."

"It was on her wrist!"

"Yeah, well. Maybe one of her friends
let her wear it." He added, "Chris said you
weren't yourself right now. Let's leave it at
that."

"Let's not," Sunny began but didn't finish.

She had stepped outside, and the door shut
behind her. Her arm pulsed from the lingering heat of his fingers.

Bronwyn had warned her. Where his children were concerned, Griffin Lattimer had a definite blind spot.

Whether or not she got her watch back, Sunny didn't intend to see him again.

CHAPTER THREE

GRIFFIN WAS STILL seething when he locked up that night. Where did Sunshine Donovan get off, telling him how to deal with his children? He cast a glance at Amanda's room.

It was after eleven o'clock, and her light still glowed through the gap in the half-closed door. Then he heard her voice.

For a second Griffin hesitated. He picked his battles these days, but with an inner sigh he rapped a knuckle against her door. "Amanda?" When she didn't answer, he knocked again.

"Go away," she said.

That sulky tone of voice drove him nuts. It was almost as if she hated him.

"I need to talk to you," he said.

"I don't want to talk."

Griffin pushed the door open. "Too bad," he said, his mind made up.

Amanda was sitting on her bed, outside the covers. She wore blue pajamas, a bunch of pink-and-lime and green-and-purple pillows piled around her. Her favorite stuffed giraffe lay cuddled under her arm, and her cell phone was in her other hand.

"Hang up," Griffin said.

Amanda's expression was one of utter disgust, but with a put-upon sigh she obeyed. "See you tomorrow. *He's* here," she told someone at the other end of the line.

He waited for a long moment, trying to choose his words with care.

"I thought we had agreed. No phone calls after nine o'clock."

"I couldn't sleep. Neither could Dixie."

Griffin almost groaned aloud. Ever since he and his kids had moved to Jacksonville, Amanda had acquired a strange new set of friends. Or, rather, one friend specifically. And she set his teeth on edge.

"Did you finish your homework?"

He didn't have to ask. Her notebook lay on the desk across the room, unopened. On top, a stack of assignment forms appeared to be blank.

"I'll do it later."

"It's almost midnight, Mandi. You need sleep."

She huffed out another aggrieved sigh.

"So, what am I supposed to hand in tomorrow? I thought my grades were important to you."

Her tone reminded him about her low average last spring but again Griffin took time to respond, his worst instincts going off like fireworks inside. For the first time he wondered if Sunny Donovan had been telling the truth. Frankly, as soon as she'd accused his daughter, he'd been too angry to think.

Not a welcome reaction on his part, but he'd thought about Sunny all evening while the Patriots kicked Miami around the football field. That was just what he needed. A woman who thought his daughter was a thief. A woman whose coloring reminded him of Rachel, someone driven—like himself in his TV anchor days.

"Your grades should be important to you," he told Mandi. "You'll be in high school next year. Four years after that there'll be college." How was that even possible? Where had the time gone? "Yes, grades matter. And in this house—"

"It's not a house. It's an *apartment*. We don't have a home anymore." She had that disdainful look on her face that made Griffin want to throw something. Not that he would.

But getting into a fight about semantics didn't seem wise.

"Look," he said, "let me remind you. I'm the adult here. You're the kid." He started toward the nearest switch plate. "Lights out. Now."

Halfway across the room Griffin stopped cold. Mandi's whitewashed dresser—something she called shabby chic—was next to the switch. And on the dresser lay a watch.

His stomach sank in a dizzying rush.

The watch matched the description Sunny Donovan had given. Perfectly. There could be no mistake. He picked it up, ran his fingers over the colorful glass beads.

"Where did you get this?"

She sounded bored. "What?"

"This watch. It's not yours."

"It is now."

"Meaning?"

"Um, Dixie gave it to me." She was clearly buying time, making up some story as she went along. "She didn't want it anymore."

Maybe a friend let her wear it. He'd said so himself. With everything in him, Griffin wanted to believe her. Only he didn't.

How many times had he heard that same tone of voice whenever Amanda was shading the truth? Right now she was plucking at some imaginary lint on her flower-patterned sheet, and her cheeks had turned an intimidating red. Her fingers trembled. She glanced at the photo album she kept on her nightstand. Next to it stood a framed picture of Rachel.

"Don't lie to me, Amanda."

She didn't respond, and Griffin had no choice but to tell her about Sunny's earlier visit. His daughter listened in stony silence.

"Why do you always think I'm guilty?" she asked when he'd finished. "It's like you want to find something wrong." Tears quivered in her voice. "You still like Josh, but you don't like me."

Mandi is not unhappy, he'd told Sunny.

Holding the watch, Griffin walked back to the bed. Her bent head spoke of guilt. Yet she wouldn't admit it. She'd tried to sidetrack him with a completely different subject.

Right after Rachel had left, the counselor had said Griffin's first task would be reassuring his children that he was still here for them. But despite his best efforts, Amanda didn't feel secure.

He had to tread lightly. True, he was deeply disappointed that Amanda had taken the watch, but he wouldn't show her how he felt. He never did. In an effort to avoid more damage to his family, Griffin struggled to maintain a deceptively calm—some would say closed-off—facade.

Yes, he was the grown-up here, the guy who had to keep things together. *Make Daddy proud.* To avoid upsetting his motherless daughter's fragile equilibrium, he had to say the right thing.

And he could be wrong about the watch. He knew he was grasping at straws, but he *hoped* he was wrong. What if she *wasn't* guilty? And Dixie really was to blame?

Griffin sat on the edge of the bed beside her but avoided glancing at Rachel's picture. He touched Amanda's chin and turned her face toward him. Her eyes, brimming with tears, met his.

"You and Josh are both my first priority. We're in this together, Mandi. We're a family."

"Doesn't feel like it," she whispered.

Griffin's breath caught. He had no idea how to answer that. "I'm sorry if I accused you unfairly." He kissed the top of her head then stood. His hand ached from the tight grip he had on the watch. "Let's sleep on that. We can talk again tomorrow."

"There's nothing to talk about," she said.

HOURS LATER AMANDA was still awake. She'd tried staring at the dark ceiling for a while after her dad left, but she could hear his words—his accusations—as if they had just been said.

It had been a long time since her mother sat on her bed, talking about the day's happenings, laughing with her over nothing at all, kissing her good-night, soothing all the hurts. Two years, sixteen days.

Why mark the stupid time, as if they still lived in Boston and Mom was just visiting her grandmother in Philly, where they used to live?

She slipped between the sheets and flopped down, squashing her stuffed giraffe and her oldest cloth doll against the pillows. She kicked off her slippers under the covers. They were too small, but only yesterday her father had said, "No money for nonessentials this month, kiddo. Maybe after payday." Amanda knew there would always be bills, lots of them from when Mom had left and run up the credit cards. Just as she knew her big feet would never stop growing.

Amanda hated them.

She hated her growing breasts, too, even though Dixie told her she'd be happy with them one day.

Amanda even hated her name. It wasn't cool like Dixie's or her other friends' in Boston or Philly. Mom had always told her it was lovely, graceful, and she'd grow into it, but Amanda hadn't heard those words in a long time. Her dad wasn't much of a talker. And when he did...

Yanking the covers up to her neck, she lay shaking in the dark.

I'm the adult here. You're the kid.

Why feel surprised that she had absolutely no power?

Your grades should be important to you.

But why? It wasn't as if she'd ever need any of the dumb things they tried to teach in school. Dixie said they wouldn't. Like those boring job talks in Aunt Bron's class. Amanda didn't plan to become a ball player or a cop or a...lawyer.

She bit her lip. She didn't want to think about bad stuff anymore.

Or about her dad.

Yet the stubborn memories kept coming. Josh had been only three when their mother took off. In sixth grade then, Amanda had been just getting used to having him around and was glad he'd finally stopped wearing diapers and sucking on a bottle.

Her father, of course, had been at work that day. He'd had a big-deal job then.

Amanda pinched herself for wanting to cry.

Even Josh didn't cry much now. She wondered if he remembered Mom, which only left Amanda feeling more alone. She remembered everything about her, even the shadows in her eyes right before she left.

In the dark she turned over, off the old doll, which glared up at her with its one remaining black eye. She groped across her nightstand for the snapshot in a porcelain frame with roses around it. Amanda ran a finger over the raised flowers, the cool glass. She didn't have to actually see the picture. Josh might forget, but she never would. She'd always remember her mom's soft blond hair. And her eyes would always be the exact same color as the blue in her favorite dishes, and her smile…

Dad hardly ever smiled anymore.

When he did, he smiled at Josh. He was always trying to reassure him.

Setting the picture down, she rolled on to her side, facing the wall. She couldn't bear to open the photo album tonight.

Fresh tears welled in her eyes. She huddled under the lavender eyelet comforter her mother had helped her pick out when they moved to Boston—like the white wicker nightstand and her dresser—but she couldn't get warm. She thought of her dad's Uncle Theo, who still lived in Philadelphia. He didn't have anyone now, and she missed him, too.

"Mandi?" Whispering, Josh stood at her door. She always kept it half-open in case he needed her. "What'samatter?"

Wiping her wet cheeks, she said, "Nothing. Go back to your room. You want Dad to wake up? He'll put you in time-out."

A brief silence made her feel ashamed. Mean.

"Daddy never puts me in time-out."

She frowned at his small frame backlit by the hallway light. "Well, he'll want to anyway."

"No," Josh said in the doorway. "He loves me."

You're both my first priority. Amanda

couldn't believe that, not after he'd accused her of stealing. Blinking, she waited until Josh went back to his room, his bare feet dancing to avoid touching the floor.

Her throat ached, and no matter how much she swallowed, it kept hurting. The tears slid down her face, dripped into her ears and on to her pillow. No wonder he liked Josh better.

No wonder he didn't smile at her. *He only pays attention to me when I'm bad. And even then, what happens? Nothing.*

That scared her most of all, as if she were a runaway train, and he wasn't trying to stop her. He hadn't stopped Mom, either.

She dragged the giraffe back into her arms and held on tight, her stupid tears wetting its baby-*stupid* face.

GRIFFIN TOOK A deep breath and rang the doorbell again. From inside he could hear raised voices, one male, one female.

He hesitated. Try the bell once more? Give up? Or open the door himself?

The Cabots rarely locked their doors.

Griffin opted for the third choice. He couldn't wait all day. He needed to pick up Josh at school soon. He'd make his apology, then go.

"Hello?" he called out. "Jack? Kate?"

Voices, louder than before, came from the kitchen, but he couldn't make out their words.

Griffin had started to edge back toward the door when Jack suddenly appeared, his face as red as Santa Claus's suit. "Griffin," he said, obviously surprised to see him standing there.

"Sorry. I did ring the bell. I'll just…"

"No, come on in." Jack turned to call over his shoulder, "Honey, Griffin's here. Any coffee left?"

Whatever their quarrel had been about, it was over now, at least for Jack.

Griffin fingered the beaded watch in his pocket.

"No coffee for me, thanks. I was wondering… Is Sunny around?"

Jack turned and rapped on the door to the den. Then he made small talk as if nothing was wrong, inviting Griffin to a cookout the next weekend. "Bring the kids, too, of course," Jack finished just as Sunny stepped into the room.

She was wearing ankle-length jeans with a white top that had little ruffles around the neck. Her feet were bare, and Griffin could see her stylish red pedicure. Her eyes, how-ever, had turned icy.

"Oh. Mr. Lattimer."

Jack glanced from one to the other, try-ing, Griffin supposed, to size up this new problem.

"I'll make myself scarce," her father mur-mured.

Griffin could hear sniffles coming from the kitchen. Kate was apparently taking it hard. Unusual, he thought, because Jack was normally easygoing.

Months ago Amanda had "adopted" Kate—who was always ready with a hug—as a sur-rogate grandmother. Josh loved to cuddle on her lap, and both his kids roared at Jack's silly jokes. Griffin and his children had spent quite a few Sunday afternoons here, always a pleas-ant break from the apartment and the endless stream of renter complaints.

Sunny sighed. "I imagine you heard," she said. "I've been hiding in the den. It's the third time since I got home."

"Speaking of disagreements…" Might as well get this over with. Griffin pulled the watch out of his pocket. "Amanda had this on her dresser. In plain sight," he said, a fact that had been bothering him since last night.

"I should have investigated first, before I jumped all over you."

She studied him. "When you found my watch, what did you say?"

"Nothing right," he admitted. "Mandi had an answer for everything. She claims her friend Dixie gave it to her."

"Which implies Dixie did take it in the first place."

"Dixie didn't want it anymore, she said. That's what I'm supposed to believe."

Her blue-gray eyes searched his gaze. "You don't?"

"I can usually tell when she's lying."

"And that's common?"

"Never used to be," he said and backed up a step. "But ever since her mother…" He shifted his weight from one foot to the other. "Ever since her mom packed up and left… yes, Amanda sometimes lies." He shook his head. "Not that I'm supposed to notice."

"Let me guess. You let her off the hook—and decided to return the watch yourself."

Griffin fell back on his usual rationale. "I know she misses Rachel. So does Josh, but he was pretty young when she took off. He doesn't have the same store of memories Mandi does."

Sunny shook her head. "I'm not buying it."

"What?"

"Listen to yourself. You're making excuses for Amanda. Again."

"Look, Counselor, all I can say is I'm sorry." He held out the watch, then waited for her to take it. She didn't touch him when she did.

Sunny's eyes chilled another few degrees. "You're sorry? What did you do—except throw me out of your apartment yesterday? I'd like to hear an apology from Amanda. She should take responsibility."

He frowned, inching backward again. "You have your watch back."

"Yes. But for some reason, taking this watch was Amanda's way of getting back at me. For what, I don't know."

"That's not like Amanda."

She stared him down and said, "I don't imagine it's pleasant to realize your daughter has a problem, but you said yourself she misses her mother. Have you talked to her about that?"

"Tried," he said. "She stonewalls me."

"And you retreat. The way you've been backing toward that door the whole time you've been here."

"Anyway," he began, taking another step that proved her right. His pulse was pounding now, slow and hard.

Sunny moved toward him. "I tried to tell you the signs yesterday, and what did you say? That Amanda wasn't unhappy. You just admitted she sometimes lies. How happy is that?"

"Well...and maybe her new friend isn't the kind I'd like her to have—"

Sunny looked exasperated. "Doesn't that tell you something? You don't do her any favors by looking the other way." She held up the watch, its beaded band sparkling in the light. "Or by returning this yourself instead of holding your daughter accountable. If she gets away with this—and it is theft—what comes next? Breaking into a store some night with her 'friend'? Knowing you'll cover for her again?"

His palms were sweating. Sunny Donovan must be something to see in a courtroom.

"Guess I'm not your candidate for Father of the Year."

"This isn't about you," she said. "I don't think you've really heard a word I said." She paused. "And of course—I'll say it for you— it's none of my business."

"Right," he said. "I didn't ask for your advice, and I've gotta go. Josh will be out of school soon."

She was still standing in the front hall when he shut the door.

He and the kids would not be coming to any cookout.

CHAPTER FOUR

As SOON AS Griffin shut the front door, her cell phone rang with a melody from *Porgy and Bess*. Why hadn't she changed it? Nate was no longer the man she would love until she died.

Sunny ignored his call…again.

Nate had made his choice. Now she was making hers. A clean break seemed the wisest course, at least until they had to deal with selling the apartment.

She wandered into the kitchen. A quick look out the windows showed a dark line of clouds heading this way, but the weather was the farthest thing from her mind. She sank on to a chair at the kitchen table and replayed her conversation with Griffin. Had she come on too strong?

She really had to stop acting like a lawyer on billable hours.

Her father was nowhere in sight, but her

mother was at the sink, clattering dishes on the drain board and muttering to herself.

"Mom, what's wrong?"

"Nothing." This being her standard answer when something was, Sunny didn't even blink. Her mother would pry every last bit of information from someone else, but getting her to open up was always a hard, if not impossible, task.

"You might as well tell me," she said.

Her mother banged a pot into the open dishwasher.

"You didn't want to talk about Nate when you got home," she reminded Sunny. "Now I should rattle on about something that doesn't need talking about?"

"Get it off your chest, Mom." She paused. "Why were you and Dad fighting?"

To her surprise her mother didn't try to pretend otherwise.

With a shaken sigh she looked out the windows at the gathering storm, then turned from the sink, drying her hands on a towel before she joined Sunny at the table. "I think we should move. Your father doesn't."

Speechless, Sunny stared at her.

"Sell the house?" she finally echoed. "But why? I grew up here. It's the only home I remember." The place she needed now, even when that meant sleeping on the old sofa bed. "You love this house," she said. *So do I.*

Her mother looked down at her perfectly manicured hands.

"Mom, you're a homebody. You enjoy spending time here and fine-tuning this room or that. Only Dad's den has been off-limits."

Her mother gazed around the homey kitchen with tears in her eyes.

"We bought this house when you were seven, and we've been here a quarter century."

"Yes, and it's still my home, too." Soon it would be the only one she'd have.

Thunder rumbled outside, making her mother flinch. "You know about the hurricane that took off our roof. Coming from the airport you must have seen the destruction all over town."

"It was pouring then. I could barely see through the windshield." Even if she could, she would have tried to avoid taking in the old neighborhoods.

"That was enough for me," her mother said. "But some of our friends, you remember the Richardsons, lost everything. And I heard Laura's mother needs to replace her entire roof."

At the mention of her friend's name, Sunny stiffened.

"They all lived closer to the beach than we do," Sunny's mom said, "but I think we should put the house on the market while it still has value." She glanced at the ceiling. Above was the partially ruined second floor and Sunny's old room with water marks running down the walls, but...

"As if you've never weathered a storm before." Sunny couldn't quite take the idea in. "Where would you go if you did sell? I mean, not that I think you should..."

Her mother's face had clouded up.

"You're on his side?"

"Mom, I know we have our differences—" one of them Sunny's long-ago move to New York "—but I'm on both your sides."

A twinge of guilt raced through her. Or was she simply making sure she had a place to hide? To lick her wounds?

Her mother scoffed. "You're a prosecutor. You always take a side." She sniffed again. "The Richardsons have gone north to live near their son and grandchildren." Which served to remind Sunny of another bone of contention. Her mother never missed an opportunity to remind her of the grandbabies she still yearned for. "They're not coming back," she said as if the Richardsons had died. "I miss them, but I think they're safer there."

"Hurricanes can hit New England, too," Sunny pointed out. A clap of thunder brought her upright in her chair. "In the time I've lived in New York, we've had ice storms, floods, a few blizzards, even a mild earthquake. I wouldn't say it's that much safer."

But her parents' argument still nagged at her. "My childhood—and Chris's—was practically idyllic." Sunny took a deep breath before she could continue. "Good schools, a big yard to play in, lots of birthday parties, long days at the beach, friends, and always the certainty that our family, unlike so many others, would stay intact." If her mother's need to keep things on an even keel had sometimes troubled her, Sunny had always felt loved. She'd had her dad's more laid-back nature for a buffer.

Now her mother seized on the word Sunny wished she hadn't said.

"Speaking of friends, you should call Laura while you're here. She still lives in town, you know. I haven't spoken to her mother in ages but—"

Sunny's aching back hurt even worse. She was so rigid, her neck was burning. "I doubt we'd have much in common, Mom. We haven't for a long time."

"But you were such good friends. What's the harm? Call her, Sunny."

"I don't think so," she said at last. This was one of the not-so-easy parts about coming back. She gave her mom a smile that didn't quite work. "Once the roof is fixed, you'll forget about selling the house. And Dad will find some new interest to pursue." The whole family called him their Project Man. "Besides, if you left here, you'd be leaving Chris and Bronwyn behind. Not to mention those grandbabies they'll give you."

She half smiled. "I'm being silly, aren't I?"

And with that, the subject was closed. For now. Sunny could already see her mother filing their talk away in some far corner of her mind where all the bad things stayed. Another minute, and she'd be bustling about again, planning what to have for dinner or starting to bake brownies.

"By the way, why was Griffin here this morning? He didn't even come into the kitchen." She paused. "I didn't realize you knew each other except from Chris's wedding."

Sunny almost groaned. "There was an incident the other day at Bron's school." She explained about the stolen watch and pulled it out of her pocket. "He returned this—but I think Amanda should have done that instead and apologized."

Her mother frowned, the worry lines between her brows deeper than Sunny remembered. "Such a nice girl," she said. "I can't believe she'd steal from you."

"Well, I'm pretty sure she did."

Her mother sighed. "I know Griffin is trying his best, but Amanda really needs her mother."

Sunny couldn't help asking. "Where is she?"

"No one knows. Apparently—and I hate to gossip—once she hit the Boston city line, there was no further trace of her. I know he's tried to track Rachel but without any luck." She added, "And as for Amanda—that poor dear."

That hadn't been Sunny's impression, but she resisted the urge to say so. To her, Amanda was like one of the storm clouds outside. "I think she needs more than her mother." She sighed. "Griffin didn't welcome my input, though."

"I'll talk to Amanda," her mother said, and Sunny could all but see her making a mental note. "There must be something we can do."

Sunny was about to answer when the first drops of rain began to fall, and her cell phone rang again. She checked the display. And almost groaned.

"I need to take this," she murmured.

Her mom's eyebrows rose. "Nate?" she mouthed, hope in her eyes.

It wasn't Nate. Instead, Judge Ramsay was looking for her, and a contempt citation in New York wasn't something Sunny could ignore.

HE WAS GOING to run away.

One of these days he'd hop in this soccer-mom van and just take off. He'd forget the daily grind at the Palm Breeze Court, complaining tenants like Mrs. Moriarty and the Grump. He'd race along the Florida highways heading for who knew where.

He'd be gone—just like Rachel.

But he couldn't ignore the voice in his head. *You're the man of the family now.*

His small son was in the backseat, staring at the rain-spattered windows. Thanks to the torrential downpour, Griffin could barely see through the windshield.

All at once his left rear tire blew. Josh whimpered at the loud bang, threatening a full-scale panic attack. Griffin flipped on his right signal, then eased the car on to the shoulder. With traffic flying past, he hit the emergency blinker switch.

"It's okay, buddy," he told Josh, breathing a little fast himself. He'd never seen rain like this. Florida really knew how to put on the show. In the rearview mirror Griffin could see Josh's pale face, eyes squinched shut.

"Are we gonna die?"

Griffin's stomach sank. "No way," he said. "You wait here. I've got to fix that tire."

Josh began to cry.

"You'll be fine. Sit tight."

He opened the door and stepped out into the rain. After his dad had died, Uncle Theo had made sure he knew how to change tires and do a lot of other fix-it jobs. Griffin scrambled in the trunk for the jack, then cranked up the van's rear end. As he worked in the downpour, he could still hear Josh weeping inside the car.

The latest storm. He hadn't forgotten his run-in with Sunny, but he needed to. What did she know about trying to get a balky thirteen-year-old girl off to school five days a week without starting another world war? In some other life he might have heeded those tough words about Amanda's behavior, but right now trying to keep his family, or what was left of it, together was all that counted. If he wasn't stepping on eggshells around his daughter, he was soothing Josh's fears.

Griffin tightened the lug nuts on the spare tire, his mouth set. Once, Rachel would have smiled at him in a situation like this, kissed him and teased Josh from his mood, but if she could always do two things at once, he had enough trouble with one.

The traffic whizzed by, rocking the van. No one was slowing down, even under these conditions. He supposed that was because it seemed to rain like crazy every afternoon.

Maybe they were used to it, but he wasn't. Neither was his son.

"Daddy?" Josh's voice came through the side window. "I'm really scared."

"I know you're scared, Josh. But everything's under control." He finished the last nut, wiped his dirty hands on his pants, then got back in the van. "Want me to put on a video?"

"No."

This was news. The best thing about the van was the twin screens that lowered from the ceiling. "How about Scooby-Doo?"

"No," Josh said again.

Griffin couldn't believe his ears. The old series was Josh's current favorite. That, and the stuffed blue creature from *Lilo & Stitch*, which he was strangling at the moment in his car seat. He'd gotten it at Disney World with Rachel's parents the spring before she left home, the week Griffin had been unable to get away from his anchorman duties at the Boston station.

"Take it easy, buddy. Stitch won't let anything happen," he said. *Neither will I*. But Josh didn't respond. Probably didn't believe him.

Cars continued to flash past their precarious place on the narrow shoulder. For an instant, he imagined the van being struck by another vehicle. Which was likely the same thing Josh was doing.

Not long ago Griffin had owned a sleek, new BMW. He'd been on his way to a network slot in an even bigger market.

A passing car blew its horn, nearly shattering his eardrum, and Josh cried out.

Water splatted against the windows like a wet rubber sheet. Mud sprayed the van. Griffin tried to find a safe opportunity to pull into his lane.

In the rearview mirror he saw tear streaks on Josh's face. His son's breath came in sharp hitches. Griffin imagined saying *Come up front with me*, holding his son tight with Stitch still in his grip. He could almost hear what Josh would say. *I'm not allowed to get out of my seat. It's against the law.* Josh was prone to the most literal interpretations, and he was right. Griffin sure didn't want to end up on the Jacksonville news tonight.

He had to fight the temptation to scoop his son on to his lap anyway, the need to feel Josh's arms tight around his neck.

This was Griffin's life now. Josh and Amanda. He didn't need a lecture from Sunny Donovan. He knew all about priorities and responsibilities, the right ones now. He tried to meet them, and sometimes did a halfway good job.

He was a long way from Armani suits and Italian loafers. These days he preferred jeans and old shirts. Even though Amanda's new friend persisted in calling him a celebrity, he didn't have to worry about making the day's broadcast at the studio in Boston.

And sitting in for anchorman Griffin Lattimer, who has the day off...

As a boy Griffin had loved to watch his father read the news on TV. But following in his dad's footsteps hadn't worked out. When Rachel left, Griffin had been forced to make some tough choices.

The rain continued to slash against the van. From the driver's seat, Griffin couldn't kiss Josh's silky dark hair or inhale his little boy's scent. Baby shampoo, red licorice, the tempera paint globs from kindergarten that blotted his Mickey Mouse T-shirt. Griffin's throat closed.

Run away? *Who am I fooling?*

If he ever left home, he'd miss Josh and Amanda until it killed him. This small, vulnerable child who needed him to be strong was all that mattered. There was no way out. Griffin was right where he belonged.

"Stitch and I have got you," he murmured to Josh.

And together, they all three rode out the storm.

BY THE TIME Sunny pulled into the middle-school parking lot, the rain had stopped.

She didn't have long to wait before Bronwyn came out of the building. She was carrying a stack of books and juggling a big messenger bag. A wayward lock of copper hair hung over one eye.

Blowing it away from her face, she spotted the Bronco. Bron opened the passenger door, then slid on to the seat, dumping her burden on the floor. "Whew. This is amazing—two visits from you within the week. I hate to disappoint you, but speaking to my class again won't be possible today. You know, the spit-ball crowd?" She gave a cheeky smile that somehow missed the mark. "School's out. Unless you'd like to help me grade fifty essays before tomorrow."

"Thanks, I'll pass." Sunny came right to the point. "Bron, I need your take on Amanda."

"As her aunt? Or objectively, as her teacher?"

"Whatever you can tell me."

"She's a bright girl who isn't living up to her potential." Bron rummaged on the floor and came up with a wrinkled paper. "This is her essay. Four incomplete sentences, eight grammatical errors, a brown smudge from what was probably chocolate milk…and virtually zero content. She didn't even address the assigned topic."

Sunny scanned the sheet. "Not a lot of effort went into this. Obviously."

"Which seems to be Mandi's habit these days." Bron sighed. "Just when I've gotten the opportunity to spend more time with her, help her adjust… I can't seem to get through." She looked away. "I practically bludgeoned Griffin to move to Florida. And now my once-adorable niece has turned into someone I don't even recognize."

"I'm sure you didn't make Griffin move. He doesn't seem that easy to convince."

Bron arched a brow. "Ah. You did speak to him about her."

"Twice." Sunny took a deep breath and told Bron about their conversations. Then she shook her head. "At his apartment he refused to hold Amanda accountable. And this morning he actually apologized for her."

"That doesn't surprise me. I warned you. Griffin's not sure how to handle her, and then there's Josh. He's always been shy, but since Rachel disappeared, I think he's afraid his father will, too. He's pretty anxious."

Sunny's heart melted. "He was the cutest ring bearer at your wedding," she said. "His anxiety isn't abnormal—from the kids I've seen in similar situations—but why doesn't Griffin get counseling? For all of them?"

"He did, for a while. Then Mandi refused to go, and Josh started wetting his pants before each appointment, and, well, they stopped going."

"A man in denial if ever I've seen one," Sunny said. "Takes one to know one, I guess. I've been a mess since Nate told me he wanted a divorce. Now I'm avoiding him, so we don't have to talk about selling our apartment."

Bron touched her arm. "Griffin doesn't have the market cornered on the hard stuff, does he?" After a moment she went on, "But he'll have to face facts sooner or later. His kids are troubled, and no amount of pretending they aren't will make it better."

"Then you agree with me about Amanda."

"I wish I didn't have to—but taking your watch was a definite signal that she needs help." She gazed off into the distance. "Maybe you can talk to Griffin again at the cookout. I'm not sure we'll be there," she added.

"When has Chris ever missed our father's barbecued ribs?"

Bron only half smiled. "Never. But there's always a first time."

Belatedly, Sunny realized that Bron's smiles had been less than genuine, and her eyes held a worry that should have registered before.

"Trouble?" she asked, tilting her head to look into Bron's downcast gaze.

She stuffed Amanda's wrinkled essay back into her bag. "Chris is jealous," she said, "of the time I spend with my girlfriends. It's upsetting things at home."

Sunny's spirits plummeted. "He's probably just upset about how the fish are running this month."

"He always tells me everything's great," Bron said, "but you're right." She smiled weakly. "This being married stuff isn't easy."

Sunny arched an eyebrow. "When Nate and I were first married, we fought like tigers. You and Chris will work it out," she said, needing to believe that.

"Why couldn't you?"

Sunny had wondered the same thing many times in the past months.

"We were too different in the end, I guess. We drifted apart in the past few years, and Nate…fell out of love with me."

Bron hesitated. "You think there's some-one else?"

"That's the classic reason, but I don't think so—not that I need to know. How's that for denial?" She paused for a moment and recon-sidered. "No, I think I'm well into the anger stage now." She told Bron about Nate's phone calls, the ones she never answered. "I'm not going to help him get over whatever guilt he may feel."

"Maybe he wants you to come back," Bron suggested.

"And maybe he doesn't," Sunny replied.

CHAPTER FIVE

"I WANT to go to the cookout!" Josh shouted, his face screwed up tight. Red spots stood out on his cheeks like a case of measles. "I wanna see Grandpa Jack!"

"Joshua, we're staying home today." Griffin tried again, using his best parent-in-control voice. Apparently his message wasn't getting through, and he felt his patience begin to fray like his nerves. "Maybe we can visit next weeken—"

"No! I need to go now!"

Griffin didn't know what else to say. With Amanda this would be par for the course, but she had stayed out of the line of fire and was talking to Dixie in her room. He could hear the low, long-suffering tone she always used.

"Josh, this isn't a good time," he said. No way would Griffin put himself in Sunny Donovan's sights again. Before he saw her, if he ever saw her, he had to get Amanda to tell him the truth about the stolen watch. Sunny's unwanted advice still rang in his ears, but since Josh had melted down in the car, his son was uppermost in his mind.

Strike two, he thought. Obviously relying on Josh to stay cute and easy to handle hadn't worked out that well.

"This is a good time for me," Josh insisted. "Grandpa Jack's waiting. He said we can play horseshoes today, and I'm gonna win." He paused. "We'll make a bet."

Josh didn't even know what a bet was. "Where did you hear that?"

"From Mandi. She says Grandpa Jack will pay me when I win."

"Great," Griffin murmured. Talk about un-asked-for advice. "The way things are going, Amanda will have you playing poker in some casino before you're ten years old." Not likely but still, she was a bad influence these days, as if she wanted to get Josh in trouble. "Remember how your sister's 'help' turned out last time?"

Josh gave him a deer-in-the-headlights look. "I don't 'member."

"Yes, you do, Josh. She told you to 'clean' your plate—on to the floor. Did you really think I wouldn't see the mess?"

Josh's mouth set. "I don't like that hamburger stuff you make."

The one-pot meat and noodles meal was one of Griffin's best efforts, his version of goulash.

"Well, that's what we had for dinner," he said. "I'm not a short-order cook. What you see in front of you is what you get that night. And I expect you to finish."

For that he got a mutinous glare. Too bad. The counselor had told him that maintaining authority was always a good choice. "Amanda is already testing me at every opportunity. You need limits, too." And until now Josh had observed them.

"At Grandma Kate's I can eat anything I want. That's what she told me," he added with a nod. "And if it rains and thunders, I don't have to be outside."

"That may be. But we're still staying home." He paused. "You won't have to be outdoors in the rain here, either. I promise."

In a flash Josh's scowl dominated his face. He took a single step toward the hallway to his room—his usual destination when he lost an argument—then stopped. His body vibrating with anger, he turned. His cheeks were purple now.

"I don't like you! You're mean!" he yelled.

The words hit Griffin right in the chest. He inhaled sharply, but before he got the chance to exhale—and try to calm himself—Amanda appeared. She didn't even recoil when Josh stomped past her, bumping her side.

"What did you do?" she asked, the freckles on her nose standing out.

Griffin struggled for the right tone, not wanting to set off another explosion. As the door to Josh's room slammed shut, he said quietly, "Your call to Dixie finished?"

"She called me," Amanda corrected him.

"Whatever," he said, using one of her favorite terms. "I told Josh we're not going to the cookout at the Cabots' house today. He didn't care for my decision."

"Oh. Fine," she said, rolling her eyes. "I suppose I'm the reason we're not going. What else?"

Griffin didn't follow her logic. But lately, Amanda seemed to think everything was about her.

"I mean, just because I had Mrs. Donovan's stupid watch in my *room*—like that proves I'm guilty—you'd be too embarrassed to be seen with me. Just because she'll be there, too—"

"Amanda."

"Okay. I *confess*," she said. Saying the word made her freckles darken. "I took her watch."

His heart began to pound. "Is that the truth?"

"Yes!" She gulped in a breath. "Are you satisfied now?"

His hands fisted at his sides. "Why would I be satisfied?"

"Because you always thought I was guilty."

He counted to three before he said, "Amanda, you know stealing is a crime. Sunny Donovan cut you some slack because you're family—her brother's niece. She hoped we could settle this among ourselves." His fists loosened, then tightened again. "I'm not satisfied. I'm ashamed of you. I haven't raised my daughter to take things that don't belong to her."

"You didn't raise me. Mom did."

He clenched his jaw. "Then what would she think?"

Amanda's chin went up. "Maybe she'd be proud of me. She stole a lot of money from *you*," she said, but her eyes didn't meet his.

It was all he could do not to sag against the nearest piece of furniture for support. What had happened to his family? He wanted to rail at Rachel for leaving, for acting like a thief, but Amanda's words had punctured his spirit.

"Yes, she did," he said at last. Another bit of truth. "But it ends there."

Amanda gave him the same blank stare he'd gotten from Josh.

"Get your little brother," he said. "He'll apologize to me for being rude. Then we'll take the three-bean salad I made this morning, drive over to the Cabots' house for the cookout, and you can apologize—in person—to Sunny Donovan."

SHE WASN'T LOOKING forward to the cookout, but at least the sun was shining. Sunny was in the kitchen helping her mother with the preparations when she heard another car pull into the driveway. Dropping her paring knife, she hurried into the front hall to peek out the window. And groaned aloud.

The van could only belong to Griffin. All the other guests had arrived and were already in the backyard gathered around the ice chest full of drinks. Sunny glimpsed Amanda in the van's front seat wearing a scowl, arms crossed over her chest. The car seat in back held a small boy she recognized as Griffin's son.

Let the party begin.

Moments later, a small bundle of energy exploded through the front door. Her dad was there to pull Josh into a hug, his sneakered feet flying off the ground. Then he set the boy down and ruffled his hair.

"Hey, Josh. Glad you could make it."

"We weren't going to come," he said with a solemn look. "But Daddy changed his mind." He broke into a smile. "Grandpa Jack, can we do horseshoes now?"

"I promised, didn't I?" Her father turned to Sunny, who was bent upon reaching the safety of the den. He reintroduced her to Josh, but after a brief handshake with Sunny, Josh ran for the kitchen, then out the back door.

"Wish I had his get-up-and-go," her father muttered.

"He's adorable, Dad."

"Sure is." Then he, too, was headed out to the yard before Sunny could resume her attempt to flee. And Griffin was in the hallway with Amanda trailing behind.

For a moment Sunny took them in. One sullen-looking girl, one too-handsome-for-his-own-good man, his dark hair glossy, those amazing hazel eyes looking grim. Then reality returned. So much for her hope he wouldn't come today.

Griffin nodded. "Counselor," he said but didn't stop. Carrying a ceramic bowl sealed with plastic wrap, he aimed for the kitchen. Apparently he hadn't forgotten their latest encounter in this very hallway.

That left Sunny to face Amanda. Or so she thought.

Without even a simple hello, her head down, Griffin's daughter rushed past her toward Sunny's mom, who was putting the finishing touches on a green salad at the kitchen island. Amanda flung herself into her arms.

"There's my girl," Sunny's mother said with a wide smile. Like Sunny, or rather vice versa, she was a hugger, and for long moments the two chattered away as if they hadn't seen each other in years. Hearing the girl laugh told Sunny theirs was a good, and probably necessary, relationship right now.

In order to maintain the peace, Sunny reversed course. Surely no one would miss her for a while, and she could collect herself in the den. Her parents' cookout was no place to tangle with Griffin.

Sunny wasn't in the best mood anyway.

She'd spent half the morning on the phone to New York again, making nice with Judge Ramsay. The contempt citation had to be dealt with, too, and now her credit card had a bigger balance due.

She was checking the transaction online when someone rapped at her door.

"Come in," Sunny called, thinking her mother needed her in the kitchen. Her dad made a big thing of grilling hamburgers and hot dogs and cooking his famous barbecued ribs, but Mom would provide the rest of the meal for more than twenty people. That meant at least a half dozen side dishes to prepare. And too many mouth-watering desserts.

Instead, Amanda peered around the half-open door.

"May I come in?" She sounded like someone headed to the guillotine. "My *father* says I have to talk to you."

Sunny nearly fell off her dad's desk chair. *Well, what do you know?* Maybe her message had registered, after all.

"Sure. Have a seat," she said, indicating the nearby sofa bed that had become her personal torture rack.

Amanda remained standing. "This won't take long," she said. Arms crossed, she glanced at Sunny's wrist, her mouth turned down at the corners. "I did take your watch. I'm sorry."

Her tone said otherwise. "Are you really?" Sunny asked.

The judge had asked her the same question earlier. And, no, Sunny wasn't sorry for her rant about Wallace Day's unfair punishment.

Amanda almost smiled. "Not that sorry," she admitted.

"Okay." Sunny stood up and folded her arms in a mirror image of Amanda's posture. "Now we're getting somewhere. Why don't you tell me why you took my watch? It's not as if you tried to hide it afterward. I saw it on you at school, and so did your friend."

"It's a *stupid* watch. I didn't even like it."

"You're entitled to your opinion. To me, it's a fun piece of jewelry. It reminds me that I don't always have to take life so seriously. There's the buttoned-down suit I have to wear for work, and then there's my little rebellion." She paused. "What's yours, Amanda?"

A shrug was her only answer, but her gaze shifted away from Sunny.

"You must have known you'd get caught," she said softly. "You even laid this watch on a bureau where your father would see it."

Another shrug. A tiny tremor of her mouth.

From the yard Sunny heard the clang of horseshoes hitting a post. Her dad's laughter and then little Josh's giggles rang out. Her parents' friends and neighbors were talking, and everyone seemed to be having a good time. Except Amanda, of course.

"In my years as a prosecutor, I've often been called upon to feel out a witness, and, many times, it's been a girl like you." She hesitated. "I was once a teenager myself," she said. "I've become a good listener."

Amanda gazed out the window toward where everyone else was having fun. Her glance, her every motion, told Sunny how unhappy she was. She had to fight the urge to pull Amanda into her arms, as she would have Ana Ramirez, saving her from Wallace Day. Saving the girl Sunny used to be.

She tried once more. "Do you have something against me, Amanda?"

Griffin's daughter looked startled, as if that had never occurred to her.

"No," she finally said in a sullen tone. Eyes still on the window.

"Then taking my watch just seemed like a good idea at the time?" Sunny's tone was wry. "A matter of poor impulse control?"

"I guess." At last, she looked away from the window. "Can I go now?"

Sunny wanted to say no. There was more here, hidden beneath the surface, but she wasn't prepared to interrogate the girl. Amanda was Griffin's responsibility. At least he'd made her admit to the theft. And she didn't seem to resent Sunny personally. Maybe she had a grudge against Career Day.

"You may go," she said. "I appreciate the apology."

Amanda made a scoffing sound. "Don't think it means anything."

The door closed behind her while Sunny was still pondering the words.

GRIFFIN TOOK HIS TIME. He helped Josh play another game of horseshoes. He hung around the cooler with the Cabots' friends and neighbors and even enjoyed the sense of camaraderie with new people who had no idea of his life before, or even now. He took his turn at the grill, searing hot dogs and seasoning burgers and slathering ribs with more sauce. Slowly, he could feel himself begin to unwind.

He'd needed this. Since the move from Boston he hadn't had much opportunity to socialize except chatting now and then with the residents. With the kids to consider, he'd had little spare time. The sum total of his circle outside of work had been Bron and Chris. Now, sharing laughter and corny jokes, he told himself that his own apology to Sunny could wait.

Chris sauntered toward him, looking around the yard. "Where's my sister?"

Bron, her arm linked with his, smiled at him. "Keeping a low profile."

"She's avoiding me," Griffin said.

But he was keeping out of her way, too. It was as if they'd made some secret pact.

"Why?" Bron asked. "Because you exchanged a few words about the watch?"

He flinched. Did the whole town know about Amanda?

"And when Mandi came outside," Bron went on, "she said she had apologized." Amanda was in a group of younger kids now, and it looked as though she was teasing— or bullying?—one of them. Griffin kept an eye on her.

"I doubt that cleared the air with Sunny."

"Well, today it should," Bron said, then dragged Chris away. Dinner was almost ready, and the heavy, mouthwatering aroma of barbecue filled the air.

"Remember," Chris called over his shoulder. "You, me, Bron and Sunny. Some night. Soon."

Yeah, sure. Like that would work out any better than his last conversation with Sunny. No matter how pretty she looked.

The back door opened. And here she came in cutoff shorts and a one-shoulder shirt, walking across the yard with a pair of bowls in her hands. Potato salad and baked beans, he saw. Griffin didn't hesitate. He jumped to relieve her of one of them and got a faint smile in return.

"Thanks. If you want to help, there's more where these came from."

She lingered at the table until he'd gone inside. When he came out again with his three-bean salad and a fresh six-pack of sodas for the cooler, she headed for the house.

When everyone sat down to eat, she chose the farthest seat from his on the opposite side of the table. Josh, however, was near Sunny, sticking close to Jack's side. Amanda was giggling with some other girls, eating dinner with them on a blanket under a big oak tree. For the moment, he was off duty.

Trying not to notice how Sunny kept her distance, he tucked into his dinner. The corn on the cob was sweet and juicy. Jack's famous spareribs practically melted in his mouth, and the spicy yet mellow barbecue sauce was perfection. Kate's homemade lemonade capped off the superb feast.

By the time everyone finished, the sun was sinking low in the sky. Griffin bused plates and plastic cups to the kitchen, scraped bits into the garbage—there wasn't much of the delicious food to be tossed—then ambled out into the yard again.

Still at the table, Josh was enjoying a huge slab of watermelon for dessert, his chin dripping juice. Amanda was with the girls under the tree, examining someone's bracelet. He hoped it didn't disappear. Jack and Chris had snuck around the corner of the house to savor their cigars with a few of the neighborhood men, but Griffin wasn't a smoker. He didn't care for the pungent scent that filled the air and competed with the lingering aroma of meat and veggies from the grill. He needed to set a good example for his kids.

Instead of joining the other men, he wandered to the corner of the back lawn for a rare moment alone. Feeling his spirit mellow, he gazed at the setting sun. Streaks of red and purple and pink spread out across the sky.

"Nothing like a Florida sunset," he said to himself.

"Better than Boston?" Sunny's voice brought his head around. She was bent over a nearby hibiscus bush with a pair of garden shears in her hand.

When she spoke, Griffin's pulse took off like a runner from the starting gate. It was one thing to help her carry food for the cookout, quite another to be alone with her.

"Boston can be good," he said, "but the show here is a lot more, well, showy." Like the afternoon rains.

She dropped the scissors, then picked up a bunch of blossoms from the grass at her feet. She was still wearing the red polish that peeked out from her sandals. "I'll leave you then, to commune with nature."

"Wait." Before he could tell himself not to, Griffin stopped her. And fumbled for an excuse. "Thanks," he said at last. "I'm glad Amanda apologized. You were right. She did take your watch."

Sunny half smiled. "And you didn't let her get away with it."

He shouldn't care that she sounded proud

of him. He shouldn't be staring at that little uptilt at the corners of her mouth. "So, what am I missing?" he said, because nothing involving his daughter was ever simple these days. "Did she even sound sincere?"

"She…tried." Sunny hesitated. "But you didn't welcome my interference before, and I doubt you've changed your mind. I'm out of the advice-giving business."

Ouch. Forcing his gaze away from her, he noticed the growing darkness. The sun had slipped lower in the sky, and the colors had bled into a deeper shade of almost burgundy that made her lighter shirt seem to glow. "I'm impressed, Counselor. Didn't imagine you'd give up that easily."

"I have my moments." She shifted the flowers in her arms. Her watch sparkled on her wrist. "I need to put these in water. They won't last long—but I keep trying. Except with Amanda," she added, then took a step away.

"Sunny," he said, "I owe you an apology myself. I didn't exactly put out the welcome mat the other day. And, well—Chris told me—I was sorry to learn about your divorce."

"So am I," she said.

Griffin blew out a breath. "You already know about my situation."

Her face softened. "You don't know where your wife is now. And—I'm treading on dangerous ground again here—that hasn't helped Amanda."

"Or Josh," he said. "She's defiant. He's fearful." Griffin told her about the flat tire, the car rocking at the side of the road every time another semi blew past. "I think he equates Rachel's disappearance with death itself, a concept he's only beginning to understand."

"I couldn't imagine leaving my children like that," she said.

His tone hardened. "Neither can I."

"But then, I don't. Have children, I mean." Sunny was all but strangling the hibiscus blossoms. "I see so many troubled kids in my work. Of course their cases usually involve violence, but the emotional damage is always severe. I wish I could help them more. But I'm rarely their lawyer. I'm on the other side of the issue—prosecuting the person who harmed someone they love."

"That's helping, too," he pointed out, trying not to notice how the fading light made her skin softly shine.

"They break my heart, though. Young girls like Amanda," she said, stumbling a little on the last, "having to deal with grown-up matters they can barely comprehend. Why would someone hurt them, their families, that way?"

The raw emotion in her voice made him study her more closely.

Yet asking probing questions was her style, not his, and Griffin didn't know why he'd felt the urge to push. He could tell she wouldn't like it.

She clutched the flowers even more tightly. "But enough about me," she said. "Or rather, my work. How do you like Jacksonville?"

Griffin had been asked that very question at least a hundred times since the move. "I like it fine."

Sunny tilted her head as if she guessed he was lying. "You don't miss Boston? And being on TV? Chris told me you'd only been in the anchor position for a year or so. You were their golden boy, he said."

"Until Rachel took off. Not to blame her for the job I have now—or the move." He paused. "In Boston, I couldn't afford to keep Josh in day care, or put Amanda in some after school program. I never finished at the station until almost midnight some days—

most days—and then they were missing Rachel. I couldn't have them missing me, which was way too familiar."

"So you quit and came to Florida." She smiled. "To enjoy the sunsets."

"To provide for my family," he replied. "To spend more time with them. Being closer to Chris and Bron is a big help, too. The kids need that support. So do I," he admitted. "Once things get resolved, we'll see."

"Would you go back?"

"To Boston? No, that door's already shut. The new anchor likes her job."

"What about the local stations here?"

"All their positions are filled," he said. "Maybe someday, when the kids are older and Josh is in all-day school…who knows what opportunity might open up? But for now, I'm a single dad."

Sunny's smile had faded. "Two years is a long time for anyone to be gone."

"That's what Chris says. But who knows how Rachel's mind works?"

"True," she said, her expression rueful. "I need to do some thinking myself. Certainly I have no idea what made Nate decide our marriage was over. But he did."

"And you're not okay with that," he said.

"Let's say it was a shock."

He could certainly relate. "So you came to Florida—" he smiled "—to enjoy the hibiscus."

"And to put myself together again like Humpty Dumpty." She told him about the Wallace Day decision and her run-in with the judge on the day her divorce had become final.

Griffin frowned. "I read a little about that case. Gruesome."

"I won't whine about the loss," she said. "The real victim was Ana Ramirez—the twelve-year-old girl he tortured then killed. I'll never get her out of my mind."

Griffin saw that look again in her eyes. Passion, determination…and something more personal. It was gone before the thought crossed his mind.

"Too young," he murmured. "I was only ten when my dad died. After that my mom relied on me. I'm not sure I was up to the job."

"Then you can understand," she murmured. He watched her collect herself, then try to shift the topic. "Well. There's always more work to be done. As soon as I get my feet under me again, I'll be going back. In a few more years I hope to run for DA."

"Talk about long work hours." He shouldn't be surprised. She wasn't going to stick around—she was a driven woman. And he was no longer the driven man he'd been. Except about Rachel.

"I don't mind hard work—or the hours." She paused. "There are too many bad guys out there. I intend to stop as many as I can."

Griffin didn't point out that she'd be stopping them after the fact. He suspected Sunny had reasons of her own to push as far as she could. And so did he. Finding Rachel would be the first step. Maybe they weren't that different after all.

As if by unspoken agreement, he and Sunny started walking toward the lights of the Cabot house. At one point she stumbled over an uneven spot in the grass, and Griffin reached out to steady her with a hand at her elbow.

Sunny jerked away to rub the small of her back.

"You hurt yourself?"

"No, I've been sleeping on the sofa bed in Dad's den. The mattress is old and thin, and it sags. Those bar supports dig into my spine every night."

Griffin walked her all the way to the house,

still feeling the warmth of her skin from when he'd touched her arm. He heard himself say, "Well, if you need a place to stay, there are a few vacancies in my complex."

"I won't be here that long," she said.

Griffin could have kicked himself. Why had he said that? And what made him reach out again to guide her up the steps with a hand at her aching lower back? At least her words were a needed reminder.

"Then good luck with your crusade." He held the door open for her but didn't meet her gaze. "Nice talking to you."

"Yes," she said, sounding equally surprised. "It was."

CHAPTER SIX

HER CELL PHONE in hand, Sunny dragged herself from the den into the kitchen, where her mother was mixing a batch of blueberry muffins. Her mom's smile abruptly died when she saw Sunny's face.

"Something the matter?"

Yes, you might say that. Sunny was still trying to make sense of her reaction to the change she'd seen in Griffin yesterday. She'd wanted to pull back from him, yet move closer at the same time.

He was attractive, she admitted, but definitely off-limits. Forget those broad shoulders and his gorgeous hazel eyes. He was, after all, married, and his focus, understandably, was on his children. Her eye was on the DA's office.

But if Griffin wasn't quite what she'd thought, neither was Nate. Her now ex-husband had just laid a thorny new issue at her feet. Pushing Griffin from her mind, Sunny waved her phone in the air.

"Nate called. Again," she said. She'd been avoiding him, along with her friend Laura, who'd apparently heard she was back in town. Had Sunny's mother tipped her off? Sunny wasn't ready to see her, if she ever would be. But for now she'd been forced to deal with Nate. "He caught me unawares."

Sunny had barely glanced at the display before she'd answered. Maybe she shouldn't have changed that ringtone from *Porgy and Bess*'s love ballad to a generic chime.

"Oh, dear," her mother murmured, folding a bunch of berries into the batter. "I knew you should have talked to him before now. I imagine he's angry."

Anger would have been surprising, since Nate's emotions tended to stay in the quiet mid-range, which only reminded her of Griffin again. Sunny laid her cell on the counter and rubbed the persistent sore spot on her back.

"We need to discuss something, Nate says." She sighed. "I thought we had already settled everything, mostly to his satisfaction."

"Didn't the court oversee all of that?" her mom asked.

"I thought so." She paced the kitchen. "What could be on his mind now?"

"He wouldn't say?"

"Mom, he didn't even sound like himself. His voice was so cold and the words he used… *'I hate to bring this up after all we've been through recently, but…'*" She sank on to a stool at the kitchen island. "At least he said 'we' this time, not 'I.'"

Her mother frowned. "You have no idea what the issue might be?"

"'Something vitally important,' was all he said. I think he expects me to hop on the next plane." Sunny saw hope flash in her mother's eyes. But she wouldn't take him back, even if he did want her. Bronwyn had been wrong about that, too. If Sunny had any doubt, this call had set her straight.

If she was being honest, as long as she hadn't answered Nate's calls she'd been able to cling to her own gauzy picture of their past.

Her mom gave the batter a last stir, then began filling the muffin cups. Her smooth, efficient motions were as much a part of her as her hair and eye color, and Sunny wanted to take comfort in the familiar sight. Instead, she jumped off the stool and started pacing again, past the bouquet of flowers on the sideboard. *So you came to Florida to enjoy the hibiscus.*

"Why does Nate do this? Just when I'm ready to step back from all the turmoil and the months of 'lawyering up,' he opens the wound again." She spun around to face her mother, who was slipping the muffin tins into the oven. "It's not as if we didn't argue over every scrap of furniture and glassware we own—I mean, owned. And here I thought we could have an amicable divorce."

"Because you let him have his way, Sunshine." Her father stood in the doorway, a scowl creasing his face. Sunny hadn't even heard the back door open. "Don't let him walk all over you again."

"Dad, I don't even know what this is about. That's the most frustrating part," she said. "I really don't care if Nate wants the rest of our CD collection. At this point I just want some peace of mind before I have to go back to work and concentrate on making my life— my career—without him."

"The divorce was the best thing that ever happened to you." Her dad plucked the empty mixing bowl from the counter and swiped a finger through the remnants of batter. "Mmm. Best blueberry muffins in fifty states, Kate."

Her mother grabbed the bowl and headed for the sink. The rushing water almost covered the little sound she made as she squirted detergent into the bowl. And Sunny's heart sank. Obviously her parents hadn't mended their quarrel. She didn't want any part of it. She didn't want to think about Griffin or deal with Nate, either.

Seeing him again, little more than a week and a half since she'd left New York, was out of the question.

Nate's tousled chestnut hair and the quirky smile she had loved belonged to her memory now, or soon would—if she avoided contact for a while longer.

"I'm not going anywhere near him," she said at last. "Why would he think I would?" But how else could she find out what he wanted?

Leaning against the counter, her dad watched her, making her blush. "Carrying a torch for Nate isn't the best idea, you know."

"I'm not torching for him. But, Dad. We were married for eight years."

"Yes, and I knew the second I laid eyes on him that trouble was ahead. Your mother might have liked him, and I can't blame her for that. He's nice enough, but Nate was never a match for you."

"Hmm. Why didn't I see that?"

"I'm sorry, but it's true. You're a far better lawyer than he'll ever be—and that worked for him for eight years. Did he ever try to lift some of the burden from you? No. All Nate ever cared about was Nate. And the few billable hours he needed to hang on to his job in family law."

"But we tried. We both did," she insisted.

"You tried more."

"Dad, if I add the two years Nate and I dated before our wedding, I gave a decade to our relationship." No wonder her mother kept hoping they might reconcile.

Her father opened his mouth, then shut it again.

"Jack." Her mom's tone stopped whatever his next words might have been.

He held up both hands. "I'm just saying."

"I do think you may be judging Nate too harshly."

But her father hadn't given up. "So what's your plan, Sunshine?"

"I should let him stew awhile longer.

Maybe then he'll tell me what this is about and save me a trip."

"And maybe you'll give yourself an ulcer."

Sunny sent him a weak smile. "Which will go nicely with my aching back. I'd almost rather face Nate," she said.

"Good idea." Her dad patted her shoulder. "Get it over with."

Except that was just it. As long as she avoided him, just as she was avoiding Laura's calls, she hadn't failed.

In court she was known for her ability to break down a witness. Her summation in the Wallace Day case—though the jury hadn't agreed with her—had been the best of her career. So far. Even her boss had said so. The man whose job she wanted in the not-too-distant future. But first...

"You're right," she finally said. Her father had a point: she needed to face this, whatever the issue was. But her mother was right, too. She had to give Nate the benefit of the doubt. "Looks like I'm going to New York sooner than I planned."

GRIFFIN HAD TO admit he was glad Monday had rolled around. That meant school for Amanda and kindergarten for Josh and a whole morning to get his ducks in order without having to juggle the kids' needs or break up their fights. While nursing a second mug of coffee, he straightened the apartment, then sifted through the usual messages from various tenants.

Since he'd already replaced the washers in Mrs. Moriarty's faucet and repainted the Grump's kitchen, Miss Carrie was first on the list. Her back patio was crumbling, and she was afraid someone might trip and fall.

Griffin worried that the little eighty-some-thing-year-old woman—who had grabbed Griffin's heart at first sight and become his favorite resident—might be the most at risk of falling.

Leaving his mug on the table, he laced up his work shoes and headed for Miss Carrie's apartment.

He'd knocked at her door before he realized it was only eight o'clock. He should have waited, given her a chance to wake up and eat her usual bowl of corn flakes swimming in half-and-half, but she answered anyway. Her big smile and halo of pure white hair—without a strand escaping its bun—made him grin.

"Morning, Miss Carrie. Sorry to get you up this early."

"I've been up for hours. A woman my age has to make the most of every day. Come in, Griffin. As a former teacher, I admire your promptness. Today's schoolchildren—" She broke off. "Don't get me started. Except for your little ones, of course. I saw Amanda and Joshua waiting at the bus stop when I brewed my coffee."

Miss Carrie liked her coffee hot and strong enough to stand up in the antique bone china cups she favored. She lived alone and didn't make much of a mess. Her living room never had a lace doily, brass-framed picture or crystal figurine out of place.

"You have a lovely apartment, Miss Carrie," he said. "After my father died, my mom and I lived on a shoestring budget. She often worked two jobs. But we always had a roof over our heads and a few nice things around, like yours."

"I imagine they were more contemporary things," she said, indicating the mantel full of family photographs, some of which were sepia prints. "But then, part of me likes to live in the past."

"That reminds me of my uncle Theo,

who was like my surrogate dad. He must have every tool he's ever bought. He never throws anything away." Griffin sighed. "But I'm afraid he hasn't forgiven me for leaving home, leaving him behind."

Miss Carrie patted him on the shoulder and said, "Coffee?"

"Thanks, but I already had a few cups." When her expression fell, he added, "Maybe later," despite the fact that his stomach burned from too much caffeine. "Why don't I take a look at that broken concrete you called about?"

Momentarily distracted, she led the way to the back door. They stepped outside. "As you can see, it's fallen to pieces. They don't build like they used to," she said, sounding like Uncle Theo might. And Griffin had to agree with her. The patio was in bad shape.

"I'll get this fixed," he said. "We can't have you risking your safety."

"It's everyone else I'm worried about," she insisted. "People my age may fall over every little hump in a carpet, but I'm not one of them. I'm steady as a rock."

Griffin smiled, determined to give her the best patio in the complex. Then he'd make a tour to see how the others were holding up.

"There'll be some noise," he said, "but I'll try to keep it to a minimum."

"Noise? If you think that will disturb my afternoon nap, young man, think again. I haven't taken a nap since I was four years old." Miss Carrie had a twinkle in her eye. "I'd be willing to bet you go to bed every night before I do. I never missed Jay Leno— or that baby-faced replacement of his. Before that, I was Johnny Carson's biggest fan."

"You're a mover and a shaker, Miss Carrie."

"Believe it," she said, then laid a hand on his arm. "Now, you'll have that coffee with me. My patio can wait a little longer."

"Well, I should really…"

"Let the other cranks wait, too," she said. "Honestly, all Walter Lynx does is complain. Last time it was his kitchen, and I'm sure he's on your answering machine today for some other reason." She paused as he opened the back door for her. "If I were you, I'd erase his message. His head will probably explode."

Griffin grinned. "You have a wicked streak, Miss Carrie."

"It's what keeps me alive." In the kitchen again she bustled about, taking one of her china cups from a cupboard, then pouring what looked like tar into it before refilling her own. Before he knew it, they were seated at the table.

He poured half the pitcher of cream into his cup, then braced himself.

"So how is Walter?" he asked, forcing a single swallow of the stuff down his throat. Griffin rarely thought of him by name.

"He's never happy. But he'll never be satisfied, so don't even try."

"Maintaining his apartment is my job. I don't get to pick and choose."

"Well, you should," she said. "But never mind Walter Lynx. Tell me. What brought you and those dear children to the Palm Breeze Court?"

His stomach tightened, not only from the acidic coffee.

We don't have a home.

Griffin tended to get by with a day-by-day attitude. He didn't care to be reminded of the past two years or of Amanda's unhappiness. But Miss Carrie was waiting, and he never liked to disappoint her, so he told her about his life in Boston.

"After my wife left, it wasn't practical to stay there. There's a lot less pressure here," he added, thinking of Sunny. *So you moved to Florida to enjoy the sunsets.* He blinked away the stubborn memory of last night.

He was safer talking with Miss Carrie, even about his past.

At least he thought so until she said, "I do admire your continued search for Rachel. But perhaps she doesn't want to be found, dear."

"Why not?" he asked through clenched teeth. "She has two great kids—"

"But if it takes a private investigator to bring her back…"

He stared at her. "How did you know I hired a PI?"

"Because that's what I would do." She paused again. "And if I found my husband at last, I'd be very tempted to strangle him."

Griffin studied her face. The lines and wrinkles only made her more appealing. She'd seen so much in her life.

"Did your husband go missing?"

"Indeed he did. Forty-some years of marriage went down the drain when he walked out. So here I am—" she smiled broadly "—living where I always wanted to be. Who needs snow?"

"You have no idea where he is?"

"Dead," she said with some degree of satisfaction. "I've seen the certificate and a photo of his gravestone on Ancestry.com."

"At least you know." Griffin rose and dumped his still-full cup in the sink. "I'd better get back to work. Including the Grump—I mean, Walter Lynx—I have half a dozen calls to answer."

She beamed. "The Grump! It's perfect."

Miss Carrie walked him to the front door, then looked up into his eyes.

"I like you, Griffin," she said. "I suppose, considering my age, I can't say that I see you as a son. But a grandson will do." She stood in the doorway as he walked down the steps. "You might think about giving up the chase, dear. If your Rachel wants to come home, she will. If not—"

He turned back. "But what if something's happened to her?" It seemed impossible that she'd vanished without a trace. He'd lost more than one night's sleep picturing her alone somewhere, helpless…hurt. Or worse. Like Miss Carrie's husband.

He almost didn't hear her final words.

"What if something hasn't?"

LATER THAT AFTERNOON, Griffin was working on Miss Carrie's back patio when a sense of foreboding made him glance at his watch. He froze. *Josh!* He'd forgotten to pick up his son at school. Josh rode the bus in the morning, but Griffin drove him home midday.

Heart pounding, he dropped the jackhammer he'd been using to remove the broken concrete. And, with his ears still ringing, ran for his car. Moments later, he wheeled the van into the school parking lot and hit the ground running. By the time he blew through the main doors, he was panting with fear and guilt.

To his relief Josh was sitting on a bench in the front office, swinging his feet. But dirty tear tracks smeared his face. He glanced up at Griffin, then focused again on the toes of his sneakers, which, like Amanda's slippers, were getting too small.

Griffin bent down. "I'm sorry, Josh." He tried to draw him close, but Josh stiffened. Griffin heard a woman clearing her throat and looked toward the reception desk where a secretary had been pecking away at a computer keyboard. Her expression was also closed off.

"Mr. Lattimer." She glanced at Josh and lowered her voice. "Joshua has been beside himself wondering where you were and if you were ever going to come for him. We were just about to call you."

"I lost track of time," he said, knowing that was no excuse. You didn't simply forget about a five-year-old boy. A picture of a stern-faced social worker from Children's Services flashed in his mind. It was one of the worst things he could think of: losing his kids, too.

"He was very frightened," the woman said, clearing her throat again. "Joshua, would you wait in the hall for your father? There's a bench just outside the door, and we can see you from in here. He won't be long."

Josh shuffled out, head down, lower lip trembling, and Griffin felt like even more of a louse. On his busiest days and nights as an anchor in Boston, he'd never left Josh sitting alone in some office, afraid he'd been forgotten like an old shoe. But then, Rachel had handled most of the parenting duties.

The woman waited until Josh was gone to continue. "If a child is at loose ends, the school will certainly watch him until a parent or approved guardian arrives. But this office is not a babysitting service," she said.

Griffin knew that.

"I said I was sorry. This won't happen again."

"I should hope not." Her lips compressed into a thin line. "We all realize, including Joshua's teacher, that your home situation has been stressful—"

"That would be an understatement."

"—and that your wife has left the family, which involves a great deal of adjustment. But Joshua is only five years old—"

"I know how old my son is. I was there when he was born."

She bristled like a hen ruffling its feathers. "And I hope you will be there for him from now on." *I would hate to have to inform the authorities.*

His mouth tightened. No school secretary was going to tell him how to run his family. She couldn't possibly understand. Tempted to tell her so, Griffin pulled back. "Yes, and what Josh needs is a solid wall of support. At home and right here."

"We have his best interests at heart," she agreed, but the words sounded like a threat, and she wasn't finished. "I must tell you that in the hour and a quarter while you 'lost track of time,' your son had a bad panic attack. The school counselor tried to reassure him, but Joshua threw up all over his clothes."

Griffin blinked. What was Josh wearing

now? He hadn't noticed anything but the sneakers. And those tears.

Another streak of guilt ran through him. Maybe he deserved the lecture, after all. How could he not have seen that Josh wasn't wearing the same Superman shirt he'd left the house in this morning?

"We maintain a small gift shop," she told him. "I've added the price of a school T-shirt to your account."

"Thanks." He turned toward the door. "Thanks for minding Josh. I'll try to do better next time."

"Let's hope there won't be a next time." She paused, then said, "Good afternoon, Mr. Lattimer. Please, tell your son he's always safe here. He needn't worry."

More advice for the year's Worst Father. She was right, of course. Poor Josh.

In the hallway Griffin hunkered down in front of him.

Josh gazed at him in accusation. "You forgot me."

"No, buddy. I just...well, yeah, I did forget but about the time, not about you."

"Yes, you did."

Griffin couldn't disagree. To a five-year-old, abandonment was abandonment, no matter the circumstance.

He held out a hand. "Looks like I owe you an ice cream cone. You deserve a treat to make up for my tardiness today." Normally, he wasn't into bribery as a parenting tactic, but Griffin wanted to see his son smile.

Josh only shook his head. "No, thank you," he said like a replay of that day in the van when he'd refused to watch a video. "I'm not hungry."

Oh, right. He'd thrown up only an hour ago.

"Then maybe a chocolate milk?" His and Amanda's favorite.

Josh looked away. "That's okay, Daddy. You don't have to buy me a treat."

The condemnation in his voice tore into Griffin's gut.

He took Josh's hand for the walk to the van. "Then let's go home. Amanda will be there soon. Tell you what. We'll stop at the store on the way. Pick up some hot dogs and fire up the grill tonight."

"Mandi doesn't like hot dogs."

"But you do," he said, buckling Josh into his car seat a few moments later, "right, buddy?"

Josh gave a long-suffering sigh. Just like Amanda.

"I guess."

Griffin slid behind the steering wheel, turned the ignition and pulled away from the school. He couldn't believe he'd left Josh waiting…all because he'd been fixated on that back patio, lost in the project the way he'd been consumed by his duties at the station. He had to stay in the moment now. For Josh.

In the rearview mirror his boy was fiddling with the action figure he always carried in the van along with Stitch. He shifted pieces around until the plastic guy turned into a sci-fi vehicle. As full of concentration as Griffin had ever been.

"Hey, Josh."

"What?" He didn't look up. Click, slam, click again. The pieces spun every which way.

"I'll never forget you," he said. "You know that, don't you?"

And Josh all but whispered the words that both saddened and angered him.

"Mommy did."

CHAPTER SEVEN

SUNNY REVELED IN the blare of a taxicab horn.
She wallowed in the rush of people. New
York was the exact opposite of Florida. Here,
impatience and excitement were everywhere
in the busy restaurants, crowded museums
and galleries. The familiar smell of the East
River on this humid fall afternoon was like
the finest perfume, and so was the heavy
scent that rose from the subway grates. On
every street the shops awaited her, the little
boutiques down in SoHo and the big depart-
ment stores in midtown—Saks Fifth Avenue
being her personal favorite. The place where
Sunny had bought all of her court-appropri-
ate suits.

Maybe being away from Florida for a short
time would help her stop thinking about Griffin and the cookout.

Still clutching her key, Sunny set down her
carry-on in the foyer of the apartment she'd
shared with Nate. After all those nights on

the sagging sofa bed in her father's den, here she was again. Everything looked the same.

"Nate?"

Sunny paused just inside the living room, high above the bustle of Manhattan. "Nate," she called again, then drifted toward the rear of the apartment and their bedroom.

He emerged from the smaller room across the hall, which Sunny had used as an office, and for a moment all she could do was look at him. Something had changed after all. His hair was more tousled than it always was, and he hadn't shaved. His blue shirttail hung from his pants. Clearly he hadn't gone to work today. "Oh. You're here. Already," he added.

Sunny's pulse hitched. Was he not alone?

Her gaze ran over him again from chestnut hair to bare feet. Seeing him hurt, just as she'd expected. And his demeanor and obvious impatience told her that he hadn't called her here because he wanted to reconcile.

Still, this had been her home. Her refuge, in a way.

"I know I'm early. My plane landed half an hour ahead of schedule. I didn't check a bag, so I was out of LaGuardia in no time. What a miracle," she said, babbling now. "I was lucky and caught a cab into town with light traffic on the LIE." She glanced at the closed office door, then the master bedroom. Nate didn't look as if he'd been working here, either. "What's going on?"

He folded his arms. "I would have told you, if you'd answered my calls."

"I did answer. Yesterday."

"Finally," he said with a quick eye roll that reminded her of Amanda.

Sunny blinked and said, "Are we really going to fight about this? Whatever it is."

Nate ushered her back into the living room. He gestured at her favorite chair across from his leather sofa, but Sunny didn't sit.

After a long moment, he sighed. "You know the agreement we reached on the division of property? There's been a change on my part. I'd like to propose a simpler solution."

"Nate, just say it. What's on your mind?"

"I want you to buy out my share of the apartment."

For a second, she didn't understand. "But—as you said—we already agreed. Our divorce is done. Correct me if I'm wrong, but according to that agreement we're to sell the apartment within a year, then divide the profits equally."

"I want to end everything sooner. As close to right now as we can."

With a fresh pang of loss, Sunny gazed around the spacious living room. They'd chosen every piece of furniture as a couple. Every picture on the walls, even the flatware had been shared. Yes, she'd been stalling about the sale. Trying to put the pieces of her heart back together before she gave up on this last reminder that they'd once been happy as a couple, that they'd planned for a future. She didn't know what to say.

They had shared a journey, a life. Sunny had felt…safe with him. Now she'd been betrayed again. For the first time in years, the past began to close around her like a pair of reaching arms…

She heard a different deep voice, coaxing her into a dark, terrifying place. *Come on, Sunny. It'll be our secret.*

"Why wait any longer?" Nate asked. "I need to move on, and so do you."

With every word her suspicions grew. She remembered Bron's remark, which had seemed far-fetched at the time. "Who is she?"

"What?" Nate shifted on the leather sofa. How many nights had they curled up together to watch a TV show or listen to music while they read?

Her voice shook. "It's obvious, Nate. I see you're not in the same emotional place I am right now, but this idea... I mean, when someone dies—" *Me*, she thought. *I could have died then. I could have died like Ana Ramirez.*

"—the grief process takes at least a year. You're not—*I'm* not, since I seem to be alone in this—supposed to make important decisions until then."

Nate refused to meet her eyes, and Sunny knew what he was about to say.

"I'm engaged."

She couldn't seem to catch her breath. Bron had been right.

"My, you work fast."

"There's no need to get testy."

Sunny disagreed. She wanted to hate him for this latest shock. "How long has this been going on?"

"Not as long as you must think," he said. "But then, how would you have noticed?" His mouth thinned with the temper he rarely let show. "If you weren't in court or at the office, you were always in the den here. With the door closed. Working."

"When we got married, you knew I'd have to work long hours. If I want to become DA by the time I'm forty, I can't afford to—"

"Find time for your husband?"

She winced. "So, while we were still married, then?"

"What kind of guy do you think I am? No," he said. "But I'd been, well, backing away from us for a while before I met her."

Sunny knew she should put an end to this topic, discuss the apartment. But if Nate could seem dispassionate, she never could.

"So. Why the rush to sell now?"

Nate met her gaze and told Sunny his new fiancée's name, but it didn't register. Her head had gone as light as cotton candy, and her ears buzzed. She could barely take in what he was saying.

He was never a match for you.

"Ironically, we met at the office," Nate said. "She was my boss's new admin, but that wasn't really her thing. I'm glad she's quit her job now. For one thing, she's a great cook." He patted his stomach. Caught up in her career, Sunny had been known for burning dinner while she pondered some legal problem. "I'm really going to have to watch my weight," he said. "Get in a few extra workouts at my club."

All Nate ever cared about was Nate.

"To set your mind at ease, I didn't start seeing her until I'd filed for divorce. By then I knew she was the right one for me."

And I wasn't. Because of that dark place. *I'm not normal.*

Nate didn't seem to notice her pain. "...And we want to start a family," he was saying. "I know that was never your thing, but we're already trying." He paused. "I want a couple of kids while I'm young enough to enjoy them. You know, play ball in the yard, teach them to ski. Put in those all-nighters walking the floor without sleep." He said his fiancée's name again, but Sunny still didn't comprehend. She'd already buried it somewhere in her subconscious. "She'll be a terrific mother," Nate said.

A hard lump had settled in her chest. "I never said I didn't want children."

"No, but you never said you wanted them now. I do."

There was no sense arguing that. She took a quick breath. "Let's get down to business, then."

With that, she could see him relax. "Well,

obviously my priorities have changed. But I'm willing to give a little. Instead of putting this place on the market, let's avoid that. You buy out my half and keep the apartment. You always did like it better than I do."

"I can't carry this apartment on my own, Nate. You should know that."

Eight years ago, soon after their wedding, they had purchased the two-bedroom, bath-and-a-half unit. They'd since built up decent equity, but she'd never expected to face this decision, this loss.

He half smiled. "Call one of your banker friends. You'll have a new mortgage by to-morrow."

"That isn't true, Nate." She counted to ten. "The apartment would have to be reap-praised, which would mean taking on a larger mortgage. Why pressure me to take this place off your hands now?"

He hesitated. With a glance toward her for-mer office, he admitted, "I was going over my accounts when you got here. We've found a house in Connecticut. Just came on the market. Won't last long. I'll need my share of this place for the down payment, for fur-niture, and we want..."

We, he'd said. And on the phone, *after all*

we've been through. He hadn't meant her at all. Sunny squared her shoulders. And hardened her heart. *Don't let him walk all over you again*, her father had said. If she'd been thinking clearly, instead of being guided by her emotions, she would have known what was coming.

"Your new house is not my problem, Nathaniel."

He tensed. "Are you crazy? This is a great deal—for both of us. Okay. Then how's this? I'll discount the price," he said, sounding desperate. "Instead of fair market value, you give me half what we paid when we bought in. You get to keep your home with full ownership, go back to your job without the hassle of looking for a new place—you'd never be able to find this kind of space—and we'll both be free."

Still on her feet, she whirled around to head for the door. "I need time to think," she said. "I'll be in touch. But don't hold your breath."

"WHAT'S HER NAME?" Bronwyn asked.

As soon as Sunny had landed in Florida— after spending one night in a New York hotel, then paying a hefty penalty to rebook her flight—she'd gone straight from the airport to Bron and Chris's house.

Sunny stirred her coffee. "I don't remember. I'm not sure I even heard it. After Nate dropped his bombshell I took off like a—wounded wife." She sighed. "No, I did hear but I forgot. I wanted to forget. Linda," she said, "or, no, Lisa."

"Sweet."

"Apparently she's some kind of domestic goddess," Sunny added.

Bron looked sympathetic. "You're wishing you had a black belt, so you could drop kick her through the window of that apartment—which, I should remind you, is still yours."

Sunny raised an eyebrow. "It's not her fault," she said. "It's mine."

"And how is that?"

She told Bron about Nate's accusations. "Not the first time he's used my career as a blunt object, but there's a certain truth to it. I did work a lot."

Sitting next to her on the sofa, Bron laid a hand over hers. "Some men have a terrible time dealing with a woman who's more successful than they are. Nate's job doesn't compare with yours." She paused. "Makes some kind of sense, really, that he's so keen to have kids. In family law he must see a ton of miserable children. Can't blame him for wanting to see happier faces at home."

"No," she had to agree. "I guess not."

"About his proposal, you're wise to take your time." Bron sipped her coffee, then set it aside. "Nate may want to buy a house, but you don't need to hurry your decision to make that happen."

"But if I drag my feet, he'll think I'm being vindictive."

"So let him."

"The worst part is, the offer isn't bad. I mean, he's right. I could never get anything in Manhattan for what we paid. Twice that might buy me a studio somewhere, but not in midtown. I can walk to work from there, Bron."

"Then you know what to do."

No, she didn't. "I wish it was that simple." Sunny played with her coffee spoon. "Nate might be willing to settle for less profit, but I'd still need to get a bigger mortgage. He acts as if I could get a new loan in a snap—which isn't easy for anyone right now—but along with that mortgage I'd also have to pay the homeowners association fee every month."

"Forget all that for a minute. It is really

quite the deal otherwise, Sunny. Nate wants to kick you the rest of the way to the curb, so he can live happily ever after." Sarcasm laced her words. "But even at a higher cost, if you can swing that, you'd be getting what you want, too."

"On one income? What if I lost my job? Making peace with Judge Ramsay was one thing, but then there's my boss, Ralph. He's determined to win another term. He might decide to crush me and my dreams."

Bron only smiled. "Sunny, don't obsess. You're the girl who came out of every test certain she'd failed and then got an A-plus."

"Who told you that?"

"Chris," she said. "He's always been proud of your academic achievements—also jealous."

"Jealous? Why? My brother never wanted to do anything but fish. I think he was born with a rod in hand. By the time he finished high school, Chris was already planning to buy his first boat and start to charter."

"And look how well he's done at what he loves. He just bought a beautiful boat to expand his business beyond fishing—once he gets it working properly." She grinned. "You were right, by the way. We talked, and my friends weren't the only thing that worried him. His charter business was off, and he was afraid we couldn't swing the new boat financially." Bron was blushing. "Anyway, we worked it out. I think I'll keep him."

Sunny smiled and threw her arms around Bron. Then she sat back and bit her lip. She still hadn't solved her own problem. If she took on the apartment by herself, and her job blew up, she'd be facing a default on the new, and much bigger, mortgage.

"Something else occurs to me," Bron said. "Are you sure you want to go back to that meat grinder in New York? You came home to sift through your feelings about the divorce—and, of course, the Wallace Day outcome—but maybe it's time for something different. Selfish suggestion," she admitted, "because we'd love to have you stay here." After a pregnant pause, she added, "And there's always my hunky brother."

"Griffin?" Sunny said. "Please. Does he look single to you?"

"Given time, he could be," Bron murmured.

"I wouldn't hold my breath," she replied. "But thanks for listening to my real estate woes."

Griffin wasn't in the market for a new relationship. *Neither am I.* Sunny had enough trouble dealing with the old one.

AFTER LEAVING BRON, Sunny drove to her parents' house. She dropped her carry-on in her father's den, then went to look for her mother. Her mom was, of course, in the kitchen putting the finishing touches on a roast. Sunny pulled her into a hug, avoiding the carving knife in her mother's right hand.

"I hate to disappoint you—" *again*, she added silently "—but it's not going to happen, Mom," she said and kissed her cheek.

Her mother drew back. "Your talk with Nate wasn't good?"

"Not very." Sunny told her about his request that she buy his half of the apartment.

Then her father wandered in from the garden. He had an uncanny ability to sense when a serious conversation—which obviously needed his input—was taking place. Was that where Sunny had gotten her gene to intervene?

"You call that a request? Sounds more like a demand." He wiped his grimy hands on one of her mother's dish towels, leaving streaks of dirt on the white linen.

"Jack, please," her mother said. "Use a paper towel."

"Sorry." He didn't sound sorry, and Sunny wondered if her parents were still arguing, though she hadn't heard any more fights about selling the house. "What did I tell you, Sunshine? The only person who benefits from that deal right now would be Nate. But if he'd take his share of the original value he must really need the cash. Why strap yourself so he and his new woman can buy the house of their dreams?"

Sunny was torn. Yes, she'd love to keep the home she'd furnished and decorated and have that short walk to work every day. Nate knew that and had used it to his advantage. But on the other hand, Bron was right. Walking into the apartment had been heart-wrenching. Did she really want to live there alone?

"Well," she said, "at least now I know." She turned to her mother, who was still fussing with the beef, adding sprigs of parsley that would only be limp by the time dinner was ready. "I guess I was never the best wife material."

Her dad put an arm around her shoulders. "Not true. Nate wasn't the best husband prospect. Good luck to him with the new one." He smiled. "No, good luck to her. If I were you, I'd tell him to find his money elsewhere."

"Dad, you're not being fair." Nate's accusations were still fresh in her mind. She had worked long hours, and she'd been hesitating about having a baby.

"Maybe not," he said. "I admit I'm biased. My only concern is for your welfare, and I think there's something you're missing here."

It didn't take Sunny long to see what that was. If she hadn't felt blindsided by her talk with Nate, she would have seen it earlier.

"If I did buy him out—and found it difficult to keep the apartment after all—I could put it on the market myself. And make a real killing."

Her father smiled. "Sure could. What did you and Nate pay for that place?"

Sunny told him and watched her father grimace. "I know, but that's New York," she said. "And in the meantime real estate there has gone through the roof."

"All the better." His gaze strayed to her mother, who was now putting a pot of peas and carrots on the stove. "If you had to sell later, you'd benefit the most."

And that was another point. The prospect violated Sunny's sense of fair play. "No, Dad.

Nate might have broken my heart, but that doesn't mean I should cheat him now." She hadn't been able to shake that sense of imbalance since she'd faced Nate in the apartment.

"Careful, Sunshine. Don't let him guilt you into making another mistake."

"But don't you see? I was the one who wouldn't answer Nate's calls. If I had, we might have settled this quickly and fairly. I did work too much. I did block him out whenever he wanted to talk about a family—all because it didn't suit my time line."

"Oh, Sunny," her mother said.

"Mom, I know you want a grandchild. I'd love to give you one. But Nate and I didn't work out, and now I'm hardly in a position to grant your wish." She gave her mom a sympathetic smile. "If only I could."

Someday. After Sunny put her life in order. Which meant dealing with the apartment. She could sort her emotions later, her own disappointment that things hadn't worked out and weren't going to.

"I've made my decision. I'm going to sell the apartment outright," she said.

"Now you're being wise," her father said. "Cut the last tie. Take your profit and move on."

"That's what's fair," Sunny said. "Nate will get more in the end, too. We'll split the profit fifty-fifty based on current market value. If that means he and Lisa have to lose the house they want now, then wait to find another one, so be it. It's the right decision for me."

Which left Sunny without a home of her own...

CHAPTER EIGHT

AMANDA HATED FLORIDA—but not always. She didn't hate it quite so much when she was spending time by the pool. She put her towel on the lounge next to Dixie's, then lay down under the hot afternoon sun. No SPF30? She could almost hear her dad giving one of his too-quiet lectures about preventing serious burns, but he wasn't around. He was somewhere in the complex fixing something or other. Big surprise. For now, she was on her own, and she wanted a tan to match Dixie's. Since she was forced to live at the Palm Breeze Court Apartments, at least for now, she wanted to belong.

There was one advantage to living here. The swimming pool was deeper than most, probably because it was so old that any newer regulations didn't apply. It was also longer than the one at Dixie's house.

Her eyes shaded by Michael Kors sunglasses, Dixie murmured, "Mmm, this sun feels good." She tugged at the top of her American flag-patterned bikini, and Amanda almost sighed. Her own suit was what her dad called "modest," appropriate for her age, he insisted. The one-piece navy blue tank made her cringe. Boring. Just like Amanda? No wonder everyone at school ignored her except Dixie.

Then there were her so-called friends back in Boston. Amanda hadn't heard a word from any of them, even her BFF—former best friend forever—all last summer. No one had bothered to text her one of those stupid back-to-school pictures either. They were all gone, like Amanda's mom.

"Did you hear what I said?" Dixie's lazy voice brought her back poolside. "I'm thinking of getting a tattoo."

"Um. Where?" Amanda asked, as if she'd been paying attention all along.

Dixie pointed to her curvy hip. "Cool, huh? It will be there, but no one will see it—unless I want them to." She had a faint smile.

Amanda snuck a glance at Dixie's coral lip gloss. She was more than ready for makeup, too, like the mascara and bronzer Dixie often wore, but Dad said no. That's all he ever said.

"I'm thinking a butterfly," Dixie went on,

"but that's so yesterday. I know three girls at school who have those. Let me see. Maybe a flower, then. Or, no, something really edgy. In black. How about a map of Florida?"

Amanda didn't think that was a good idea, but she didn't say so.

"I'm not getting a tattoo until I'm eighteen," she said.

Dixie groaned. "Don't tell me. Your *father* wouldn't approve. I'm glad my dad lets me do whatever I want."

Amanda had no answer to that, either. She rolled on to her front to make sure her back tanned, too. "You should have heard my father when we went to that cookout," she said, voice muffled by her folded arms.

"He actually made you apologize about the watch?"

"He totally did," she murmured. "I still haven't recovered."

For a long moment, there was silence. In the distance Amanda heard the growl of a lawn mower. Why even bother? The grass here, unlike the soft green carpet of lawn in Philly or Boston, was coarse and weird-looking even if it did smell good. And it wasn't her dad mowing. It was that boy he sometimes hired for the easier jobs around the complex. Dixie had noticed him earlier. She'd made sure he saw her, too.

"I wonder what your dad would think if you dated that lawn guy," Dixie said, as if she'd read Amanda's mind. "I bet those ear gauges would go over well. Not."

Amanda lifted her head to look at Dixie. "Ear gauges?"

"You don't know? Those black discs people put in their earlobes. They make a hole, and it gets bigger with every set of discs you get. I hear it hurts. A lot."

"Gross."

"I can't believe you didn't see them." Dixie smiled. "But then, I guess you were focused on the rest of him." She paused, lowering her sunglasses so she could meet Amanda's gaze. "How many boys have you kissed? Tell the truth, Mandi."

"Not that many," she said, crossing her fingers that Dixie wouldn't guess the truth. "I like to save that for guys I'm serious about."

Dixie laughed. "Now I really don't believe you. We're not talking about some peck on the cheek at a birthday party," she said. "I mean real kisses."

Amanda merely stared at her, not knowing what to say. She'd never been on a date.

Even her mom had said she was too young for anything but a group outing with chaperones. Who even thought about that these days? Only her parents.

Dixie dropped the subject.

"What about smoking, then? Have you ever done that?"

"Who hasn't?" Amanda said, trying for her best jaded tone. She sat bolt upright, adjusted the too-wide straps of her tank suit, then headed for the pool. "I'd rather take a swim."

Dixie was right behind her. "See those two guys coming this way?" They had left the nearby cabana, a ramshackle building no one ever used, and spotted Dixie. Or was that one guy looking at Amanda? She tried not to blush. Were they smoking in there? Dixie said, "Let's see if they want to play Marco Polo."

She did a swan dive into the pool's deep end before Amanda could move. She doubted her dad would want her talking to the older boys. But then he was still working on one of his maintenance projects—as if he didn't miss his big job in Boston.

Amanda took off running and cannonballed into the water. Her father would never know.

LATER THAT AFTERNOON Sunny sat across from Laura Carson. Seeing Nate had made her realize she couldn't keep ignoring Laura's calls. While she was in town, she had an obligation to see her, at least once. Laura had been her best friend. They had been inseparable. Like Amanda with Dixie.

"How does it feel to be back here in the 'burbs'?" Laura gestured at the shaded restaurant patio. Neutral territory, Sunny had hoped. Laura still had the same dark hair, but she didn't wear it in a ponytail now. Her brown eyes shone as they always had. She looked content, unruffled. "This is a far cry from the corridors of power in New York City." She hesitated. "Car pools, Cub Scout meetings, soccer practice, ballet lessons. Welcome to my world."

Her words reminded Sunny of how far apart they'd grown. Laura had married right after high school. She had three kids now, two boys and a girl, and her husband was a cop. When Laura showed her some pictures on her smartphone, Sunny tried to suppress her envy. Laura's neat home, on a quiet, tree-lined street not far from Sunny's parents' house, obviously suited her.

"It's a good world," Sunny said, "except for

the lumpy bed in my father's den. And I'm not exactly walking the corridors of power."

"No swanky law office with a gorgeous view of Manhattan?"

Sunny almost winced. The one window in her small office gave her a view of a brick wall. Her desk chair creaked, and she'd been eyeing Ralph's corner suite for years.

"Actually, as a government employee, the only swanky law offices I see belong to the defense lawyers or judges. That's a far more rarified atmosphere, believe me. You should see my office," she finished. "The only good thing about it is the wall of bookshelves crammed with legal volumes." She waited a moment, then asked, "What happened to your dream of being an archeologist?"

Laura twirled the straw in her iced tea. "I didn't even get to college." Her smile grew wistful. "But I'd already met my Mr. Right, and let's say I was ready to have my own home. Even at eighteen." With a small frown she studied Sunny. "I was sad to hear about your divorce, and from what you've said about selling your apartment, I guess that's still going on."

"Yes," she said. "Nate's furious that I won't buy his half of the apartment. Perhaps he'll see reason after some time's passed. I wish we could resolve this without his losing the house he wants in Connecticut, but I doubt a sale will happen in time."

"So. What's next?"

Sunny had been avoiding the topic all through lunch. She'd put on a good face for Laura's benefit, staying clear of anything more than catching up and the sale of the apartment. Which, of course, would mean going back to New York soon to clean out her belongings. After her boss's call earlier, that seemed like an omen.

"I'm staying here. For a while longer," she announced.

Laura's face brightened. "You don't look that happy, but from my standpoint that's wonderful." She toasted Sunny and said, "We can be 'ladies who lunch' more often and talk about everything we've missed for—gosh, how many years has it been?"

Sunny knew exactly. She guessed Laura did, too.

"I left home for good two weeks after my college graduation," Sunny said.

"Ah, yes. Law school at Harvard was waiting."

"And, as it turned out, Nate," she said. They'd met her first week there.

Laura's smile faded. "But, Sunny, that's not what I meant. Our friendship had petered out years before you went to college. No, even before high school."

Sunny had been Amanda's age when she began to withdraw from their friendship. She still felt guilty for leaving Laura behind and not being able to explain why.

Sunny wanted to set the record straight. But that would mean hurting Laura even more than she already had.

"You know how girls are at that age," she said, thinking again of Amanda. "How fickle they can be."

"But we were so close." Laura's eyes darkened. She smoothed a hand over her simple summer dress. Its subtle print in cream, taupe and black suited her coloring and her still-trim figure. The years had been kind to her. Sunny was glad. Yet the hurt in Laura's eyes gave Sunny another twinge of guilt. "We did everything together," Laura said.

Not quite. A shadow seemed to pass over her, and Sunny's palms grew damp.

"I'm sorry, Laura. I ended our friendship at a difficult time for me. I didn't mean to hurt you," she said. And the past swept over her like a tidal surge.

Nine years old, Sunny is long-limbed and skinny. She sits down on a bus stop bench to rest before walking the last few blocks. On such a hot afternoon it's not easy pushing the wicker baby carriage her grandmother gave her, now piled with Sunny's dolls and all their clothes. An older woman smiles, asks her about them. Then, before she has a chance to answer, the car pulls up at the curb. And Sunny's heart begins to pound.

"Need a ride?" The man leans over to smile at her through the window.

"No," she says. "I'm fine. Almost there."

He won't take no for an answer. "It's too hot to walk. I'm going your way."

The woman on the bench studies them. But despite her frown, she doesn't say a word and neither does Sunny. What else can she do? He's already put her carriage in the trunk, then slammed it shut.

Sunny has no choice. She gets into the car. Again.

Sunny felt overwhelmed by the memory until Laura's voice pulled her back to reality. "My parents kept asking why you didn't come around anymore. Remember my mom's Saturday morning baking marathons?"

Sunny's mouth watered. Or was it the fact that she felt nauseated? She was afraid she'd be sick and embarrass herself.

Her voice quavered. "She made the best cakes and pies. And her breads were to die for. But I think her doughnuts were my favorite."

"Mine, too! Right out of the deep fryer she'd set on the kitchen counter. You and I would hover too close to the heat, waiting for the first ones to be done."

There. A better memory. "I loved her doughnut holes with sprinkled sugar."

"Yes! I'd almost forgotten those," Laura said.

Sunny shifted on her chair. She swallowed. And for a moment they were friends again. "Does she still bake?"

"Not as much," Laura said, "unless the kids are at her house."

A cold shiver ran through her. But what else could Sunny say? If she didn't ask the question Laura was expecting... "How are your parents?"

"My mother's fine." She hesitated, then added, "She and my father divorced, though, right after I got married. And after their split, my father—"

"I'm sorry," Sunny said again, her pulse racing.

"Don't be." Laura reached for her hand. "Let's put whatever happened behind us. We'll start over," she said with a tentative smile. "How long do you think you'll be here? Sleeping on your dad's sofa bed?"

Ralph's earlier call ran through her mind again. She told Laura about the Wallace Day verdict, her original reason—one of them— for coming back. "Apparently Day is unhappy about his 'sentence.' My boss says he hasn't adjusted to the facility upstate. Believe me, it's pretty fancy, more like a spa or country club than a prison. I guess Day didn't count on being in there with a bunch of 'loonies.' His word. But instead of blaming the jury for sending him there, he blames me. I think he's figured out that his defense backfired. He could easily end up spending more time in that facility than he would have in prison."

"Is he violent?"

"Oh, yes. I don't think Ana Ramirez was his only victim…" She paused. "He threatened to do the same to me."

Laura shivered. "Sounds like this guy needs a straitjacket."

"No, I still think he's sane." She took a breath, feeling too close to Wallace Day again and, with Laura there, to her own past. "I have to admit, the things he said rattled me." She took another breath. "For now, I'm to keep a low profile. My boss is afraid he'll get to the press again and they'll have a field day with the story."

Laura squeezed her hand. "Makes my gig as suburban soccer mom look pretty good, Sunny."

She couldn't disagree. "I'll be telecommuting from here. For now."

"Lucky you."

Sunny wasn't so sure. She wondered if even a padded cell could keep Wallace Day from getting to her if he really wanted to.

In the cramped nook that served as Griffin's office, he sat at his desk, going over the day's disastrous events. He'd nearly completed the repairs to Miss Carrie's patio when he heard laughing and shouts coming from the pool.

Amanda and Dixie had been playing Marco Polo with two boys—one, seventeen, the other, eighteen. Griffin had sent them packing, and Dixie had followed soon after. No way was his thirteen-year-old daughter going to "hang out" with those much older guys.

Now Amanda was pouting in her room. If she was on the phone with Dixie, they were whispering. From the kitchen the smell of cooking hamburgers, onion and garlic filled the air.

He clicked an icon on his laptop and Facebook appeared. Dozens of messages and posts scrolled on the screen. Griffin hadn't checked his account in days, but now he had a fresh sense of purpose.

"Josh," he called, "turn down the volume, okay?" His son was watching a video on the iPad in the living room. "I'm trying to work."

Griffin created a new private message, selected one of Rachel's friends from a list, and began to type. Hi, Deb. I was wondering... have you heard from...

The doorbell rang.

"I'll get it," Griffin said because Josh was already scrambling off the sofa. If the boys from this afternoon stood outside, Griffin would deal with them more harshly this time. Ready for battle, like one of Josh's Transformer action figures, he opened the door.

Griffin couldn't wipe away his frown fast enough, and Sunny took a quick step back. She was wearing a green-and-white sundress paired with a light apricot sweater. Not much protection from the cool evening breeze, but the sweater showed off her lightly tanned forearms. Florida seemed to agree with her.

"Bad time?" she asked.

"No." He moved away from the door. "Come on in."

Seeing her, Josh abandoned the iPad. He bounded off the sofa into the small entryway. "Hi, Mrs. Donovan! Are you and Grandpa Jack having another party?"

She shook her head and smiled. "Not this weekend, Josh. But my dad says you can come over to play horseshoes anytime."

His face lit up. "Anytime?"

"Yes."

He turned to Griffin. "Right now?"

"Not now, buddy. It's almost dinnertime. Take your movie into your room, okay? I need to talk to Mrs. Donovan."

Whatever she wanted, he couldn't quite get over his surprise that she'd shown up on his doorstep.

He waited until Josh had gone to his room with the tablet before he ushered Sunny into the living room. She looked tense, which made Griffin uneasy, too. "Amanda's not in trouble, is she?"

"Not at all."

Griffin didn't agree—after the pool party she was in plenty of hot water with him. But Sunny clearly had something else on her mind. Instead of continuing into the living room, she glanced toward his laptop. The cursor was still blinking on the message form.

"I am interrupting," she said. "I won't keep you."

"That's okay. Burgers aren't done yet." He took a closer look at her and noticed dark circles under her eyes. "You okay?"

"This hasn't been the best few days," she admitted, then looked at the computer again. "But obviously, I've caught you at a bad time." She turned to go. "I'll come back tomorrow."

"No, now is fine. Great, in fact." He started toward the desk to shut down the laptop. "Have a seat in the living room. Be right with you."

Griffin had intended to get them both something to drink, but she followed him toward the kitchen as if she wanted to say what she'd come for, then leave. Instead, she stopped at his desk.

"I was about to launch a new investigation," he said. "Playing private detective isn't one of my skills, but that's what it will take to find Rachel. I haven't done much lately. It's time to see again if her friends have heard from her."

"I'd think digging into someone's life would be second nature to a television journalist. An A-list news anchor."

"Ex-anchor," he said with only a twinge of regret.

He sat down, and she leaned over his shoulder, her light perfume reminding him of fresh-cut flowers. "Facebook?"

"Why not? It's the source of all information these days—even for the media. It's also one of the first things recommended by any article on how to find someone." Griffin turned and almost brushed against her. He felt the heat rise in his face. "I bet you're a pretty good investigator yourself, Counselor."

"I've done my share." She paused. "I'm about to do it all over again."

"You're going back to New York?" Already? The news didn't sit well. But she wouldn't have come here merely to tell him goodbye. They weren't exactly friends, even after their talk at the barbecue.

"No, I'm staying. Temporarily." She told Griffin about Wallace Day and her opportunity to telecommute. "My boss wants me to review some upcoming cases before trial while I'm here. So it seems we're both using technology to get the job done."

Easing away from him, she turned her back on the computer screen. "I didn't mean to pry... The reason I'm here is... I'm putting my apartment on the market and I...." She didn't go on.

Griffin allowed himself a light touch on her arm. But Sunny didn't continue. "And?" he prompted.

She gazed around the room, then at the blinking cursor on the computer.

"In a minute," she said. "Do you have any leads about your wife?"

"Nothing but dead ends."

"Where else, other than her friends, have you looked?"

"The usual," he said. "Made a police report in Boston, first thing."

"But there wasn't much they could do," she guessed. "Rachel's an adult. She was free to go wherever she pleased. It's not against the law to disappear."

Griffin had given the police everything he could. Photos of Rachel, a description. The places she might go, the people she knew. Nothing had turned up. "I registered with a bunch of websites, services with databases on missing persons, but that didn't work, either."

"None of her friends could help?"

"Nope. No one had seen her or talked to her then—or since. So far. Her Facebook account's still active, but she never posts. I've called hospitals, coroners, put up fliers in Philly, Boston and here…no luck," he said. "Once we moved to Florida, I let the PI I'd hired go."

"What about the local media?"

Griffin sighed. Rehashing his many efforts to find Rachel only reminded him that so far he'd failed. "Played that card, too. They seemed willing to spread the word, but Rachel's never lived here, and after one slot on the evening news—as a professional courtesy, I suppose—they lost interest. My station in Boston did the same. With no evidence of foul play, it's hardly a big story. It's not as if someone snatched her off the street or from the grocery store." He paused, half unwilling to admit the truth. "The honest answer?" He took another breath. "She left the house—and us—then kept going. If something happened to her, I haven't found any record of it."

"I'm sorry, Griffin." She looked at him for a long moment. "Good luck with your search. I'd better be going. It smells as if your dinner is ready."

Before he could take in the fact that she was leaving, she hurried toward the door. At the last second she turned and nearly ran into Griffin.

"Whoa," he said. "You didn't come here to listen to me talk about Rachel."

"Oh. Right," she said as if she'd forgotten. Griffin watched her ease the kink in her lower back. "I was wondering, since I'm selling my place and planning to work from here... I'll need somewhere to stay." She paused, then must have decided to go for it. "Do you still have a vacancy?"

CHAPTER NINE

"WHERE DOES THIS GO, Sunny?"

Chris's question brought her mind back from another place. Wiping a hand across her forehead, she bit her lip and looked around the apartment a few times before tilting her head to the left. Her bedroom would be just the spot for the hand-painted chest she'd picked out years ago for the New York apartment. This smaller one-bedroom unit at the Palm Breeze Court suited her current needs, yet Sunny was already having second thoughts.

Living near Griffin and his children, seeing him every day, might not be the wisest choice. For a woman who made big decisions without a qualm, Sunny was waffling now, even over the small ones.

"Unless you think it would look better in that corner of the living room," she said to Bron, who had paused in the middle of the room. Chris was holding up the other end of the chest.

"Make up your mind, Sis."

"I'm trying." She sank on to the sofa, exhausted. In the past week she'd made another trip to Manhattan. Cleaning out her share of the furnishings, choosing which to ship to Florida and which went into storage, not to mention trying to avoid a grouchy Nate, had taken its toll.

"Better pick soon." Bron eased her end of the chest down on to the floor. "My muscles are screaming."

"You offered to help," Sunny reminded her with a smile. "And I'm more than grateful. If Mom and Dad had come today, he'd take over, Mom would fuss and I'd be a nervous wreck."

"More than you already are," Chris murmured.

"Bedroom," Sunny said, pointing to the other end of the small apartment. "See? My mind's made up."

After the chest was in place, Chris wandered back into the living room, where Sunny was arranging books on the built-in shelves. A set of law volumes, some do-it-yourself decorating books, and a shelf of fiction.

Chris peered over her shoulder. "Grisly," he said with a mock shudder.

"I like thrillers. True crime, too."

"No wonder you became a prosecutor. But isn't this a busman's holiday?"

If he only knew. Sunny had her work cut out for her reviewing those upcoming trials, and she was still having nightmares about Wallace Day. Chris left her to her task, then headed for the next piece of furniture in the U-Haul van.

She and Chris had driven the rental truck from New York, and to her surprise the trip had been fun. Her brother knew how to tease her out of any mood, and by the time they'd reached Florida, she'd even stopped wanting to cry. Progress of a sort.

She set another book on a shelf and turned back to the open box. Then from outside she heard Chris's voice.

"Hey, Griff. Just in time."

A minute later Griffin's broad shoulders filled her doorway, and he and Chris walked into the apartment. Each of them carried a stack of boxes. "Clothing," her brother said.

"Bedroom. Thanks." She was supposed to

be standing by the door, directing each load as it came in, but she'd gotten distracted.

Part of her wanted to pack everything back up—the part that was actually willing to sleep on her dad's sofa bed for the duration—but she knew she needed to settle in and begin this next phase of her life. Whatever it turned out to be.

Sunny hated uncertainty.

When Griffin passed by a little too close, she quickly sidestepped him, and he frowned. "Wasn't going to touch you," he said with a glance at her face.

Sunny schooled her features into a calm mask. "I'm not worried. Why would I be worried?" she said, but her heart was beating faster.

She watched him for a moment, letting her eyes rest on his strong shoulders and the long line of his back. Griffin was a good man. He'd look out for her, just as he did for all his tenants. It might be nice having him around. But he had his own burdens to bear—and that endless search for Rachel.

A few minutes later he came out of her bedroom with Chris, the two men sharing a laugh about something.

"Truck's empty," Chris told her. "You're

moved in now." He paused. "Let's all have dinner somewhere."

"Chris, I have plans," Sunny said.

"What? Arranging and rearranging your law books?"

"Sorry," Griffin said with another glance at Sunny. "The kids are waiting. Maybe another time," he added—Sunny thought—to be polite.

Bronwyn hugged her. "C'mon, Captain," she said, pulling on Chris's shirtsleeve. "We need to stop at your parents' house. By now your mother's in a grief state because Sunny left home. Again. We'd better try to cheer her up."

Sunny watched them walk down the sidewalk to the truck. Chris would return it and they'd pick up Bron's car, which she'd left in the U-Haul lot. She supposed they would urge her parents to join them for dinner, which did make Sunny feel better.

She hadn't intended to scuttle Chris's idea. He'd meant well, and it was just dinner. But she wasn't sure she'd made the right decision about this apartment.

At the moment, listening to her parents quarrel almost had appeal.

GRIFFIN DRIED ANOTHER pan, then passed it to Amanda. She put the cookware in the lower cabinet without saying a word.

Since he'd short-circuited the pool party, she'd hardly spoken to him. Griffin's questions about homework, school, next weekend's pep rally—really, football in eighty degree weather?—and what they should get Josh for his birthday, which fell right after New Year's, were often met with silence. He was becoming used to her occasional grunts and shrugs.

Good thing she didn't know he'd taken down the license plate number of the car those two boys had been driving. If necessary, he could call a cop friend for information about them.

He tried again.

"You think Josh would like that insect-collecting kit we saw the other day?"

"Maybe."

"It comes with a book, too. He can't read yet, but you or I could read it to him."

"Wow. Just what I've always wanted—to tutor a five-year-old."

It was the most she'd said to him in days. "Amanda. Don't take your bad mood out on your little brother. Or me."

She was clearly itching for a fight. He set the next pan he'd been drying on the counter. "What's the problem?"

"Do you have any idea how humiliating it was when you made Dixie and the boys leave the pool? Everyone at school has been whispering behind my back." She slammed the cabinet door. "Pretty soon Dixie won't even talk to me!"

If the kids were talking, they'd learned about the incident from Dixie. Griffin glanced toward the hall. Josh had already gone to bed, and Griffin didn't hear anything from his room, but that didn't mean Josh wasn't listening. "Keep your voice down. To be honest, Amanda, I don't care whether Dixie talks to you. She's not the kind of friend you should have."

"Why not?"

"She's...well, she seems older than you are—acts older, at least."

Her cheeks turned pink; she knew what he meant. The older boys. No one was going to win this argument. Still, he'd had his fill of tiptoeing around her silence. They hadn't shared a pleasant meal since before the Cabots' cookout—and her admission about

the stolen watch. Which reminded him of
Sunny.

As of this afternoon, she was living here
at the Palm Breeze Court. That presented all
sorts of possibilities—and dangers. He liked
Sunny, and for that reason he'd been right to
avoid dinner with her, Chris and Bron. He
had Amanda to deal with right here.

He cleared his throat. "It's not only how
Dixie acts…it's her attitude. And those boys
at the pool—"

"They must be wild. They'd probably force
me to do all sorts of *inappropriate* things.
Why didn't I think of that?"

Griffin would have snapped at her, but
he kept quiet. He could tell by the way her
eyes avoided his that she had her doubts, too.
Something else was going on with Dixie,
something she wouldn't tell him about.

He made a mental note to mow the grass in
the complex himself. The kid with the holes
in his earlobes had seemed okay, but he didn't
want him around Amanda either. Was that
simply a precaution or blossoming paranoia?

"All I'm saying is, why not spend time with
other girls at school, too?"

"I have Dixie." Abandoning the dishes, she

marched into the hall, then called back. "We want to go to the mall on Saturday. Will you drive us?"

Griffin stared after her. He would drive them, if only to be sure that's where they were going. He didn't trust Dixie not to have some other plan. And the girls would have to agree to a pick-up time. That wouldn't win him any friends, but he wasn't going to let his thirteen-year-old child run the show.

Too bad, though, that every issue these days seemed fraught with conflict. If he pushed too hard, he would lose her. Like Rachel.

Down the hall Amanda's door closed, not quite a slam but not soft enough to keep from waking Josh, either. Griffin winced.

When he didn't hear Josh get out of bed, he went to his desk. If only he could find Rachel. At the computer he searched for any responses from her friends. The first was from Boston.

Sorry, Griffin. I still haven't heard a word. How can she have just disappeared? I miss her, too. Take care. The evening news here isn't the same without you.

His old job, his old life, seemed farther away with each day. The second message from a friend in Philly didn't make him feel any better.

I wish I had good news for you. But the last time I saw Rachel was at lunch a few weeks before you moved to Boston. If I do hear or see anything, I'll let you know. Hugs for the kids from me and Tony.

Griffin sat back in his chair. During the first year without Rachel, he'd kept in touch with her friends almost every day. But then he'd left town, and her trail—such as it was—had grown even colder. He'd all but stopped being able to force himself to pursue the same list of family and friends and acquaintances.

They'd all moved on with their lives.

Still, Josh needed Rachel. So did Amanda. He turned to the keyboard again and hit the one name on the list he'd been avoiding for months. Uncle Theo.

Rachel and Theo had been close until the move to Boston. In the old neighborhood near Philly, Griffin and Rachel had lived in his mother's house right next door to Theo.

They'd all gone back and forth as if there weren't any walls between them. Theo had been there when the kids were born. He'd just taught Josh how to use a toddler-sized hammer when Griffin's new job offer came in.

A month later, Griffin and his family were in Boston. Theo was on his own.

Not that Griffin and Rachel hadn't begged him to relocate. Theo had refused. He'd never approved of Griffin's broadcasting career, just as he'd always been resentful of his brother, Griffin's father, becoming a journalist instead of a tradesman like Theo. Griffin's move to Boston, combined with that earlier "betrayal," had cut their last ties. Griffin hadn't spoken to him in…he didn't know how long.

He started to write an email, then stopped. He owed his uncle more than that, and Theo checked his ancient computer only once in a while. Griffin reached for his phone. Better to try him direct.

To his surprise, Theo answered on the first ring.

"Hey," Griffin said, trying for a hearty tone of voice. "It's your long-lost nephew. How are you, Uncle Theo?"

"Still hurt," he said. "Florida treating you any better than Boston, Hotshot?"

"It's different," Griffin said, wincing at the nickname. "Tell me about you."

"Still here. Same old place. Those people who bought your mother's house have torn out the whole back wall. Put in a glass slider and a big patio. Every Saturday night they throw a party. A man can't get any sleep."

His voice threw Griffin back into the past they'd once shared. His mom had wanted a newer house in a better neighborhood, but the sale had fallen through when his father died. For years she'd struggled to hold on to the old house and what was left of their family. Uncle Theo had always been there to help Griffin try to become the man she needed him to be.

"Remember when you taught me how to build that birdhouse? I was all thumbs. Now Josh wants to learn."

"A balsa wood kit from the discount store." Theo paused. "It's still out in the yard—not your mother's. Mine. I rescued it," he said, "before those new people moved in."

Griffin didn't know what to say except, "Thanks."

Theo broke the short silence. "How are the kids?"

"Growing up," he said. "Amanda looks more and more like her mom." He frowned, discomfited as always by the reminder. "She's been a handful…" *Ever since we moved*, Griffin thought. But he wouldn't admit his frustration with her or remind Theo that he'd walked away from his uncle's support. "Anyway. I was wondering…"

"I haven't heard from Rachel, Griff."

"Yeah," he said on a wave of disappointment. "I figured that. Just thought I'd check. The neighbors ever ask about her?"

"All the time, the few who are left. They ask about you, too. But the neighborhood's changing. The old people—like me—are dying off, and new ones, like those two next door, are moving in. Renovating, tearing down… Would you believe the old place on the corner is a pile of rubble now? Gonna be a new house there, three stories, four thousand square feet. It'll gobble up the whole yard."

"You working on the site?"

Theo ran his own small construction company. He built decks and did repair work, like Griffin now, but sometimes he put up a spec house or two to make money. "Not me, no. They have a big-time architect, huge crew," he said, "but I got enough to keep me busy." He added, "What are you up to?"

"Well, as manager—and chief maintenance guy—at the apartment complex where we live, I'm never bored."

There was a longer silence. Then, "I didn't think you'd last a week in that job, Hotshot."

"I remember everything you taught me, Theo." To his surprise, he had.

Theo laughed. "That's a far cry from the birdhouse or that paper route...even from your first real job as my assistant until you decided to bail out and become a news junkie."

Griffin cleared his throat. "Everything has its time, Theo."

"Kind of tickles me in a way. You being back on the job."

"I am," he said. That fact always surprised him, too.

He and Theo had run out of small talk, and always there was that gulf between them. Theo's disappointment that Griffin hadn't followed in his footsteps; that Griffin had somehow driven Rachel away.

"You'll keep your eyes and ears open? At some point Rachel might appear on your doorstep."

"My ears and eyes are always open. I'll let you know."

"Thanks, Uncle Theo."

Griffin had done what he'd needed to do, but Theo obviously hadn't forgiven him. For an instant he fought the urge to beg his uncle to come to Florida to help. To be with the kids.

He hung up with a fresh sense of guilt.

The search had never been easy. With time it was only getting harder. How was he ever going to find her?

Good luck with your search, Sunny had said.

That only reminded Griffin that she was living here now, where he might see her every day. He imagined her lying by the pool, her sunglasses concealing the look in her eyes. Or carrying grocery bags from her car to her apartment, her legs moving smoothly—away from him. Another woman who didn't seem to welcome him in her life.

Just like Amanda. Just like Rachel.

"How do you like it?" Sunny asked.

She turned a circle in her living room, trying to see the apartment through her mother's eyes. Not bad for a short-term rental. She'd even leased a car because she couldn't keep borrowing her father's Bronco. In just a few days, she'd made a new, if temporary, home.

Her mother was her first visitor. Sunny had pulled out all the stops, baking chocolate chip cookies—the kind that came in a roll from the grocery store—and making sun tea as soon as Mom had phoned to ask if she could stop by. They hadn't yet sat down to enjoy the refreshments, since the grand tour had been her mother's first order of business.

Sunny couldn't help wondering if that was the only item on her agenda.

"I like it," her mom said. "I miss having you in the house, but I've told your father a hundred times to get rid of that old sofa."

"It must hold a special place in his heart."

Her mother scoffed. "So does the house—and our still-missing roof."

Sunny shook her head. "They haven't fixed it yet?"

"All the roofers are swamped. Ours is apparently not high on the list." She paused. "I do wish they'd gotten to us before now. You could be in your old room and—although this is lovely—you wouldn't have to pay rent."

Sunny indicated the nearby dining nook, which—following Griffin's lead—she was using as an office. "This works for me," she said. "I even started my case reviews this morning." And she'd managed to get some of her old mojo back.

Her mother frowned. "I'm glad the DA suggested you stay here."

"I'll be keeping out of Ralph's way, too," she said. "He didn't seem to blame me for the result in Wallace Day's trial, but ours isn't the easiest relationship."

"Maybe you'd be wise not to challenge him, Sunny. There's no need to run for DA in the next few years. You're younger than he is. You can afford to wait him out."

"Not if I want to keep my career on track. Spending time as an assistant DA was fine in the beginning. I need to take the next step up or get left behind."

Her mother sat on a stool at the counter. "You know how proud I am of you, how proud your father is, too. But are you sure about this?"

"The day I arrived in Jacksonville, no, but things have changed. Our apartment went on the market today. If I'm lucky, it will sell soon—and I'll be rid of the emotional baggage I've collected over the past year. I'll be ready to do my job at a higher level."

"Well," her mother murmured. "I know nothing about the law. I've only met your boss once or twice—last year at that office Christmas party in New York—but be careful, Sunny. You have nothing to prove with me or your father."

Sunny put the cookies on a plate. "I'm not trying to prove anything," she said.

Her mother shook her head. "You could have had a good law practice right here." She paused. "Something drove you to New York years ago."

"Yes, Mom. The job I wanted." Instantly she regretted her sharp tone of voice. She poured two glasses of sun tea, then joined her mother at the counter. "Let's talk about something else. How's the battle over your own move going?"

"It's not," she admitted. "Why your father refuses to see reason, I can't say. But I'm ready for a change. I've been clearing out closets ever since the hurricane—and it's quite freeing." She tilted her head to the side. "You've just done that with the apartment. Maybe you should consider a total relocation, too."

Her mother knew how to circle back to the topic she really wanted to discuss. "I did think of that at first," Sunny said. "After Nate announced he was through with our marriage, and after the Day verdict…" She smiled to lighten the moment. "Then I got home, found the roof over my old room gone, and ended up on the sofa bed. If that wasn't enough to chase me right back to Manhattan, I don't know what would be."

"Now you're mocking me."

"No I'm not. But, Mom—" she tried again "—do you really want to leave the house— the place you've lived for much of your married life—and start over somewhere else? Believe me, it's not easy. You'd need new doctors, a new dentist, another bank, a financial advisor…and that's only the small stuff."

Her mother sipped her tea, then set it aside. "Sometimes we have to begin again," she said. "For me, that time is now, while I'm young enough, healthy enough to undertake a major move." Like Nate, having kids with Lisa? "You've already cut some ties in New York, Sunny. Is it that hard? Selling the apartment?"

"Hard enough," she said.

"Nate has moved on. So should you. By the

way, how did you get a three-month lease for this apartment?"

"I twisted Griffin's arm," she said. "We started out at a year, which is the usual, then negotiated to six months, and finally I nailed him down for three. He had four vacancies until I walked in."

"Rentals can be difficult in the shoulder season. But what if you don't stay even that long?"

Her mother hadn't missed the lack of clutter in the new apartment. Sunny had unpacked very few photographs—none with Nate—and she'd left most of the mementoes she did bring in their cartons.

"If I need to leave sooner, I'll pay off my lease." She hesitated, choosing another cookie from the plate. "In the meantime, you know you're always welcome." Sunny's pulse missed a beat. "If you need to get away—for any reason—you can stay here."

"Thank you, dear." Her mother looked puzzled. "Why would I need to get away? From your *father*?"

"No, of course not." She didn't know what had made her say that. But, all at once, it had seemed important.

"Sometimes I don't understand my own

daughter," her mom said, "but I also wonder…"

Sunny hesitated before asking, "Wonder what?"

"Whether it's me who might need a safe place—or you." Her gaze softened. "I wonder if you're running toward something after all—becoming DA—or if instead, dear, you're running away."

CHAPTER TEN

AFTER HER MOTHER LEFT, Sunny gave up trying to review more files from those upcoming trials. She pushed away from her laptop, changed clothes, then went out to the pool. Now this was an amenity she could get used to.

The fall weather was still hot, and the sky was a brilliant blue. Normally, on a weekday in late afternoon, the area would be empty; the younger residents were at work, and the older people rarely sunbathed. But today she wasn't alone.

A mother was playing with her baby in the shallow end. Sunlight sparkled on the water's surface. The air smelled of hibiscus and the multihued bougainvillea that was everywhere. Sunny exchanged a few words with the woman and admired her child before moving on. She chose a nearby lounge, intent upon relaxing. Had her mother come too close to the truth?

Instead, you're running away.

She laid her towel on a chaise—and heard giggles. Near the deep end of the pool, Amanda Lattimer and a friend occupied adjacent lounges. The girls were huddled together, forming an arch. Hiding something between them.

None of my business.

But the whispering continued. "Come *on*, Mandi. Before my stepmom comes."

Amanda watched the gate to the pool area for a minute, then shifted her gaze to the buildings that surrounded it.

"I can do it," she said. "I'm just not sure I should. If my dad sees us—"

"He won't. Remember? He picked your brother up at school, then took him to the dentist for a checkup. He won't be home for at least an hour." A flash between the girls caught Sunny's attention again. "This is our best chance."

There was no reason to intervene. Sunny had tried that once, and she wouldn't soon forget the incident with the watch. Most of all, she wouldn't forget Griffin's first reaction, his refusal to even consider that his daughter might be headed for trouble. Amanda's less-than-heartfelt apology still stung a bit, too.

Sunny looked away from the teenagers. She had enough to worry about. The apartment sale, her half-renewed friendship with Laura and her shattered relationship with Nate, the trial reviews. Then there was Griffin. *Don't get involved.*

The giggling grew louder. The other girl snorted. Sunny saw a glow from the tip of what was certainly a cigarette. She was on her feet before she even thought of doing so. She walked around the pool's concrete apron to the two lounges.

"Amanda."

Shocked hazel eyes—Griffin's eyes—met hers. "Oh. I didn't see you."

"Did you think this was a wise choice?" Sunny asked. She glanced at the other girl. Dark-haired and brown-eyed, she looked a few years older than Amanda. "I don't think we've met," she said and held out a hand. "I'm Sunny Donovan."

"Dixie." She didn't add a last name. She didn't shake hands.

Now that she'd stuck her nose in Amanda's business, she had to make some decision. Had Dixie urged her to try a cigarette just as she might have pushed her to take Sunny's watch?

What if, long ago, the woman at the bus stop had intervened? And saved Sunny from another bad memory?

For a moment she stood over the two girls. The lit cigarette dangled from Amanda's hand. Defiant, as Griffin had said of her? Or simply frozen in place?

"Let's talk to your father," she said at last. "Come with me."

Amanda sputtered. "But—but—"

"He's not home," Dixie put in, but Sunny didn't acknowledge her. She plucked the cigarette from Amanda's fingers, marched across the concrete apron and plunged it into a bucket of sand. When she turned, the girls were whispering again, casting looks at her with every few words.

"Do you have a ride home, Dixie?"

"Yes," she said, lower lip thrust out in a pout. "She's on her way."

Quickly Sunny checked their surroundings. The young mother was still there at the shallow end of the pool, taking note of the exchange. But Sunny didn't feel comfortable asking her to watch Dixie. Prepared to wait with her until her ride arrived, she told Dixie, "You can see Amanda tomorrow at school."

But Dixie had glanced toward the parking lot.

"She's already here."

As soon as she left, Amanda whirled on Sunny. "This is not your problem! I'm not some little kid you can push around."

Sunny didn't reply. As soon as they had left the pool area, Amanda's shoulders slumped. Her face looked green.

"Are you feeling sick?" Sunny asked gently.

"I'm never sick. I'm not a baby."

Oh, yes, you are. The thought came to Sunny as quick as the flare of that cigarette. Smoking wasn't life-threatening unless it became a habit. But an image of Wallace Day's victim flashed so clearly in her mind that Sunny missed a step. The two girls—Ana Ramirez and Amanda—weren't only close in age. They were both vulnerable children.

Shaken, she guided Amanda along the path lined with hibiscus bushes and palm trees to Griffin's apartment. "Do you have a key?"

"I didn't lock the door."

Sunny couldn't imagine Griffin allowing

that lapse of security. She sighed. She would have to mention that, too.

Sunny was determined to stop Amanda from risking herself. Whether or not Griffin welcomed her advice.

GRIFFIN STOOD AT the kitchen counter, wishing he were anywhere but here. Boston, maybe, when everything had still been the same. Timbuktu. Didn't matter. "I hate to admit it, but you were right," he said to Sunny.

"I don't take any pride in that."

"No, you warned me, and I didn't heed the warning."

Sunny perched on a stool at the counter where the kids ate their cereal every morning, but she and Griffin were the only ones here now. More bad luck for him. He tried not to look at her. And failed.

Sunny's face was flushed from her earlier scene with Amanda, and his daughter's tear-filled, angry words rang in the air between them. Minutes ago Amanda had slammed her door hard enough to rattle the windows. He'd talk to her again after they all calmed down. Which left him with his own embarrassment and Sunny.

She was still wearing the white cover-up

and modest black swimsuit she'd worn to the pool, probably expecting to have a quiet hour or so in the sun. Maybe she'd wanted to read a book. Or work on her laptop...yeah, that was more like her. Her hair was piled on her head, shiny blond strands escaping the clip she'd used to contain them. Griffin tried to clear his head. This wasn't about his attraction to Sunny or the fact that it couldn't go anywhere.

Too bad that Sunny had run into Amanda and the ever-problematic Dixie. Griffin didn't know what to do. Ban Amanda from seeing her again? Move her to a different school?

Rachel, he thought. *Why aren't you here?* She'd always meted out the discipline.

"Wish I'd handled that better," he said. "I managed not to raise my voice, but ever since she turned thirteen—" He sighed. "It keeps getting worse," he added.

"I shouldn't have said anything," Sunny murmured. "Now she thinks you and I are both against her. Any hope I had of helping is obviously gone." She paused. "Amanda was right. I was butting in where I have no business being."

"Wrong, Counselor." He leaned against the counter, facing her. "You only got in-

volved because of that first incident with
your watch—and that wasn't really the first.
Weeks before, Amanda had several warnings
from Bron about not handing in her homework, being late for class. Even skipping
school once." He shook his head. "Maybe
she and Dixie were out in the parking lot,
smoking."

"No, I think today was a first for Amanda."

"But with Dixie around, she'll try again."

"Amanda knows right from wrong. We
shouldn't—I mean, you shouldn't—just
blame Dixie. What do you know about her?"

"Not enough," he said. "She lives in a
pretty nice neighborhood. Big house, neat
lawn, a couple of expensive cars in the driveway. But I've never seen or talked with her
parents. They're always busy, Dixie says,
whenever I come to pick up Amanda."

Sunny thought for a moment. "You should
call them. Arrange to meet—size up the situation—then decide whether the relationship
with Dixie should continue. Or not." Sunny
took a breath. "Oh, and here I am, giving
more advice. As if you couldn't figure that
out for yourself."

"No, that's okay. I could use help."

She half smiled. "Cut yourself some slack."

She glanced at her sparkly watch. She was getting ready to leave again. "You're a good dad," she said, "but you've never had a teenage daughter before."

"Thanks. I've had a five-year-old, though, and believe me, the male version is easier in every way." Josh was in his room now, too, playing with his army men. Or had he been more affected by the scene earlier than he let on? Maybe instead, he was lying on his bed, crying into his pillow, with Stitch clutched in his arms.

Griffin would check on him. Right after he started dinner. Tonight would be simple, at least the menu would be. But he couldn't face another meal with Amanda glaring at him or Josh looking at his plate, flinching any time he heard an angry word. Griffin considered Sunny and the light blush of color in her face. From the sun or Amanda, he couldn't tell.

If that was a tan, it made her glow. He tried—and failed again—not to look at her mouth. That little uptilt made him crazy. In the next second he gave in to weakness.

"You like chili?"

She blinked at the abrupt change of subject. "Yes. I like chili." She sounded as if she were reluctant to admit it. And give him an opening.

"Stay for dinner. I need reinforcements."

DINNER WAS DELICIOUS. Even though her stomach had been tied in knots when they sat down to eat, Sunny had downed two bowls of chili. A crisp green salad and corn muffins had completed the menu. Griffin wasn't a half-bad cook, certainly better than she was. *How could you not like a man who cooks*?

When she told him so, he grinned and said she was probably just as good.

Sunny rolled her eyes. "Most nights Nate and I ate separately because I worked late. If I got home early enough, my best effort was probably chicken breast tenderloins in some kind of marinade—whatever the refrigerator held at the time—because they cooked in a jiffy, served with a bagged salad from the store. Bottled dressing." Griffin had mixed his own tonight with balsamic vinegar and a pricey-looking brand of olive oil. She couldn't help but be impressed.

"Don't get too excited," he said. "The chili's Rachel's recipe, and the oil was a Christmas gift." He slanted a look at Sunny. "I've been saving it for a special occasion."

Sunny could feel the color in her face deepen.

As they shared dish duty, their shoulders kept bumping, and she tried not to look at him too closely. Every time their gazes met, his hazel eyes gave her a jolt. But all too often she felt that gaze on her as she rinsed plates, and Griffin placed them in the dishwasher.

Sunny tried not to mind the latest reference he'd made to his wife. Had he meant that as a reminder that he was off-limits?

Bad enough that she'd agreed to have dinner with him and his kids in the first place. As at the cookout, Josh had taken to her readily. Amanda, not so much, but she'd clearly been instilled with manners and had said little—nothing else inflammatory—during their meal. Afterward, she'd helped to clear the table, then vanished into her room while Josh could be heard splashing, talking to his plastic dinosaurs in the nearby bathroom. She wouldn't have stayed except that Griffin's invitation had been offered with a pleading expression she couldn't seem to refuse.

Or was it that simple? She'd also been curious. What was his family life really like? Was there some obvious reason why Amanda was acting out, other than teenage hormones and missing her mother? Some reason Rachel had simply taken off one day? And left her children behind.

"How's your search going?" she asked. "Any news?"

Griffin shook his head. "None of Rachel's friends have heard from her."

"Do you think they'd tell you if they had?"

In the midst of taking another plate from her, his fingers grazed hers, and he cocked his head.

"You think they wouldn't?"

"It's not unusual," she said, wondering how the light brush of his hand could send such electric signals along her nerve ends. "In my work you knock on someone's door, trying to find a valuable but elusive witness, and everyone clams up." She ran another dish under the water. "The witness, often a close friend or family member of the victim, could be hiding in that apartment or house, but the person being asked 'don't know nuthin'.'"

"Your line of work sounds like a whole lot of fun."

"It has its moments," she said. "What will you do next about Rachel?"

"I talked to my Uncle Theo the other night. It's always in my mind that she might show up someday in more familiar surroundings. She never did care for Boston. Too much traffic, too much noise, too many crowds. When we moved there, she lost her whole support group, including him." He wiped his hands on a dish towel. "Rachel was close to my mother, too, before she passed away." He paused. "But she always had this—I guess you could call it—restlessness. If she was done roaming, she might come back to the old neighborhood, to the house where we first lived. Theo's place is next door."

Sunny was still feeling that tingle just under her skin. "I already know why you left Philadelphia," she said, "but what made you decide on Florida—other than Bron?" Moving here hadn't furthered his career. Quite the opposite. And Sunny remembered her sister-in-law saying she felt guilty for dragging him here.

"Bron went to college at Florida State. Then she met your brother through a friend— and that was that." He paused. "Theo wanted her in Philly, so they don't speak now. Bron and I are each other's only family. And I wanted to normalize the situation as much as possible." He shut the dishwasher, then steered her into the living room, one hand at the small of her back. "Coffee? Dessert? We have ice cream—and ice cream. That's Josh's favorite."

Sunny felt as if her skin were on fire. "No, thank you. I'm fine." She looked toward the front door. Now that they'd finished the dishes, she didn't feel right being alone with Griffin. "I should go. I have a ton of work waiting."

Griffin didn't try to keep her. "I remember how that goes," he said, then walked her to the door. "I need to get Josh out of the tub before he's shriveled from head to toe. Thanks for staying. I'll try to deliver my lecture on the evils of smoking sometime tomorrow." He waited a few seconds, then added, "Oh, and I'll make that home visit to Dixie's parents."

"Good idea."

"It was yours," he pointed out.

With a smile Sunny stood in the doorway. Outside, another balmy Florida evening was in full swing. She could hear the palm trees swaying, their fronds rustling in the light breeze, a far cry from the constant wail of sirens through the skyscraper canyons of New York. She did miss the city, but if she overlooked the hurricane threat here and her darker memories, this wasn't a bad place. And dinner had gone better than she'd expected.

She could smell the woodsy scent of Griffin's aftershave, see the five o'clock shadow on his jaw. She should move. Step away.

"Thanks for dinner," she said instead. "If I'd stayed in my apartment, I would have eaten a tuna salad sandwich at my desk."

"And played Tetris or Free Cell on the computer?"

"Guilty," she said. "How did you know? Although I'm more addicted to Pinterest right now." She hesitated. "No, tonight I would have tried to work."

He smiled. "In the past two years I've learned to balance work and real life. You know what they say. 'Too much work and no play makes Jack' or Sunny…"

"A workaholic," she finished. Maybe she was dull. Maybe that was another reason Nate had ended their marriage. Tonight she'd had no business interfering with Amanda or sticking around Griffin's family while they ate. She had no business standing here like this, wondering how it would feel to have his arms around her. She should go. Now.

Griffin leaned against the door frame and

looked down at her. After a long moment, while Sunny held her breath, his gaze lowered to her mouth. And his eyes darkened, the brown rim around his irises all but blocking out their hazel color.

"So. You liked the chili, huh?"

As he spoke, she felt his warm breath against her cheek. She could smell the clean scent of his skin. "I liked the chili. It wasn't too hot. Just spicy enough."

His tone dropped even lower. He leaned in a little. "You like some heat."

"Yes. I do," she said, sounding breathless.

His gaze returned to hers. And stayed. "So do I."

After a moment, Griffin blinked and straightened, as if telling himself to keep away, but his voice stayed warm and a little husky.

"Guess we have something in common," he said, as light as another touch.

Sunny couldn't answer. Her pulse was thumping—in awareness or alarm?—as she stepped out into the night. It was something all right, something far removed from the children or Rachel. And even, for Sunny, from New York.

She just didn't know what to do about it.

CHAPTER ELEVEN

GRIFFIN WAS STILL thinking about Sunny the next morning when he removed the wooden frame for the new concrete on Miss Carrie's back patio. He couldn't stop remembering that slightly uptilted corner of her mouth. And the easy way they'd been able to talk. For the first time in a long while he'd enjoyed that simple companionship, being…together with someone. No, with her. She was far more than just the big-city lawyer he'd first met. She had a good sense of humor, too. Maybe they were becoming friends, but that wasn't all—for him anyway.

Which wouldn't be fair to her. Lingering in the entryway, he'd come that close to kissing Sunny. He still wanted to. And where could that lead? When he thought about it, she had seemed just as interested in him, if equally unsure. With the kids and Rachel to consider, he'd be crazy to take this thing with Sunny any further. He'd be violating his own standards for a woman who didn't intend to stick around. If she got close to his kids, then left...

"Nice work. Didn't know you were a jack-of-all-trades."

Startled, Griffin glanced up to see Chris standing there, grinning.

"By the time Miss Carrie gets back from her crafts group, she'll be able to use her patio." He stood and dusted off his hands. "Playing hooky today? Thought you'd be out to sea by now, Captain, trawling for shrimp."

Chris made a face at the well-worn dig. He didn't like shrimpers. "My charter canceled this morning." He shook his head. "If he didn't book a full day with me at least once a month, I'd tell him where to take his business."

Griffin swept off the new patio, then started moving Miss Carrie's porch furniture back in place. The pot of chrysanthemums he'd bought her on impulse would look great in the corner by her door. Chris pitched in, shoving the last chair close to the side table. With every motion, Griffin felt last night and the image of Sunny in the doorway recede further into memory. But not all the way.

"Done," Chris said. "I was wondering...

you and Josh want to come out with me today? He's been begging me to take him on the boat." Chris gestured in the direction of the nearby marina. "My new one's a real monster. A forty-six footer. I got quite a deal on her, probably because she burns marine fuel like a house on fire. I'm going to try something different," he went on, "honeymoon and sunset cruises. Just got her running right again. It's time to try her out."

"Can't. After I pick Josh up, I've got to do more patio repairs. Six more apartments to inspect, and I'll be caught up again."

Chris shifted from one foot to the other. "That include your new tenant?"

Griffin didn't need that reminder of Sunny and last night. "You mean that lady from Alabama?"

"Not *that* lady. My sister, you jerk."

He stalled for time. "You helped her move. You probably know more than I do. Her patio looked fine to me, so unless she calls about a plumbing problem, I doubt I'll see her."

"You're a bad liar, Griffin."

He felt the tips of his ears turn hot. Like some boy Amanda's age.

"Okay, go ahead and have your laugh.

She stayed for dinner last night. She likes my chili."

Chris laughed. "And here I just wanted you to get out now and then."

"No, seriously. She liked the chili I made." Teasing her about it had seemed far safer than doing what he'd wanted to do. What he shouldn't even be thinking about now.

"Well, well," Chris said. "The beast has come to life."

"Don't start, Christopher. Your sister and I are neighbors. That's all. Pretty soon we won't be. She'll be gone, and someone else will b-be living in her apartment."

Chris cuffed his shoulder. "Look at you. Stammering like a teenage boy."

My thought, exactly.

"Tell you what. Since you've decided to have a social life again, Bron and I are going to the Seaside for supper next weekend. Why don't you two join us?"

Griffin hesitated. Was he actually considering that? "Chris, I'd need a babysitter, and the budget's tight this month."

"I bet Mom would be happy to stay with the kids. She'll say it's practice for when Bron and I finally make her a grandmother." He paused. "Sure doesn't look as if Sunny will, the way things have been going."

"What *things*?" He couldn't do dinner. Eating chili with his kids there wasn't the same thing as a night out with a woman who wasn't his wife. Chris should know better, even if the invitation was for a casual get-together. "Why don't you go catch some shrimp?" he finally said.

Chris wagged a finger at him. "If you and Sunny ate together last night, why not dinner with Bron and me?"

"For one thing, Amanda's in trouble again," he said. Even changing the subject to his daughter seemed preferable to letting Chris go on about Sunny. Then he thought of her nearness the night before, the way her hair had smelled, the way he'd wanted to sift it through his fingers to see if it felt as silky as it looked. "Since you're determined to talk about your sister—Sunny caught Amanda smoking."

"Get out," Chris said. "Amanda?"

"That was her name, last time I checked. She and her friend Dixie were at the pool yesterday. Sunny saw them and brought her home."

Chris blew out a breath. "That's not good, Griff."

"No, and neither are her grades. She 'forgot' to show them to me last night. I found them sitting by the coffeemaker this morning. Amanda rushed off to get the school bus before I could react."

"Being a parent is hard. I'm not sure Bron and I should go there." He sighed. "What are you going to say to Amanda?"

"No idea," Griffin said. "I'll play it as it lays."

"If you need backup, let me know." Another pause. "Or I'm sure Sunny would be glad to help. That's kind of her stock in trade."

"I don't think so." At the moment he almost resented her for catching Amanda smoking, bringing her home. Staying for dinner. Tempting him to abandon his principles. "I'll handle it."

Griffin's hands were shaking. Chris watched him set the pot of mums beside Miss Carrie's door. "With Amanda in lockdown, and you busy with all these patios— how about I get Josh from school for you, then take him with me?" He waved a hand at the blue sky, making his case. "Gorgeous day," he said. "Might be good to get the kid away from home for a few hours."

Chris was right. Let his son enjoy an afternoon of fun. He would love Chris's new boat. But Griffin hesitated to say yes. Would Josh be okay? In two years he hadn't been out of Griffin's sight very often. Except for kindergarten half days, he was usually right here.

Chris continued to make his case. "I'm only going over to another marina. Nearby. One of my other boats is being fixed, and I want to check on it."

Not far at all, then. Probably not even out on the open ocean. Griffin rubbed the back of his neck.

"Okay," he finally said. "I'll call the school." Bron and Chris were already on the list of people who were authorized to pick up Josh, though Griffin dreaded talking to that office secretary again.

As soon as he completed the call, Chris gave him a thumbs-up.

"Stay safe," Griffin said with a glance toward the dead-flat sea in the distance. Not a wave in sight. No wind at all.

"You know I will." Chris wandered toward the parking lot, then called back. "Oh. If you ever want to book a nice sunset cruise, let me know."

Griffin watched him head for his truck. Chris was solid, reliable. Josh would be all right. And in his absence Griffin would keep picking up the pieces of his dysfunctional life until it made sense again. A process that didn't include Sunny.

THAT EVENING SUNNY sat across from Bronwyn, her mind somewhere else. Today's conference call with Ralph was still troubling her. She'd been fretting when Bron met her for an early dinner.

"Wallace Day has been ranting again," she told Bron. "That earned him a short stay in solitary confinement—which caused more threats. Somehow he got to the press, and the New York papers have run with the story. Apparently it's turning into a real smear campaign. Against me." Sunny glanced at Bron and felt guilty for running on about Wallace Day. Bron was already upset, too.

Chris had taken his new boat out early that afternoon but wasn't back yet. Bron had become increasingly worried. She looked out at the darkening sky. Another half hour, and dusk would become night. Sunny's attempt to distract her, even about her own problems, hadn't worked.

"Have you heard from him?" she asked.

"Not in the past hour. I hate to bug him, but he didn't have a charter today. He should be back by now."

"Chris has been piloting a boat since he could reach the controls. I don't blame you for worrying, but I'm sure he'll be fine."

Bron clenched her teeth. "I could wring his neck."

"You'll get your chance. He'll be on dry land again before we finish our salads. Did you tell him where we'd be?"

She didn't answer Sunny's question. "I'm so scared! And he's not alone," she said. "He took Josh with him."

Sunny winced. This was not good news. She grasped Bron's fingers and held on tightly. "Chris won't let anything happen to either of them," Sunny said. "Any minute now he's going to stride through that door, windblown and laughing with Josh."

Bron tried to smile. "That's why I picked this restaurant near the marina. He won't have far to go. I asked Kate and Jack to join us, but they had something else on their schedule tonight." She paused. "I think they were meeting with a contractor about their roof. At last."

The waitress took their drink orders, then left menus on the table. Bron appeared to study hers, though Sunny knew she always ordered the same meal here. "I think I'll have the broiled red snapper," she said in a teary voice.

"What a shock."

Bron didn't laugh. "Do you think I should call your parents?"

"No," Sunny said. "Mom will get upset, and you know how she's been since the hurricane. She and Dad are probably battling right now about selling the house. Let's wait."

"You're right. Sorry, I'm rapidly becoming a mess."

This wasn't like Bron at all. Sunny patted her hand. "You handle dozens of students every day. You're one of the most collected people I know." Or at least she'd learned that since she'd come home. "For my part, having you as a sister-in-law and a friend has made the aftermath of my divorce a bit easier to bear."

"My shoulder is always available if you need to lean—or cry—on it." But her voice shook, and right now Bron was the one who needed comfort.

"If I were in your place, I'd feel the same." Sunny sipped her Coke and snuck a look out the window. Despite her words, and her confidence in Chris's ability, she was worried now, too. "I'm not in the same place, of course." She drew her hand back, then rearranged her silverware beside her plate. "Actually, I don't know where I am."

"You're in Lucille's Diner," Bron said weakly.

"Ha-ha." Hoping to distract her, Sunny asked about school and, unable to stop herself, came back to that morning's call with Ralph. "I already had plenty to do here, but now he's also assigned me to prepare another high-profile case." She added, "At least I'll be too busy to think about Day."

"Sunny. What if you looked for another job?"

I wonder...if you're running away from something, her mother had said.

"You mean, let Wallace Day know he's chased me away? No. And it's not as if there are other firms I could join in New York. If I jump ship at the DA's office, I wouldn't have a chance at moving into Ralph's job."

Which wasn't the most important thing to be talking about, and Bron was only half listening. Her gaze kept darting to the door, then to the window, then back again.

The few customers who had come in for the early-bird specials were paying their bills, then shuffling toward the door.

Bron and Sunny were now the only people left in the restaurant.

Their meals came, but neither of them felt like eating. Sunny picked at her green beans. At least another half hour had passed. *Where was Chris*? Now Sunny, too, kept glancing at the restaurant entrance.

"Maybe you should try him again," she said.

"The last time I called, it went straight to voice mail."

"What about his communications equipment? A ship-to-shore radio, or something. Isn't that required by law?" Sunny asked. "He's probably on his way in now, though. He might pick up a cell connection closer to shore."

Bron punched in his phone number again. She left a brief message, sounding desperate. "Chris. Call me. Please." She set the phone beside her plate and blinked a couple of times. "He's never been this late before. Not without a charter. He's usually home around sundown."

Sunny wouldn't say so, but she was becoming frantic, too. The sky was so dark it could be midnight instead of early evening. Yes, her brother was a great captain. He was young and fit, always athletic and stronger now from his years on the sea. He loved his boats, almost as much as he loved Bronwyn. He would bring this new one home, too. Yet there were sometimes treacherous riptides here. During her years of growing up, more than one sailor had been carried off course by strong currents.

Not knowing what else to do, she made another weak attempt at conversation, this time about Amanda's smoking incident.

"Oh, no," Bron said, her eyes glazed as if she were still in some other place, envisioning Chris floundering at sea. "I thought she was doing better. Her grades in my class aren't the best, but she has been handing in her assignments. And no more missing watches. Now this. Smoking?"

"Yes, and when I took her home," Sunny admitted, "Griffin put off talking to her about it. I really wish he hadn't but he offered to feed me, and since I had nothing in my refrigerator, I decided to let him."

Which hadn't been the best decision she'd ever made. Now the image of him leaning against the door frame, looking as if he would kiss her, his steady gaze on her mouth, was stuck in her mind. Or it had been, until she'd started to fixate on Chris and Josh. At least she'd pushed Ralph from her thoughts at last.

"You can let Griffin feed you again on Sunday," Bron said.

Sunny stared. "What makes you think that?"

"Chris was going to ask him to come with us—and you—to the Seaside. They have great lobster."

Sunny tensed. The Seaside was a favorite of her parents, but, like that day at the bus stop, she didn't think she could ever go back there. She often wished she had spoken up then, but even the thought of doing so had been traumatic. "Thanks for thinking of me, but, no."

She was about to say something else when the door flew open again. A tall man rushed in, bringing the briny smell of the sea with him. Sunny's relief was so strong she leaped from her chair. So did Bronwyn.

Then Bron stopped, like Sunny, halfway to the door. It wasn't Chris. The man pushed back the hood of his sweatshirt and Sunny saw her father's too-pale face. He sounded winded and all but choked out the words.

"Just had a call from the Coast Guard. Chris," he said. "His boat. He—"

"Dad." Sunny caught his arm. "What happened?"

Her father shook his head. "He sent out an SOS about an hour ago. He's lost, Sunny." He gathered Bronwyn close, muffling her sobs. "He and Josh are lost."

CHAPTER TWELVE

GRIFFIN HAD WANTED TO pick his moment with Amanda, but the vague sense of something wrong followed him down the apartment hall. Maybe he shouldn't have let Josh go with Chris. It wasn't that late, just after dark, not even Josh's bedtime yet. But why wasn't he home?

A nearby marina, Chris had said. How long could it take to get there, find out about the boat that was being fixed, then turn around and head back to port?

Amanda had already taken her lengthy nighttime shower and was in her room, the light showing under her door. All day he'd been planning what to say to her about the smoking incident. Now was the time—before Josh came home.

Unfortunately, he couldn't remember a word of his speech. He knocked at her door and pushed it open when she said, "It's not locked."

Wing it, then, he thought. *Take your mind off Chris and Josh.*

Amanda was sitting up in bed. Wearing one of her crop tops with PJ shorts, she had her arms wrapped around her knees. The covers had been pushed to the end of her bed. Her hair, still wet from her shower and looking shades darker, trailed over her shoulders. A few drops of water clung to her freckles. She also wore an expression of impending doom that seemed to mirror his. Apparently she'd been dreading this, too.

She gave Griffin one of her aggrieved sighs.

"Hey, baby." He walked past the dresser where he'd discovered Sunny's watch. Tonight its surface held nothing but a hairbrush and some of those elastic things she used for ponytails.

"I'm not your baby. Josh is the baby."

"Have it your way, Amanda." So much for the friendly approach. Okay, then. "Question—why cigarettes, kiddo?"

"Cigarette. One," she said.

"Whether it's one or a dozen, buying cigarettes—or having someone else buy them for you—when you're underage isn't legal.

You've been making some pretty poor choices lately."

She rolled her eyes. "Please. Don't bring up Sunny Donovan's watch again. You sound just like her at the pool." Amanda buried her head on her knees.

They were getting nowhere fast. "Then how about those grades that appeared this morning by the coffeemaker? When did they come?"

"Yesterday," she said.

"That the truth?" Or had she been hiding them for a week?

She raised her head. "Are you calling me a liar?"

Here we go, he thought, wishing he could remember his speech. It had been wise and understanding, the words to be spoken in a low, nonthreatening manner. He should have rehearsed some more.

"Look, Mandi. I'm not going to run through the reasons why you shouldn't smoke. I'm sure you've heard that lecture at school. It's unhealthy. Maybe you and Dixie should find some other means of entertainment." He never thought he'd say what came out next. "Email some other friends…hang out on Facebook," he said.

Amanda gave him a disdainful look. "That is so yesterday. Besides, we were only relaxing at the pool."

"Smoking relaxes you?"

"Dixie said it would."

"That isn't what I asked."

She lay back on her pillows, squashing her one-eyed doll and the stuffed giraffe she'd had since she was a baby.

"I didn't think it was relaxing, no," she said at last. "Is that what you want to hear?"

"This is not about me, Amanda. I'm not the thirteen-year-old who was caught smoking."

"You can ground me. Go ahead. I don't care." As if he needed her permission.

Griffin saw her gaze falter. She wasn't as sure of herself as she let on.

"I'm curious." He watched the spray of freckles across the bridge of her nose turn a shade darker. "Where did you get that cigarette pack?"

"Dixie took it from her dad's car."

"Was that how you got the idea to take Sunny's watch? Does Dixie make a habit of stealing?" Sunny was right. He would definitely visit her parents.

Her lower lip formed a pout. "No."

"Do you think she's a good friend? A good influence?"

Another sigh. "Yes."

"Well, I'd be happier if you thought about that some more."

Amanda pulled the giraffe from beneath her and flung it across the room. It landed on her carpet with a soft plop. "Why are you trying to destroy our friendship?"

"If it means saving you from developing a nasty habit, keeping your grades up, preventing you from doing things that will someday get you into real trouble, then I'll do anything I can to end that friendship."

She flipped over on to her stomach and pulled one of her many pillows over her head. "I wish we'd never come to Florida! I wish we still lived in Boston—or next door to Uncle Theo."

How could he get through to her? This long-legged, coltish girl who was growing up in front of his eyes, growing farther away from him with every passing day—just as he'd told Theo. Sometimes it seemed as if those freckles of hers were the only thing left of the child he remembered.

Griffin sat down on the edge of her bed, but she scooted away. "Mandi, I know the move was rough on you—on Josh, too—but after Mom left I couldn't keep my job in Boston and take care of you guys. You like being near Aunt Bron and Uncle Chris, don't you?" But that only reminded him that Josh wasn't home yet.

Maybe Griffin should have gone along, after all. He could have used a few hours of fun with Josh, some time away from the complex and all the problems that kept cropping up. He would have known where Josh was now. He'd have been with him.

Griffin had other responsibilities, though. He always had. One of them was Amanda.

"I like Aunt Bron," she said at last. "I love Uncle Chris." She hesitated. "But they're not Uncle Theo. They're not Mom!" The last word was torn from her.

Griffin tipped his head back to stare at the ceiling.

"Aw, Amanda." When he looked down, her back was quivering. Her shoulders shook. The two people she had loved most were gone from her life. At least for now. *Rachel...dammit, Rachel.* He didn't know how to comfort their daughter when she needed him most. He never knew what to say. "You miss her a lot, huh?"

"All the time. Josh doesn't remember what she looks like unless I show him a picture, but I do." She glanced at the album that was always on her nightstand. "I remember everything."

"I remember, too," was all he said.

"Then why isn't she here?"

"I don't know, honey. I wish I did."

"Was it something I said? Something I did?" she asked in a plaintive voice. "The day before she left she told me we were going to shop for school clothes. Then you had to take me instead. I had to wear that gross blue skirt the whole year."

"I don't claim to be a fashion expert," he said, trying to lighten the mood. He'd probably been numb when he picked that one out. "No, it was nothing you said or did. For reasons of her own, Mom decided to leave."

Her tone pleaded with him. "Why can't you find her?"

"I've been trying, Amanda. You know that. I just contacted all her friends again. I'll talk to the police detective in Boston—though they have no reason to reopen her case. Oh, I almost forgot to tell you. I talked with Uncle Theo." She rolled over to face him. "He asked about you and Josh, of course."

Her face brightened. "How is he? Is he okay?"

"Yeah. Sounded a little lonely, I guess." *Still angry with me.* Hurt, Theo had said, making their rift feel even worse, and more permanent.

"He should move here with us."

"I've tried that. He won't budge. You know how he likes his house."

They shared a quick smile, and Griffin realized that his daughter had shown interest in someone other than herself. She'd given him a flash of the Amanda he knew. In that instant she was the sweet-natured little girl who had loved without reservation.

"But, Dad. What if Mom comes back? To his house? Or to Boston? And we're not there? She doesn't know where we live now."

Griffin flinched. She'd probably been worrying about that since the move. "Theo knows. So do your grandparents." Rachel's mother and father had turned their backs on him after she'd disappeared. They blamed Griffin. Gradually, they had even stopped sending letters and gifts to the kids, as if the connection was too painful to maintain. But they had his number, too, so to speak.

"Don't worry," he said, smoothing a hand

over her still-wet hair. It looked like a sleek otter's pelt. "I'm on the job. We'll find her, baby."

She didn't protest his use of the endearment, and Griffin set aside any thought of discipline for the cigarette tonight. That could wait. In the distance he heard the doorbell chime, and his stubborn sense of unease kicked up again.

Who could be at his door? He hoped it wasn't Walter Lynx. But, no.

Josh must be home. At last.

He rose from the bed. Griffin picked Amanda's stuffed giraffe off the rug, then handed it to her. And, his insides beginning to unwind, he went to answer the door.

THE LIGHTS WERE on inside Griffin's apartment. But was no one home? At this time of night that didn't seem likely. Amanda must be doing her homework or getting ready for bed. Sunny dreaded telling him why she was here.

She raised a finger toward the bell just as the door swung open.

For a second she and Griffin gazed at each other, their almost-kiss the other night suddenly between them again. But his beautiful hazel eyes looked fearful, and she could almost see him thinking: What was she doing at his apartment now?

"Sunny," he said as if disappointed.

"May I come in?"

"Sure."

She stepped into his small entryway, an exact replica of her apartment.

Sunny tried to steady herself but her heart kept pounding. He must have seen the terror in her eyes. He looked behind her as if he expected someone else to be there. Josh, of course.

"Something wrong in your apartment?"

"I don't know how to say this," she began, remembering her father's white features at the restaurant. The Coast Guard call had shocked him to his core. Shocked her and Bron, as well.

"What's happened?"

She tried to collect herself. The words were choppy. "Chris was on his boat."

"I know that." Griffin swore under his breath. "Josh went with him."

She watched his face turn gray as the possibility of disaster set in. "They were supposed to come in by six-thirty. Bron and I were waiting to have dinner with Chris at the marina—" She broke off, knowing she was making a hash of this. "The Coast Guard called my father." She told him the rest in jerky stops and starts. "That's all I know right now."

"I shouldn't have let him go." Griffin was about to say something more when Amanda appeared, carrying her stuffed giraffe, her eyes dark and troubled.

Griffin sent Sunny a look that said *don't make too much of this in front of her.*

And Sunny's heart went out to him. She'd said what she came to say, but that wasn't all. There was no way she'd leave them here to worry.

"Come with me. We'll all wait at my parents' house," she said, trying to keep from shivering. "Bron's already there."

As soon as Sunny walked in her parents' door, Bronwyn rushed toward Griffin. He caught her close, murmuring words Sunny couldn't hear but that didn't seem to comfort. Her dad spoke to them, then kissed Sunny's head, disappeared into his den and shut the door. He would monitor the phones.

"I'll make sandwiches," her mother said too brightly. She put an arm around Griffin's daughter. "Will you help, Amanda? Bron, dear? It's better to keep busy."

With a nod, her gaze solemn, Bron broke away from Griffin, then followed Sunny's mom and Amanda into the kitchen. As usual, despite her own obvious fear for Chris, Sunny's mother had managed the situation smoothly.

Sunny might have smiled, but she couldn't. Every nerve in her body seemed to vibrate. It wasn't as if Chris didn't know how to handle any boat...but what if tonight he'd run out of skill? Out of luck?

Griffin put his hands on her shoulders. "You're shaking. Sit down. You want something to drink?"

"Thanks, no."

He sat on the sofa beside her.

Sunny welcomed his warmth as she hoped he welcomed hers. His little boy was missing, and Griffin already looked drawn. When Rachel disappeared, he must have been half out of his mind, but at least she was an adult, and as far as anyone knew, able to care for herself. Josh could not.

What if something had happened to Chris? If he was hurt, even unconscious, Josh would be out there, alone.

She laid a hand on Griffin's larger one. "I can't imagine...you must be terrified."

"Close," he said, his hand tense under hers before he turned it to link their fingers. His shoulders were set as if waiting for a blow to land.

"It's not the same," she said, "but I haven't felt this way since Nate came home and told me our marriage was over. For him." No, she had an even worse memory, one she wouldn't share. "My whole life changed in that one instant."

Griffin's jaw clenched. "What is the Coast Guard doing to *find* them?"

"They have boats out, of course, looking for them. Chris's distress call came in over two hours ago. It wasn't quite dark then," she said. "It won't be that easy to spot the boat now."

"They have radar, don't they?" Griffin shifted, his shoulder brushing hers. Though he rarely showed emotion, she recognized anger now as a defense. "I feel helpless. There's nothing we can do but wait. It's like torture."

He was right. And here she was, tucked up against Griffin when she hadn't yet faced her growing feelings for him. Now they'd been joined by fate during a family crisis. Because, yes, he was family, too. At the restaurant, Sunny hadn't thought twice before she'd offered to tell him about his brother-in-law, his friend. And Josh. She didn't want him to learn, like her dad, from a telephone call.

"I keep thinking about Josh, remembering things," Griffin said. "What if—what if they *don't* find them? What if he doesn't come home—"

She blinked back the sting of tears. "Of course they will, Griffin."

He returned the light pressure of her fingers. Sunny could see him try to shake off his fears. With a rueful glance, he changed the subject.

"I spoke with Amanda earlier tonight. About the smoking. I'm not sure we got anywhere, but she ended up talking about her mother." He told Sunny what she'd said. *What if Mom comes home...and we're not there?* "I'm always surprised by the things the kids say," he finished. "She sure made me even more determined to track Rachel down."

Sunny's throat tightened. She relished the strength of his hand, but what could she say to help? Of course she wanted him to find

Rachel. But if he did, their attraction would be impossible, even more inappropriate than it already was. His family would be whole again. Sunny hoped she'd be back in New York by then. But this was now. And she'd keep on holding his hand.

Griffin gazed at the far wall where the fireplace stood cold and empty. "Amanda told me she remembers everything about Rachel. Me, too," he said, "but when I started to talk about her laugh, that expression she used to get... I didn't say any of that."

"Why not, Griffin? That might have helped her."

"I couldn't."

Sunny had no trouble talking to Amanda even when her help wasn't wanted. Why couldn't Griffin? He'd even avoided talking to her about the smoking until tonight. But then, there were things Sunny wouldn't talk about either. How could they take this friendship to another level, if that were even possible, unless they were open with each other?

"I couldn't tell her because... Amanda worries that Rachel won't be able to find *us*." After a long moment he went on. "But I wonder how I'll feel if she does." His gaze held hers. "Crazy, huh? Here I am, emailing her friends, calling the detective on her case, talking to Theo, but maybe I'm not doing everything I can. Maybe I'm just going through the motions."

"I doubt that," Sunny said, seeing her chance, "but you must feel a lot of anger at Rachel. Mixed emotions. I know I do about Nate. Rachel left you and the kids flat, and you don't even know why." She paused. Did he? "There's your family, then there's your marriage. The kids' worries are heartrending but simpler in a way."

"I guess."

Sunny sighed. She squeezed his hand again. "Griffin, talk to me." When he remained silent, she said, "Did you have any idea Rachel planned to leave?"

His gaze faltered. "I don't think so. No."

Still, something seemed off here.

"There were no signs at all? Rachel didn't disconnect from you, from the children or her friends? Pull away from her parents? Your Uncle Theo?"

With his free hand he rubbed the back of his neck. "In Boston, we didn't get together as much with mutual friends, but we'd moved and I had the new job." He paused. "When we lived in Philly, she used to meet her pals for lunch all the time. But after the move, not as much—she was still new to the city and didn't know many people."

"Did she get rid of any mementoes? Pictures? Special possessions? She wouldn't want to take anything with her that might point to her former life."

"Like in Witness Protection?" He frowned. "She took a bunch of stuff to Goodwill a few weeks before she left, I think. But a lot of that was clothing the kids had outgrown. She did that every season."

"Then she gassed up her car and hit the road?" Her mother had said as much.

Griffin nodded. "Two days later the police found her car in a parking lot at her favorite mall—the same place she'd planned to take Amanda shopping for school clothes. I'd forgotten until she mentioned that tonight." He went on, "Rachel had left the registration in the glove compartment. The keys were in the ignition."

"And the doors were unlocked."

He sent Sunny a look. "Familiar, huh?"

"There are other indicators—backing away from social media, for instance."

"Another sign I missed?" He cleared his throat before he went on. "Lately I've been thinking…the kids believe that if Rachel comes back, everything will be the same again. For me, it's different." He shook his head but didn't continue.

Her pulse skipped. Did he mean his feelings had changed because of her? And the growing awareness between them?

"I've gone on without her," he said, his voice low and unsteady. "I had to for the kids, but as time goes on—and other things happen—" He glanced at Sunny but then stopped as if he'd had enough of talking about emotions.

He released her hand, then got up to cross the room and lay a fire on the hearth. Even though the weather had stayed warm, there seemed to be a chill in the air tonight—like the one in Sunny's heart. For long moments there were only the sounds of logs being scraped from the pile, a match being struck. Then a cozy flame began to crackle and glow, orange and red and electric blue.

After a time her mother appeared with a huge tray of sandwiches. Amanda followed with a pitcher of iced tea. Bronwyn carried bowls of potato chips and green salad. They set everything on the table with plastic plates.

"Here we are," her mom said. "There's coffee in the kitchen. We all need to eat."

Everyone did, but with her thoughts still on the confidence Griffin had shared for once, Sunny wondered if the rest of the family could taste anything. She couldn't. She ate anyway. If she didn't, her mother would fret, and she had enough to worry about.

Sunny's father called the Coast Guard again and again. Around 2:00 a.m. Amanda cuddled up beside Griffin. "What if they don't come back? Josh must be so scared."

"I am, too," Griffin admitted.

With tears in her eyes, Amanda wandered into the den, and Griffin soon reported she was sleeping on the lumpy sofa bed with the stuffed giraffe she'd brought along held close.

The house fell silent.

Bronwyn joined Sunny and Griffin on the sofa. She sat on the end closest to the fire as if she couldn't get warm even under the blanket Griffin, seated in the middle, had laid over her. She and Bron must have looked like bookends.

Sunny's father, with his cell phone glued to his hand, went upstairs for a while. Her mother soon followed.

Around four o'clock, Griffin's arm stole

around Sunny's shoulder to pull her closer. As he did the same for Bron and sighed, he and Sunny exchanged glances, but the look held something more than fear. For a man who backed away from any show of emotion, he had opened himself to her a little tonight.

They were each facing another possible loss, and, like Griffin, so many memories ran through her mind. Chris, in her favorite photo of him at three, an adorable little boy like Josh. Her brother on his high school graduation day, tall and solid with that beaming smile, that sparkle in his eyes.

Once Bron had fallen asleep, Griffin leaned closer to Sunny. He drew her face toward him and—as if he'd guessed at her memories of Chris—softly pressed his mouth to her temple, then again. The comforting touch was so light Sunny wondered if she had imagined it. With another sigh, he tucked her head into the crook of his shoulder.

They were both thinking the same thing now. Chris couldn't be gone. Josh either. They couldn't, not like Rachel.

AMANDA HUDDLED UNDER the blankets on the sofa bed in Grandpa Jack's den, thinking about Josh. *Where is he?* She loved Uncle

Chris—she'd told her father so earlier tonight—but Josh was only a little kid. He didn't like the dark or thunderstorms, although, thank goodness, there wasn't one tonight. Only a light breeze had riffled her hair when she got out of the car. She shouldn't have been so mean to him.

No matter what her dad had said, this must also be her fault.

Amanda had made her mother leave. Now Josh was gone, and maybe he wouldn't be coming back. *Ground me*, she had said about the cigarette. She could still remember the bitter taste of tobacco in her mouth. Sunny had been right. It had made her queasy.

Why did she keep doing things she shouldn't? She couldn't seem to help herself. If Josh didn't come back, she would be to blame for him, too.

Amanda listened for Grandma Kate's voice from the other room, then Grandpa Jack's, but didn't hear them. She heard Sunny's. Now and then she heard Aunt Bronwyn. But it was her father's deeper voice that, finally, made her begin to drift off. She shouldn't have been such a brat tonight when he tried to talk to her.

Amanda wished she'd said the right things.

If they hadn't argued over Dixie, she might have shown him her favorite pictures in the album of her mother. Of their family, all together then. *I remember, too*, he'd said. Her dad never said much, but he had tried, and having a little brother wasn't always the worst thing she could think of.

Please, bring Josh back. I'll never tease him again.

That was her last thought before she tumbled into sleep.

By DAWN SUNNY knew her mother must be in the kitchen again. The scents of toast and butter and an omelet, redolent of green peppers and onion, floated through the air, overwhelming even the lingering ashy smell from the fireplace.

Sunny didn't realize she'd fallen asleep until she jerked awake, her mouth watering. She wasn't hungry—had anything happened with Chris while she was dozing on the sofa?—but apparently her stomach disagreed. Beside her, Griffin was stretching the kinks in his back. Good grief. Had she actually gone to sleep next to him? The blanket spread across the length of the sofa told her she must have.

At the other end Bron tossed and turned, as best she could, in her small space. She had just blinked her eyes open when Sunny's father burst into the room. His face looked as pale as it had the night before, but his eyes were wide, and he was waving his cell phone in the air.

Sunny held her breath, waiting for what she hoped would be welcome words, afraid in the next second they wouldn't be. Then her dad broke into a shaky grin.

"They've found them!" he said.

CHAPTER THIRTEEN

THE CELEBRATION TOOK place a few nights later. On Sunday evening the Seaside was already filled to capacity when Sunny arrived. Some people watched the wall-mounted big screen TVs that blared different sporting events. A few couples tried to entertain their young children with crayons and place mat puzzles while waiting for their meals. The Cabot/ Donovan/Lattimer table, or rather, two tables pushed together in the center of the room, was all laughter and teasing. Her chair was the only one empty.

Her gaze went straight to Griffin, as if he'd sent out some signal. Tonight he looked relaxed and even happy. Remembering the tense night they'd shared and his oh-so-light kiss on her temple, Sunny looked away.

With Chris in the place of honor at one end of the table and her father at the other as the family patriarch, she would have no choice but to sit between Josh and Griffin.

For a second she stood beside the hostess desk. Could she do this? She'd considered not even coming, but here she was. She wouldn't have chosen the Seaside for this occasion, or any other, but this was Chris's party. Josh's, too. Finally, she made her way to the tables.

This was not the dinner Chris had intended. Griffin's children were part of the party. So was the rest of the family. And for them, she'd have to put her misgivings aside, the bad memories of this place that she'd hinted about to Laura but always kept to herself. She tried to pick up on the conversation in progress. Griffin was teasing her brother in that gruff way men had with each other.

"Just be glad you're sitting here," he said, "surrounded by people who love you. Every last one of them," he added as if Chris didn't have a thousand other friends. "That bandage on your head should serve as a reminder. You got lucky."

"Spending that night on the boat, dark as pitch everywhere, the generator not working and my communications out, was an experience. Right, Josh?"

Sitting as close to Chris as possible without being on his lap, Josh nodded. The event, which had shaken everyone else, including

Sunny's brother, seemed to have had surprisingly little effect on him. "We had a 'venture."

Bron leaned over to kiss Chris's cheek. "Were you thinking about me?"

"Every minute." He wasn't smiling now.

At the other end of the table her mother's attention suddenly focused on Chris. She'd been talking to Amanda but never seemed to tire of hearing about the rescue.

He cradled Bron's hand in his, then kissed her knuckles. "Especially," he said, "about our wedding day. I kept seeing you in your white dress with the sparkles, and those pearls in your hair..."

Bron teared up. "Aw, you're so sweet."

Sunny's father cleared his throat. "You had trouble with that boat's engine from the day you bought it."

"Wish I'd known that," Griffin muttered. "I would have kept Josh home."

"Dad's exaggerating. He was never in any danger." Chris grinned at Josh. "After the engine conked out, we were just rocking and bobbing. Weren't we?"

Josh nodded again. "It was like a 'musement park ride."

"True, my man. Or a haunted house.

Couldn't see a thing. Could we?" As if on cue, the little boy grinned. His uncle was clearly his hero. "Didn't faze us a bit, did it, Josh?" That seemed to delight them both. "I figured we'd get out of there sooner or later, one way or another, but it was a long few hours, believe me. We ran into some wind, then fog for a while." He winked at Josh. "Good thing I had my first mate with me."

Sunny could have kissed him. He'd kept Josh safe. He'd also made sure the experience didn't leave emotional scars. Chris had turned it into an adventure, all right.

"Then dawn came," he went on. "Fog still lay on the surface of the water, and it messed with the Coast Guard's radar, but when it got light, they were finally able to spot our boat. They towed it to the marina, then took Josh and me to the ER. I was sure glad to see you guys walk into the hospital," he said to his father.

"We couldn't wait," Sunny's mother murmured. "Could we, Bron?"

"Not another minute," she said, resting her head against Chris's shoulder.

Sunny's dad glanced at her mother with a teasing light in his eyes. "You didn't need to come along, Mama—and let everybody see you blubber all over the place."

"Jack Cabot. Once a mother, always a mother."

Their good-natured bantering made everyone laugh again, helping to relieve the tension. The story was told over and over, always with Chris's light version of events so as not to alarm Josh.

Sunny studied her brother. At one point in that long night he'd been knocked off his feet and slammed against the wheel. The bandage on his forehead covered a cut that had required stitches. A scan had revealed a slight concussion, so Chris had spent one night in the hospital for observation. Because of him, though, Josh didn't get a scratch.

Beside Sunny, Josh kicked at the table leg. He had one concern after all.

"That's a big bandage," he said, frowning.

Griffin laid a warm hand on Sunny's shoulder to lean past her. "Josh, it's okay. You don't need to worry."

Their meals were served. And he proposed a toast.

"To Josh—to Chris's health." Griffin paused, his glass held high. "And to the fact that he has a head as hard as stone."

Sunny raised the soda she'd been nursing all evening. She was glad she'd come after all. How could she not show up when the celebration was for her one and only brother? She couldn't imagine being without him. And from what she could see, Amanda looked equally grateful that Josh was safe.

Despite her relief for Chris, Sunny kept glancing at the short, dark hallway that led to the restroom. No way would she use it tonight. Or ever again. She set the glass aside, still half full, to focus on her meal.

To her surprise, Griffin chatted with her throughout dinner, as if he felt no awkwardness after the night they'd spent together. Sunny welcomed the distraction. That night at her parents' home, while they'd waited to hear about Chris and Josh, had changed the dynamic between them again. So had his admission about Amanda and his tangled emotions toward Rachel. If they were friends now, that was all either of them needed. All Sunny could handle.

Because she sat closer to Josh, she helped to cut his meat. He was becoming her new little shadow, which was another concern. As much as she liked him, it wouldn't do to let herself get too close, then have to walk away. Griffin's kids had been hurt enough. Still, she was here now, and Josh might need more help.

"Do you want me to open the straw for your chocolate milk?" she asked.

Josh smiled. "No, I'm a big boy. But thank you."

"You're very welcome."

She asked him about kindergarten, what he was learning, and whether he could already write his name.

"Yes," he said. "I know all my colors and my numbers. Wanna hear me?"

"Josh," Griffin said in a warning tone.

Sunny smiled. "No, I'd like to hear him count. Go ahead, Josh."

He made it to twenty. After that it was twenty-eleven, twenty-twelve....he sounded like Bilbo Baggins in *The Hobbit*. What a little dear he was.

"He's still working on it," Griffin said, smiling.

She leaned close to whisper in his ear. Her shoulder bumped his more solid one, reminding her of their unplanned sleepover. "He's delightful."

"Yeah. He sure is." He shot a glance at Amanda, who was talking nonstop to Sunny's mother. "My daughter's having a good time, too."

He said that like a prayer of thanksgiving.

"Things do get better," she said.

"Different," he agreed. He gazed at Sunny with an expression she couldn't read. Her shoulder felt too warm after touching his.

Sunny was almost glad when he left the table to take a telephone call from someone at the Palm Breeze Court, but she hadn't counted on Josh needing her while Griffin was gone. Josh had to use the bathroom, and he wanted Sunny to take him. How could she refuse? Josh was jiggling on his chair. She stood on legs that were suddenly shaky, then took his hand.

Her pulse began to skip beats, and her chest already felt tight. Outside the men's room she waited in the too-dim hall, wanting to pace with a growing anxiety. Had the Seaside owner never heard of brighter light-bulbs? Josh was old enough, he had insisted, to go in by himself, but Sunny wouldn't let him. She'd checked the men's room for him to make certain it was empty. Safe. But why was he taking so long? Her knees felt weak, and the memory washed over her again, plunging her back from the dark hallway into the past she could never outrun, never forget. The same memory, among others, that had sent her running to New York.

She and Laura are in the Seaside ladies' room together—until Laura leaves to return to their table. The door opens. Someone hits the wall switch, and the lights go out. In darkness, alone, Sunny begins to panic. And he's there...

A DOOR SLAMMED, the memory shattered by the sound. Sunny gasped. Josh was standing outside the men's room, flapping his hands to dry them. "I'm done."

"Okay. Good, Josh." She led him back to the tables, trembling all the way. She shouldn't have come after all. She should have made some excuse—any excuse. Chris would have forgiven her.

Thankfully, Josh had appeared before she recalled the rest, and no one seemed to notice how shaken she felt. But then, she'd had plenty of practice at covering up. By the time the night wore down, and her parents made their goodbyes, Josh was slumped in his chair, ready for bed.

"I need to get them home," Griffin said. "Come on, kids. School night."

Chris and Bron had tumbled into their own world, their eyes only for each other. "Hey, lovebirds," Sunny said, forcing a smile. "Party's over. Take your bride home, Chris."

He grinned. "Best idea you've had all night." When he stood, he had to steady himself with a hand on the table. He wasn't as okay yet as he thought, but he'd put up a good front for Josh. Bron was there to slide her arm through his, subtly guiding him from the restaurant.

As everyone drifted toward the exit, Sunny walked behind them. Passing the restroom again, she kept to the far side of the hall and felt her pulse hammer hard enough to be heard.

In the parking lot, hugs and kisses were shared. Promises made to get together again soon. Relief over Chris's survival had reminded everyone, including Sunny, that such gatherings were always fragile. This one might never have happened, just as she might not have gone home that other night long ago. Surrounded by family, she thought, *all right. I did this. I came here. Nothing happened this time. Laura didn't leave me.*

Turning abruptly from Chris and Bron, she walked into Griffin's chest. Plunged back into memory, she nearly fainted. All the air rushed from her lungs. "Oh! Sorry."

Embarrassed by her overreaction, she was about to move away when Griffin caught her hand. Could he tell how panicked she felt?

He didn't seem to. He even smiled. "I just put Josh in his car seat. Amanda's almost asleep in front. I came back to…" Sunny wasn't expecting what happened next. He tugged on her hand a little, and she lost her balance, ending up against him with her head tucked in the warm spot between his neck and shoulder. As if she'd found a refuge there, like the night they'd waited for Chris and Josh to be found. Griffin smelled of the fresh night air. "I wanted to say good-night, Sunny."

"Good night," she managed. "It was fun." *Nice talking to you.*

The words meant nothing. They were merely a small politeness. His children had good manners because he did, too.

But then, as she stepped away, he drew her back, and as if she were walking through water, Sunny glided into his arms. To her surprise, even with that old memory still playing in her mind, she had no desire to pull away. She could have stayed there forever—except that his children were nearby. He framed her face in both hands and pressed his mouth to her temple, as he'd done at her parents' house, before he moved lower to plant a quick kiss on her cheek, and finally at one corner of her mouth. Sunny at last drew back. "We really shouldn't..."

Griffin only smiled, his hazel eyes shining, before he rested his forehead on hers.

"Rain check," she thought she heard him say.

THE NEXT AFTERNOON Sunny stared at her laptop without actually seeing the screen. She had a real life. Why was she wasting time on a fantasy that couldn't be? Surely Griffin hadn't said what she thought he had.

Why would he kiss her like that?

Always, Rachel was in the background, and if she knew Griffin at all, he'd honor his marriage vows. Which made last night, and the bond they'd shared when Chris and Josh were missing, even more of a puzzle. He had two children to consider. Sunny was newly divorced and, in her own way, still encumbered. *Rain check*. Besides, she wouldn't be here that long.

Sunny straightened in her chair. Never

mind the way her senses reacted whenever Griffin touched her. She had work to do. She opened up the new case file. Sunny didn't like the looks of this trial, but while she was cooling her heels in Florida because of Wallace Day, it was the case she'd have to prepare—one with another insanity defense. This defendant had a history of misdeeds going back to before he turned thirteen, but he didn't hold her interest for long. Soon, she was closing the file and opening another.

Wallace Day's folder with the transcript from his trial. Maybe she could find out where she'd gone wrong. Correct her mistakes and this time get a conviction for someone else.

Sunny scanned Day's mug shot. Not flattering, but none were.

He wasn't a bad-looking man, if you didn't know what he'd done. Day would appeal to many women, but Sunny shuddered every time she saw that grainy photo. He was younger than she always expected him to be. Still in his twenties, he had long dark hair and almost-black eyes. Tall, dark, and dangerous, he'd made a career early on—like this defendant—of swindling people. Day wasn't averse to robbery, but stalking young girls had become his style. Sunny had never seen a smile like his, sly and mean.

As she skimmed a police report, her skin crawled.

How many men like Wallace Day were walking around? Preying on innocent girls like Ana Ramirez? And once upon a time like…

The blood drained from her limbs again.

With a snap Sunny shut her computer, then glanced at her beaded watch. She'd made little progress on her new trial prep today, but now she needed to…take a swim. As if to run from her memories and Wallace Day, she was out of the apartment in record time.

Taking advantage of this perk had become a daily habit. The pool water glinted in the sun, clear and blue. The temperature was in the low eighties.

After a few laps she dried off, then stretched out on a lounge. She was drifting off, the sun glowing red behind her closed eyes, when she heard voices.

Opening one eye, she spied Amanda with Josh coming through the gate. Both in brightly colored swimwear, they had beach towels slung over their shoulders, and Josh was bouncing with eagerness to get in the pool. At whatever he was saying, Amanda rolled her eyes.

Josh spotted Sunny, headed straight for her and flung himself into her arms.

"We had a good time yesterday. Didn't we?"

"Yes we did."

"Leave her alone, Josh." Amanda stood by Sunny's lounge, her expression cold. Not a good day for her, then, but at least Dixie wasn't here.

"He's fine," Sunny said, relishing the feel of warm little boy against her as she had at the party. When he pulled away, her arms felt empty. "You two planning to enjoy this beautiful day with an after- school swim? How lucky are you to live where there's a pool? In New York I never—"

Amanda frowned. "Florida is stupid. I don't care about the pool."

Sunny stopped herself from rolling her eyes, too. She'd seen Amanda enjoying the pool with Dixie. But maybe swimming at the Palm Breeze Court was a reminder that Amanda had left her home in Boston behind. Philadelphia, too.

With a sigh Sunny lay back on her lounge. Then she sat up again.

"Where's your father?" She didn't think Amanda was old enough to be left in charge of her five-year-old brother near the water.

Amanda eyed her with suspicion. "He's somewhere," she said. "Fixing something." As if that wasn't a good use of his time. "I think Mr. Lynx called again. Or maybe Miss Carrie. I'm not sure." Her expression said, *Why do you want to know?*

"I'll keep an eye on you then, if that's all right. Until he comes back."

Without answering, Amanda walked off, towing Josh with her. And muttering. Sunny could guess at her thoughts. She didn't need supervision. She was a teenager. Sunny was a busybody.

Still, she couldn't ignore them and simply hope Josh would be safe.

Pretending to read the magazine she'd brought along, she watched Griffin's children splash and call to each other, their voices amplified across the water. A few minutes later, though, Amanda suddenly climbed out of the pool.

Panic rang in her voice. "Come out, Josh. Now."

Sunny sat up. What was wrong? Despite her command to hurry, Amanda walked slowly to the two lounges she'd chosen—as far from Sunny as possible. Hastily, she rubbed her towel over her wet swimsuit, water dripping from her legs. "I said get out of the pool! I have to go."

"Amanda?" Sunny called.

The girl turned toward her. For a second she hesitated.

"Can you watch Josh?" She didn't wait for Sunny's answer. "I'll be right back."

Sunny almost smiled. She'd already been watching them.

Amanda didn't look back. She rushed through the gate, letting it clang shut behind her, then started toward Griffin's apartment. She must need a bathroom. There was one here in the old cabana, but Sunny wouldn't use it, either. Today the Seaside was too clear in her mind.

Or maybe Griffin had warned Amanda not to use that bathroom. Like the Seaside, the space had only one entrance and wasn't well lit. Someone could easily lurk there. Without Griffin nearby, Amanda wouldn't be safe.

Sunny slipped into the water. Josh had taken a seat on the edge of the pool and was dangling his feet. He inched ever closer to jumping in.

She held up her arms. "It's okay, Josh. You can swim with me."

"Can we play ball?" He glanced behind him. A big blue beach ball rolled gently back and forth by his lounge.

"Go get it. Then I'll catch you."

She guessed they had played for about ten minutes, chasing the ball and laughing as they tried to scramble through the water, before Amanda came back. If she'd seemed a bit pale before, she looked white now.

Sunny caught the ball. "Hold on, Josh." She swam to the side of the pool to look up at Amanda. "Are you okay, sweetie?"

"No."

Had she been smoking again? "Anything I can do?"

"I need my mother. Not you."

Oh, dear. Sunny took a closer look. Amanda had been wearing a red tank suit when she left the pool area. Now she wore black shorts and a yellow tee. Her chin quivered, and she hugged herself tight as if she were chilled.

"Do you have a stomachache?"

"Not really. No," she murmured.

She lifted pleading eyes to Sunny, as if to say *you know*.

Oh. Of course. She shouldn't be surprised. After all, Amanda was thirteen. Sunny glanced at Josh.

"Sorry, hon. Pool time's over." She climbed out, then offered a hand to help Josh from the water. "Let's all go to my apartment. I need to help your sister."

The relief that flashed in Amanda's eyes told Sunny she was right. At a critical moment like this, even her support was welcome.

CHAPTER FOURTEEN

SUNNY DIDN'T EXPECT the good feelings between her and Amanda to last long. But for now, the girl gave Sunny a grateful look from her cozy spot on the sofa.

An analgesic had helped her mood, too. Cramps were no fun at any age.

Josh, who had no idea what was going on, had just settled with Sunny's iPad to play a movie when the doorbell rang. They'd been at her apartment for less than an hour.

Griffin stood outside, his face a study in parental concern. Sunny wanted to smooth the frown from his forehead, erase the worry in his hazel eyes, but kept her hands to herself. She had called him once the crisis was resolved only to say where his kids were. She'd left the details for later.

"How's Amanda? She okay?"

Sunny stepped outside and shut the door. Briefly, she told Griffin about Amanda's special occasion. "She'll need female supplies.

I'd be happy to pick them up, if you like. Please, don't mention it to her."

"She's embarrassed."

Sunny smiled. "She's also immensely proud of herself. Dixie, she informed me, had the same first experience a year ago."

"Dixie," he repeated with a glance at the front door.

"Come on in. Josh and Amanda are each having a glass of lemonade." She opened the door, then paused. "You might as well all stay for dinner. I owe you one. But just so you know—it won't be chili."

"I made enough for ten families," he said. "We always eat that stuff for days."

"Then you'll be glad for tonight's tacos with guacamole..."

"You make good guac?" he asked, his eyes alight and warmer now.

"I do," she said. "I guess that's my specialty, other than chicken."

Was she getting herself into trouble here? She'd invited him before she'd stopped to think. Her new connection with Amanda must have made her feel bold. Well, too late now.

While she cooked, he told her he'd had a long day. "Apparently the Grump has a squir-

rel living in the space above his bedroom.
I promised to get the exterminator here tomorrow."

"The Grump?"

"Walter Lynx and his constant complaints about apartment 12C. I keep wishing his lease would run out and he'd decide
to move." He took another sip of his lemonade, and Sunny studied his face. Was he
waiting for—expecting—her to leave, too?
How much would he care if—no, when—she
did? "Unfortunately, he's a landmark tenant,"
Griffin went on. "Been here since the place
opened. Which, I suppose, is why he thinks
he can tell me how to do my job."

"You do it well, but this must have been a
big change for you after TV."

"Makes more sense than you might think,"
he said. "When I was a kid, I worked for my
Uncle Theo. He taught me how to fix toilets,
paint walls, rebuild broken patios…and in
my teens I did some roofing work for him.
I didn't expect to be able to say this when I
first moved here, but I actually like what I
do now. Most of the time." He set his glass
down. "I sure don't miss wearing a tie every
day."

"Another thing we have in common,"

Sunny said, swimming in dangerous waters again. "I left all my courtroom garb in New York. All those suits are in boxes in a storage unit in Queens." She smiled. "Navy blue, charcoal gray, but never black. Too severe— and that's reserved, by some unwritten rule, for judges."

"I never thought of that. Same goes in TV. Some colors don't work well with the camera."

"Dressing for trial is also an art," she said. "No loud colors, please. I must have a dozen pairs of sensible dark pumps with low heels. No Jimmy Choo spikes."

His eyes darkened the way they had in the Seaside parking lot last night. "What a shame."

Rain check. Sunny decided to drop this topic before she got lost in the memory of those light kisses.

"About toilets," she said, going with the first thing that came to mind. "The cabana at the pool needs work."

"Or an order from the city to condemn," he said, shaking his head.

"A coat of paint would do wonders." Although Sunny doubted that would be enough. "And better lighting," she said, her heart skipping a beat. *He slips inside the restroom. Shuts down the lights…*

As if he shared the memory, Griffin's smile faded. "No wonder Amanda took off from the pool as if someone was chasing her. The place must seem scary."

Sunny's pulse hitched again. "That is another worry. If she—Dixie, or any other woman—went in there, and someone unsavory was nearby, she could be trapped." She paused. "That sounds like paranoia, but it's not. You wouldn't believe the strange things that happen." She couldn't go on for a few seconds. "If nothing can be done with the cabana, maybe it would be best to tear it down. It's an eyesore, really, when the rest of the pool area is so pretty."

"Another project. I'll put it on the list," he said, "right after Miss Carrie. She needs a new kitchen floor. The old stuff is worn through in front of her sink." He paused. "Mrs. Moriarty would like to have her apartment rewired. That's beyond my capability, and I doubt management will agree, but she keeps trying. I've had six calls from her since yesterday."

"Never a dull moment."

Sunny smiled before she realized how

comfortable she felt talking with him. Like her daily dip at the pool, these cozy dinners with Griffin and his children were getting to be a habit. He was relaxing in his seat at the counter as if he belonged here, lived here. As if they were any normal family catching up at the end of the day. But how many families had a husband, a father, who looked like Griffin Lattimer?

Griffin took his time before posing a question. "What about your job? Would you ever reinvent yourself? Take a lesser position somewhere or start a new career?"

"No," she said. "I don't think so."

"That was quick." He frowned. "Then you'll be going back soon."

"Not before my lease is up." She smiled to keep things light. "I wouldn't want my landlord to take me to court."

He didn't smile back. "I'm not your landlord. I'm the maintenance man."

This conversation was heading for even deeper waters, reminding Sunny that she wouldn't stay. Shouldn't. "Besides," she admitted, "I can't go back just now." She told him about Wallace Day's solitary confinement, then the latest round of media coverage that was dragging her name through the mud, and watched Griffin's frown deepen.

"How dangerous is this guy, Sunny?"

Laura had wondered the same. Head down, she focused on the two ripe avocadoes for her guacamole. Methodically, she peeled and chopped and mashed.

"Very," she said at last. "But I'll be safe here."

His gaze stayed on her. Griffin couldn't care—could he—that she would soon pick up her old life? Return, when the coast was clear, to Manhattan? His focus would be on Rachel and his kids.

It wasn't until after they ate that Griffin brought up that topic again. "While you're here, Counselor—" he lowered his voice "—what's your take on my finding Rachel?"

Sunny glanced toward the living room, where Amanda was still making the most of her pampered state, lying on the sofa with a teen magazine she'd brought in her beach bag. She had earbuds on, listening to her iPod. Josh wore superhero earphones and was playing some video game on Griffin's cell. Neither of them even looked up.

Not knowing what to say, Sunny perched on a stool at the counter beside Griffin with two mugs of steaming decaf coffee and a plate of cookies between them. Like an old married couple, she thought, although she and Nate had rarely shared an evening like this toward the end. Did Griffin want her opinion as a lawyer or as a woman who was beginning to like him far too much?

"I hope you do find her—of course—and she comes home."

"You know what I said the other night." He tilted his head toward the living room. "I'm not sure how that would work out."

She tensed. Maybe, Sunny thought, he should tell Amanda and Josh about his growing ambivalence toward Rachel. As he should have admitted his feelings to his daughter the night Chris and Josh vanished. Instead, he'd stayed silent. That didn't bode well for a relationship with Griffin, even if one was possible. Nate, despite his quiet nature, would have told their children everything. But they didn't have children…because of her.

This was not territory she wanted to invade, but she did have experience to share. Sunny tried to soften her tone. "It must be hard to know Rachel had a plan to leave you—but that's how it usually plays out."

"And I didn't see it coming."

"She wouldn't have wanted you to," Sunny said.

Griffin took another cookie from the plate but didn't eat it. He turned it in his fingers. "The other night," he said, "I started to tell you…this is purely hypothetical, understand…but I've started thinking about divorce." He paused. "With Rachel missing, I have no idea how I'd even go about that."

Sunny's head swam. Divorce? He wanted her professional view, then. "There's a statute of limitations," she finally said, "because Rachel is a missing person—but I don't know what the term is in this state. I'd have to check." Not that she was offering, exactly.

"And after that?"

"You'd need to fill out forms at the city clerk's office here. I assume this is now your state of residence." When he nodded, crumbling the cookie in his hand, she went on in her best courtroom voice. "Then you would put a notice in the classified section of the local papers, a public notification of your intent to dissolve the marriage."

He cast another glance toward the living room to make sure Amanda and Josh were still occupied. "That's it? I already posted a notice in Boston soon after Rachel left that I wouldn't be responsible for any further debts. The credit card balance was enough."

"No, that's not all," she said, "but those are the first steps. If she doesn't turn up or protest the divorce, it's pretty simple from there. Depending on the state."

Griffin didn't comment, and she touched his forearm. The muscles were steely, his shoulders hunched. There was still something he hadn't said. Sunny sensed there always was.

Finally he sighed. He sifted the cookie crumbs onto the almost empty plate. "This isn't so simple," he said, "and no one else has seen this—but Rachel even left a note on the front seat of her car." He paused. "I'd show you, but I don't have to. I memorized every word long ago."

Sunny's breath caught. Now they were getting somewhere. Griffin had probably buried the importance of that note all this time.

"It was short and to the point," he said, his voice husky. "'I'm going away, Griff. I need to—but I'm okay. Tell—'" his voice faltered "'—tell Amanda and Josh I loved them.'"

She was half afraid to ask. Afraid she hadn't heard right. "Did you tell them?"

"No," he said, almost whispering now. "I couldn't. They've never seen it."

They should have, but Sunny knew why they hadn't. This time it wasn't because Griffin tended to bury his emotions. It wasn't because Rachel had used the past tense about her own children. *Loved,* not *love.* That was bad enough.

It was the rest of her message that he'd locked inside for two long years. She hadn't mentioned Griffin.

Rachel Lattimer didn't love her husband.

It was what he'd been hiding, even from himself.

So why was he still trying to find her?

LATER, GRIFFIN TOOK the kids home and put them to bed.

Then he sat in his darkened living room. And thought about Rachel.

By now, maybe she had a new name. Everything about her might be different. The kind of house or condo or apartment she lived in. A small town instead of Philadelphia or Boston or New York. Her hair color might be brown now or black instead of dark blond like Amanda's. She could be wearing contact lenses to change her eyes from blue to green.

Everything, he thought.

He should stop trying to find her.

If only he had shown the kids that note as soon as Rachel left home. That note in her handwriting had meant Griffin wasn't a suspect with the police, but it would have hurt his children too much. Just as it still made him ache.

He shouldn't have confided in Sunny either. Asked her about divorce.

They'd enjoyed dinner again tonight. Why spoil it? He remembered the way the overhead lights had shone on her hair and made her tanned skin gleam. They'd had some good conversation, too, with only a brief glitch when Sunny admitted her job in New York was the most important thing in her life. Which shouldn't matter to him, even though Wallace Day was making her work more difficult. Griffin didn't like that at all.

Still, he was grateful that she'd helped Amanda with her new status as a young woman. He liked the way Sunny treated Josh like the special little boy he was, making Griffin yearn for a family life that was whole again. And how she'd sat beside him at the counter, their bodies almost touching. Trusting.

Then he'd ruined it.

In sharing that note, he'd told her the secret that had been eating him up for the past
two years. Just as bad were his actions in the
parking lot at the Seaside. He'd kissed her
with Amanda and Josh close by. If Sunny
hadn't pointed that out, he might have really
lost his head.

Rain check, he'd told her.

There would be none, though.

Because of Rachel, he had his demons to
slay, and if he didn't miss his guess, so did
Sunny. Whatever they were.

THE NEXT MORNING, Nate called.

"This isn't what I'd hoped for," Sunny said,
disappointed by the low numbers on this first
offer. She wouldn't let the apartment go for
that price. "That's not enough."

"Why quibble? We're still hoping to get
that house in Connecticut. You're standing in
my way. In the interest of post-marital har-
mony, why don't you—"

"Nate, there's a lot at stake here. I want to
make a counteroffer."

"At full asking price, I assume." He added,
"Which the buyer will refuse."

"Undoubtedly. However, that will send a

clear message that we're insulted by their low-ball offer and encourage them to raise the ante. The market in New York is robust. Units in our building have commanded good prices. Look at the comps, Nate." She sighed. "Like you, I did hope the sale would go fast, so I can buy something for myself," she admitted, trying not to think of Griffin and leaving Florida, "before I get busy at work again."

Sunny mentioned Wallace Day then Ralph. She heard Nate sigh in the background.

"I've seen the stories. Maybe you should stay there. Permanently."

Wow, the opinions were really stacking up on that score. First Bron, then her mother and even Griffin, though she hadn't figured out his reason for asking. But was Nate worried about her? Sunny doubted that. He'd never been supportive of her goals. Of her income, yes, as her father had pointed out.

"Stay here? That's not in my plans."

No matter how much she liked Griffin, no matter how much she liked his children, staying wasn't in the cards.

But Nate hadn't given up. "And here I hoped you'd succumbed to the glorious Florida weather and decided to leave New York behind."

Sunny winced. He must want to scrub her from his life completely. That only reminded her of last night. The note. And Griffin's search for Rachel.

She wondered about the things he still hadn't said. *Maybe I'm just going through the motions.* Or maybe, because of Rachel's note, he couldn't face more hurt. Which brought her back to Nate.

"Let's talk instead about an offer you would be comfortable with," she said.

To her relief he didn't argue, and they discussed the counteroffer. Then, while she had the chance, Sunny decided to confront another issue. Their broken marriage. Her guilt. She didn't know why Griffin's wife had left home, but some clarity with Nate wouldn't hurt.

"What happened to us, Nate? It's more than possible, as you said, that I worked so hard I had nothing left to give—and you got tired of waiting for me." Just as Griffin must be weary of waiting for Rachel to come home, weary enough to consider divorce. "You're right that if I'd put off having a family for much longer, that wouldn't have even been a possibility."

Helping Amanda yesterday had reminded her that her ability to have a child wouldn't last forever.

"Of course I never expected to be divorced."

Nate hadn't said anything. For a moment she wondered if he'd hung up.

"Sunny," he finally murmured, "you and I are done." Then, after another long silence, he dropped an emotional bombshell.

"Lisa's pregnant?" Sunny echoed. She felt like a fool for trying to understand their divorce.

"Did we set a land speed record, or what?" She could hear the pride in his tone. "Two months of trying, and I learn I'm going to be a daddy. So," he said, "you can see that selling the apartment is even more important now. I emphasize the word *now*."

"Don't put this on me, Nate."

"You were the one who insisted we go ahead and sell. I'm still amazed you didn't want to keep the place for yourself."

"I did love the apartment. But time changes things. So did our divorce," she pointed out. Over the past weeks, as Bron had suggested, Sunny had come to think of the apartment as a painful reminder of the years when she and Nate had been happy together. But he wouldn't budge now.

"I need the money from this sale. I'd sell for pennies on the dollar if it was just up to me."

"It's not. Both of our names are on the mortgage. Not Lisa's," she added. "I'm sympathetic to your wishes, but we need to hold out for a more reasonable offer. I'm as eager as you are to get this behind us." Sunny held her breath for a moment. "I don't want to end our relationship with anger. Or bitterness. This is the last thing we'll do together," she said, and heard the break in her voice. "Let's give the listing another week or two. Then, if necessary, I'll agree to lower the asking price."

"You'd better," he said. "Or I'll stand in the doorway when the next buyer comes here— and lower it myself!"

He hung up before Sunny could respond.

CHAPTER FIFTEEN

SUNNY HADN'T WORKED well all morning. Her new trial prep had hit a serious snag, and she kept going back to the Wallace Day files instead.

Obviously, it was time to get out of the apartment again.

In the past weeks Sunny had worked out a new schedule. Mornings were for work—when that was working out. Late afternoons, when the swimming pool area was still empty, she reserved for herself. This new habit suited her better than she might have expected. It even felt decadent. Indulgent.

I hoped you'd succumbed to the glorious Florida weather.

She finally had. What would the staff at her office in New York think?

As she closed the pool gate behind her, Sunny smiled to herself.

No one would believe it.

She hardly believed the change in her attitude. Every now and then she had the sense that she'd been missing out before, maybe for a long time. And not only because in New York she never had the chance to work on a tan.

What if she did stay? What if Griffin got that divorce from Rachel? And stopped looking for her? For a moment she entertained the notion of another lifestyle completely. Enjoying more dinners with Griffin and his children, getting closer to Amanda—if she could—and being able to cuddle Josh every day. Where, and how far, could her relationship with Griffin go then? But Sunny paused. If she stayed, she would never become DA, never find justice for all those victims…

A sound nearby caught her attention and Sunny froze with her towel in hand, about to lay it on her usual lounge. Someone was in the cabana.

In a single heartbeat her pulse went flying.

Sunny looked around. She was alone. Not even that young mother was here with her baby. If someone came out of the pool house, would Sunny have time to run? *Don't be silly.* It was probably a mouse scurrying through the cabana's gloom.

A second later, Griffin stuck his head out.

"Hey," he said. "Glad you're here. I need your take on something."

She hesitated. If she didn't walk over to the cabana, she would look foolish.

He gave her a winning smile. "I've been thinking about your suggestion."

For a moment, her legs weak, she couldn't imagine what he meant. She was still lost in the illusion of danger, in her own daydreams of Florida and having the family she'd put off for so long.

"Oh," she said. "The tear-down order." Sunny walked over, trying to show him she wasn't alarmed by the surprise of his presence. After all, he was the maintenance guy. He had every right to be here.

"Not a tear down," he said, motioning for her to follow him into the cabana. "Look at this. I've been thinking—not only could this structure be saved, it could be a great asset to the complex. As you said, the rest of this area looks good."

Keeping her distance, Sunny edged into the dark cabana. She didn't like enclosed spaces, and this one reminded her of the Seaside. She knew her fear was irrational, but she couldn't seem to convince her body not to react in fright.

Griffin didn't notice. Caught up in his new idea, he gestured at the space around them. Not only dark but clammy, the room seemed like a dank dungeon and smelled of mold. Sunny couldn't stop the shiver that ran down her back.

"Ugh," she said and turned to leave.

"Wait." He touched her shoulder. "I know it's a mess right now, but you have to see the big picture here." Could he feel the thud of her pulse under his fingers? She could certainly feel the warmth of his hand, but even that didn't ease her discomfort. Neither did his soothing tone of voice. "If I lighten the space up—paint this old bead board paneling white, take down these ancient dropped ceiling panels and expose the beams—this cabana will look twice as big." He steered her toward the small bathroom. "I can knock out that back wall to expand the space in here—"

Sunny was no longer even trying to listen. It was all she could do not to hold back, dig in her heels or run. With a hand at her lower spine, Griffin crowded into the bathroom behind her. His body seemed to shut her in, even though he hadn't moved more than an inch or two closer. It was wrong to feel so afraid. She wouldn't move and let him know she was. But her heart pounded, as if to leap from her chest.

"—then, see? This bathroom becomes more usable," he was saying when she turned around, "complete with an outdoor shower right here." He thumped the wall in the corner of the room, and Sunny almost jumped out of her skin.

She couldn't stop the memory. It was all right here, in front of her again, even more vivid than on the night of Chris's party.

She and Laura are in the Seaside ladies' room. Sunny is having trouble with her hair—as usual. She changes the style almost every day. So does Laura. They're giggling about it as Sunny grapples with the elastic band for her ponytail. Laura's hair, hitched high and centered, looks perky. Fine. But then, impatient with Sunny, she glances toward the door. "Our burgers will be there by now. Hurry up. They'll get cold."

"I can't. Every time I get it almost right, my hair slips out somewhere."

Laura's mouth sets. "I'm going back to the table. Don't take all night."

"Laura." But she's already gone. Abandoning the stubborn elastic, Sunny throws it in the trash. Her hair spills free around her

shoulders. Maybe it looks okay this way instead. With a growing sense that she needs to hurry, she looks toward the door. Lingering is never a good thing. Her heart is skipping now. She doesn't like being alone too long. Laura has abandoned her.

She rushes to the door. But before she gets there, someone else comes in. Silently, the door closes, boxing her in. Then the lights go out. In darkness she feels the first lick of real panic.

A hand touches her. Sunny starts to scream, but nothing comes out. Like that day at the bus stop when he loaded her doll carriage in his trunk, he has already covered her mouth... Sunny is trapped.

Sunny blinked the world—the old cabana—back into focus.

Griffin was still talking. "Tile will be better in here. This mold in the corner will be gone." He plowed on, his voice filled with enthusiasm. He sounded happier, more engaged than she'd ever seen him. "The residents will be able to wash off before and after they use the pool. I'd like to put a long vanity on this wall, supply some hair dryers, lotions—"

"Shampoo and conditioner..." She tried to share his eagerness, to calm herself with the mundane words. "Like in a spa." But the memory was still with her. All she could think, or feel, was fear.

Unaware of her growing panic, he grinned. "I'm no designer, but maybe you could help with some other ideas." She forced herself to concentrate.

"What if we picked a nice ocean blue for the walls instead of all white? White trim would really pop then. Some soft green accents? A plant or two?" She stepped away. "A few pretty baskets would warm up the space. They could hold towels and you'd need a hamper for the used ones…"

He tilted his head. "You in then, Counselor?"

"I'm busy with trial prep, but I'll help if I can." Of course she would. In helping others, she forgot about herself. That fear.

"Won't be full-time." He grinned again. "But I'd really welcome your input."

The idea was a good one. Sunny loved her afternoons at the pool, and not having to go home whenever nature called would be a bonus. *If* she could make herself use the new cabana.

But for years she'd been able to mostly hide her fears. Moving to New York had helped, and she'd even survived the Seaside again, thanks to Josh. Besides, she wasn't staying. Her earlier visit to fantasyland was just that.

"Well…"

Griffin took that as a yes. "I'm going to sketch these plans," he said. "I'll need the go-ahead from the management company and the group that owns this complex. If they all agree, we'd have to hire an architect for the blueprints. But this can only add value. Maybe an enhanced pool area will take care of the empty units I have."

Her legs threatened to give out again. Sunny didn't know how it had happened, but as Griffin explained his ideas for the cabana, their positions had become reversed. Now he was blocking the only way out. He was in the doorway, as if ready to go call the management, and she was standing in the center of the small room. She couldn't get past him.

Fresh terror gripped her. She knew he'd never hurt her, yet all she could see or think of was being trapped here.

"Sunny?" Griffin was standing over her now, broad-shouldered and far stronger than she was. Sunny had gone as stiff as a post. Griffin slanted his head to study her. His hazel eyes looked serious. "You all right?"

She could barely breathe. No, she wasn't all right. She would never forget that night when she'd been trapped, hurt…what had she ever done to cause that?

"I'm fine." Her breath came in short little gasps.

"You don't look fine, Sunny."

But his soft tone didn't help. He moved as if to hold her, nothing more than that, but…

The lights had gone out. In the darkness he came at her.

Sunny flinched as if someone had struck her. She put one hand out like a traffic cop.

"Stop!" Her heart was beating like a wild animal caught in a snare.

Beyond thought or reason, using a strength fueled by adrenaline, she shoved Griffin aside.

And ran.

SUNNY WAS STILL shaking early that evening. How would she ever face Griffin again? He must think she was crazy. When the doorbell rang, she almost didn't answer. Then to her surprise, Amanda was there.

To her even greater shock, she wanted to thank Sunny.

"I don't know what I would have done

without you the other day," she said, her gaze on her flip-flops. "I was pretty freaked out by what happened…and I had Josh with me… and, well, I'm glad you were there."

"I'm glad I was, too, Amanda."

For a moment Sunny even forgot the panic she'd felt in the cabana, the fact that she had run from Griffin. She stopped trembling.

"Want to share a smoothie with me?" she asked. "I just got out the blender."

Amanda shrugged. "Sure."

They went into the kitchen. "Does your dad know you're here?"

"I said I was coming over, and I'd be back soon." She paused. "He has to take some new floor tiles to Miss Carrie's tonight so he can start there tomorrow morning. He took Josh to 'help,' so I don't have to hurry," she said.

Now this was a new experience. Not only was Amanda in a good mood, she seemed eager for some girly talk. That worked for Sunny. Sipping their mango smoothies a few moments later, they sat at the counter, where Amanda talked about her little brother and school and, finally, Dixie.

Obviously the friendship had been troubling her.

"I like Dixie," Amanda said, playing with

her straw. "We have fun together—but she sometimes talks me into doing things I don't want to do."

"You both want to be cool." She smiled. "I was the same way at thirteen."

"Really? Were you one of the popular kids?"

Sunny shook her head. No, she'd been the damaged one, the girl who for years had been afraid to walk down a deserted street alone— or go into a dark space. "I was a geek. It was your Uncle Chris who always defined the word 'cool.'"

Amanda grinned. The smile lit up her whole face.

"I love Uncle Chris. He doesn't treat me like a baby."

"Ah. And your father does," Sunny said, seeing where this was going. "So did mine. He does still. It's the way dads are. Might as well enjoy it."

"Really?" Amanda said again, sounding skeptical but intrigued.

"Trust me. When you get older, it stops being annoying."

That didn't go over as well. "I don't think it will," she said. "Sometimes I want to…" She flushed. "I almost said, 'leave home.'"

"Like your mother."

Amanda twirled her straw. "I couldn't do that. Not to Josh." Her eyes met Sunny's. "He would cry again. A lot. I used to be mean to him," she said, "just so he'd stop thinking about Mom." She paused. "I couldn't leave my dad either. He…"

Sunny gentled her tone. "He what, Amanda?"

"He wouldn't say anything. But I think he needs me, too. Right here."

"I'm sure he does." Sunny wished he'd express himself more, and that was putting it mildly. By holding back, Griffin was missing opportunities to heal his children—and probably himself. But who was she to talk? She couldn't seem to heal herself. After today in the cabana, how could they ever have a relationship?

"This has been a hard time for all of you," she said. "I work with girls your age. I've seen a lot of bad times for them, too." The ones who survived. "If there's anything I can do to make things easier for you, please, let me know."

Amanda sipped the rest of her smoothie and stared at the kitchen wall. Finally, she said, "Do you think I should stop being Dixie's friend?"

"I don't know her, Amanda. What do you think?"

Another long pause. "My dad doesn't like her, but I think she's okay."

"If I were you, I wouldn't be quick to do whatever she suggests." For a moment Sunny didn't go on. What if she'd refused to get in that car years ago? What if she'd punched her abuser—as she'd pushed Griffin today—then run? "Dixie is probably just testing you. So the next time, try saying no. It may be she'd like you to be the better influence on her."

"I'm not going to smoke again," Amanda said, wrinkling her nose. It had a pretty spray of freckles across its bridge that made her seem even younger. "I thought that was gross."

Sunny laughed, then patted her hand.

"You're all right, Amanda. Don't let anyone tell you you're not."

She thought that over. "I'd be even better," she said, "if my mom came home."

Reminded of Griffin's refusal to show Amanda the note, Sunny let that sink in for a few seconds. "Is that why you've been testing your father the way Dixie tests you?"

Amanda flushed. "I don't know. I never thought of that."

"Then maybe you should."

Sunny had the impression Amanda had something more on her mind, but she wouldn't push. For a while longer they talked about easier topics. Clothes—what new fashions were cool and which were not—then about the boy at her school who, she thought, liked her although he never said a word.

After another telling pause, Sunny asked, "Anything else?"

Amanda hesitated. "Well, I guess you know about those guys at the pool. My dad made them leave—but I still see one of them."

"At school?" She smiled. "Wow. Two boys."

"No, Tommy graduated last June. I see his car at school, though, when he picks up his youngest brother. There are three of them. And he…always looks at me." She rolled her eyes but with a shy smile. "Dixie calls him my stalker."

Ah, the teenage years. "Do you like his attention?"

She shrugged. "I guess. Sometimes. He's cute."

A stalker? Sunny felt her heart leap, then forced herself to take a deep breath. That must be teen-speak for a boy who liked you. There was no need to pass on her own fears.

Sunny smiled but said, "Well, just remember to trust your instincts." She walked her to the door. "Thanks for coming by, Amanda."

"Could I come again?"

Sunny gave in to the impulse she'd had when they first met—and hugged her. Maybe this fragile connection with Amanda was one of the things Sunny had been missing in her life. "Yes, please."

Amanda surprised her again by hugging back. For a moment, she even clung, her cheek pressed to Sunny's shoulder. When she pulled back, her eyes sparkled with unshed tears, but she was smiling.

"See you," she said, then disappeared into the night.

"See you," Sunny murmured, watching her walk between the two buildings toward her father's apartment.

Well. What do you know?

SUNNY WAS AVOIDING HIM. Griffin knew it, and for the next few days he let her because when she'd pushed him away in the cabana he'd felt shaken, too. She hadn't just flinched. She had panicked. She had run.

He knew now that her demons must be worse than he'd imagined.

But what could he offer her, a woman he couldn't get out of his mind, when he wasn't free? He shouldn't have even mentioned divorce. Sunny had already been hurt by her ex-husband and something more. And then there were his kids. And soon, Sunny would leave. Still, right now he was going to take her advice.

Griffin stopped the van in Dixie's driveway.

Her house was easily three times the size of his apartment. A combination of stone and brick, it rose several stories to a multileveled roof. He went up the wide flagstone path to the front door. On the porch were pots of mums and petunias mixed with some sort of trailing ivy, an artful arrangement that made his neglected flowers pale by comparison.

Griffin rapped the brass door knocker a couple of times.

When a woman answered, he blinked.

Dixie's mother looked much too young to have a teenage daughter. Blonde and willowy, she also had a welcoming smile.

He offered a hand. "I'm Amanda Lattimer's father. Griffin," he added.

The smile disappeared. Her eyes had turned wary, as if she expected trouble, and

Griffin recognized that look. With Amanda he was always ready to hear the worst.

"It's good to meet you," she said at last. "I've been meaning to call. Is there some problem?"

"Not at all." Not right now. They could get to that later. "But I wanted to put a face— mine—to the guy Mandi and Dixie call *him* or *he* all the time."

She relaxed a bit, then held the door open. "You sound like my husband—Dixie's father." She guided him from the entry into a large, tastefully furnished living room. "This is my first year as the wicked stepmother. Frankly, I'm not quite sure what I'm doing."

Griffin couldn't have agreed more. "It's a tough age," he said. And decided there had been enough pleasantries. She offered him a seat, but he remained standing. "I won't take much of your time," he began, then he plunged right in, "but I wonder if you know about the girls smoking at my apartment complex pool."

"Smoking?" She shook her head. "Dixie?"

"And Amanda," he said. "She claims it was your stepdaughter's idea."

Her gaze cooled again. "I understand that

girls this age are keen on experimenting. Do you think it's more serious than that?"

"I hope not. I've already talked to Amanda."

"I'll talk—or her father will—to Dixie."

"Apparently the cigarettes came from his car."

She frowned and stared at her hands. "He's trying to quit. He allows himself two a day. He wondered where they went, but neither of us even thought of Dixie. He blamed the missing package on the people at the car wash. She's usually an easy child to deal with." The frown deepened. "This is a first for us."

Are you sure? Griffin wanted to ask.

"My daughter is just into her teens," he said. "According to her, she and Dixie are nearly a year apart. Amanda can be moody and even obstructive at times."

He explained about Rachel's disappearance and the effect it had on Amanda.

"She's still trying to make sense of what happened, but at the moment she's not only difficult—at times she's also very biddable."

Dixie's stepmother didn't miss the implication.

"You wanted to check out Dixie's background. Her family. Make sure Dixie is a suitable friend for your daughter."

"Well, yes." He rubbed the nape of his neck. "I'm sorry to have done this so clumsily. I don't mean to accuse Dixie—"

"Do you want to know something even more awkward?"

Griffin nodded.

"We've been meaning to talk to *you*. My husband is convinced that Amanda is the instigator." She paused. "We try to keep tabs on their whispered conversations. Their *schemes* have seemed harmless enough. Now I wonder."

Griffin could only stare at her. This was a switch.

Dixie's parents, worried about Amanda.

An *instigator*? Sure, she often tattled on Josh or teased him until he screamed, but that was big sister-little brother stuff. The watch incident had troubled him, but Amanda hadn't taken anything since. That he knew of. Smoking? Amanda claimed she hadn't liked it. And all Griffin heard, day after day, was Dixie-this and Dixie-that. Had he misread the whole situation?

Are you calling me a liar?

"I didn't want to upset you," Dixie's stepmother said. "You're right about this being a hard age. We parents are caught in the middle."

Griffin was already edging toward the door. He'd said his piece. Instead of being reassured about Amanda's friendship with Dixie, he felt stunned.

She opened the door for him. "We'll be talking to Dixie. Tonight."

"I'll talk to Amanda," he said.

Again.

CHAPTER SIXTEEN

SUNNY HAD STAYED away from the pool area—
and Griffin—for several days. She'd worked
full-time and unsnarled most of the pretrial
snags she'd come across. Wallace Day's file
had helped her see where she'd gone wrong,
and this prosecution was shaping up. Then
her boss called.

"Donovan, it's Ralph."

"Yes. I know." She almost smiled. The
DA seized every opportunity to mention his
own name. Or to remind his staff, including
Sunny, that he was the one in power?

"I have something to tell you," he said.

For an instant she wondered if he was
going to fire her. But the only blot on her
win-loss record was Wallace Day, which
couldn't be enough reason. Then he spoke
again and Sunny tensed.

"As you already know, your friend Day
didn't like solitary. But those smear stories

have gotten much worse. And this office doesn't need the publicity."

Sitting frozen at her desk, Sunny didn't respond. *Keep looking over your shoulder, Donovan. One day I'll be there.* How could he blame her for the verdict in his trial? Sunny had lost. Maybe he wasn't sane after all.

Ralph cleared his throat. "I hate to say this, but Wallace Day has been talking about escape. It's unlikely, but if he somehow found a way, he's saying he'd come after you."

Sunny glanced around the apartment—her temporary home. She'd felt safe here. Wasn't she?

"Don't let the stress get to you. I need you. Keep your head down there and work on that trial prep," Ralph said. "I don't think there's any immediate threat, but I didn't want you to read about this in the papers without hearing first from me."

He hung up, and Sunny sat paralyzed in front of her laptop, trying to set her world spinning right on its axis. When her doorbell rang, she jumped. Wallace Day was still in custody. He couldn't be at her door now. Ralph had only given her a heads-up. *I need you*, he'd said. Could it be he was really worried about her? Saw her as his successor? She peered through the security viewfinder, and her stomach tightened anyway.

"Griffin." Keeping him out seemed childish. And she didn't want to be alone right now, even though he must think she was a little crazy. She pasted on a weak smile and opened the door.

"Hey," he said as if she hadn't kept out of his way for days. "Wanted to come by and show you my sketches. I'm waiting for the owners of the complex to weigh in, but I've already talked with management." He went into her dining area to lay the drawings on her desk. "They're not opposed. Take a look."

Sunny waited for him to step aside. He frowned but said nothing. She leaned over the plans. "These are beautiful. I love this larger area where people can sit and relax."

"As you've probably noticed, many of the residents here are older," he said. "They like to socialize at the pool in the morning but don't stay in the sun too long." He glanced at Sunny, whose Florida tan was coming along nicely. The warmth of his gaze almost melted the ice inside her. "This would give them a shady area." He pointed. "If I can get approval for an AC unit, it could go right there.

Not too noticeable, and with the advantage of also being a heating element. On cooler days people could get warm inside."

It was as if they were on two different planets. Griffin with his ideas for the cabana, Sunny hearing Ralph's words echo in her brain. She forced her gaze back to Griffin's plans.

"Have you thought about using this space for a meeting room, too?"

His face brightened. "Great idea. There's already a residents' association. But the clubhouse isn't much better than the cabana, so they normally meet at someone's apartment."

A long silence followed. Fighting her sense of being vulnerable again, she studied his drawings while becoming even more aware of his nearness. She loved the light, fresh scent of his aftershave and the way his five o'clock shadow gave him a rugged, totally masculine look by the end of every afternoon. She liked a lot of things about him.

Griffin rolled up the papers, then placed his hands on her shoulders and slowly turned her to face him, as if he expected her to run again at any moment.

"I'm glad you showed me those," she said, still wanting to jerk away.

"But you're not glad I'm standing in your space." His tone softened. "You weren't exactly glad the other day, either. What is it, Sunny?"

The question she'd been dreading. She wanted to duck out from under his hands, but his touch heated her too-cold skin. Now she was the one who couldn't communicate. She couldn't meet his gaze. Couldn't tell him what had happened just before he rang her bell. What had happened at the Seaside long ago or on the street.

"I've been busy."

Griffin sighed. As if in defeat, he broached a safer topic. "I talked to Dixie's mother. Stepmom." He told Sunny about their meeting. "Nice woman, but she thinks Amanda is the one directing the show. That it was Amanda who urged Dixie to smoke."

Sunny tried to gather her wits. "That can't be true. Dixie took the cigarettes from her father. How would Amanda get them? You don't smoke. And Dixie had the pack when I saw them. Sounds like a cover story to me."

"All I know is, hearing it made me feel lousy. Like I haven't made any headway with Amanda." His gaze was intent. "To be honest, I'm tired of being the bad guy."

Sunny blushed and looked away. "Griffin, let's not—"

"Go there?" he finished for her. "Where should we go, then?"

She spun away from his grasp, as if she might evade the memory of Wallace Day's threats, too. But Griffin walked around her until they were facing each other again. "The other day at the cabana. You ran. I want to know why."

"I ran because—" She couldn't think of a plausible excuse. She was trembling again, her gaze searching for an escape route. She crossed her arms. "I don't have to explain myself to you. I didn't choose to stay in that cabana. That's all I'm going to say."

He shook his head. "Who knew I was such a dangerous character?"

"Griffin, I wasn't afraid of you. I didn't mean that."

"Then what do you mean? Because I don't get it," he said.

Sunny said nothing. She felt as if she were being choked.

"No," he added, "that's a lie. I could tell something was wrong, and I wanted to hold you…kiss you. I'm tired of pretending, even to myself, that I don't."

Still chiding herself for her silence, Sunny struggled not to panic again. Remembering that other time, those times, when she'd felt trapped and helpless and terrified. And now, as Ralph had said, Wallace Day was still threatening to come after her.

"We didn't start on the right foot about Amanda," Griffin went on. "But over time I've figured you felt the same attraction I do." He shrugged. "Not to sound like some pathetic loser here, but I thought you should know."

"It's not you," she managed at last.

She hadn't meant to hurt his feelings. Or to mislead him. Yes, there was an attraction between them, one that couldn't go anywhere now. For either of them.

Griffin shook his head. "Look at you right now. Arms folded across your chest like someone's going to strike you."

Griffin grasped her shoulders again, his touch light. Sunny tried to back out of reach, but he wouldn't let her, and after a moment she gave up. She went limp in his arms, like a marionette whose strings had been cut.

"Sunny," he murmured. "Were you like this with Nate?"

"No," she said. "Nate was…" She ran out of words. "We were fine," was all she said.

"You weren't fine, or you wouldn't be here now. Neither were Rachel and I."

His hands moved along her back. His fingers grazed the nape of her neck. And Sunny shivered. "Did you trust him?"

"I thought I did."

"If it wasn't Nate, who was it, Sunny? Every time I go to touch you, you flinch. If it's not me either, who scared you? Who hurt you?"

She tried to twist from his grasp. He must feel her shaking. She couldn't tell him about Wallace Day or…anyone else.

"No one," she said. "Maybe I'm more neurotic than I ever imagined."

She certainly felt that way right now. But Griffin didn't believe that, either. He didn't let go.

"You're the least neurotic person I've ever known," he murmured. "We'll let the rest go for now." He waited until she relaxed in his arms, her breathing becoming slow and steady. Sunny sank ever deeper into his embrace, wanting so badly to stay there. "I need you to know," he said. "I would never hurt you."

Then he raised her head, looked into her eyes, and slowly, inch by inch, brought his mouth to hers. And still, she couldn't tell him. Couldn't move away. Sunny kissed him back, and clung.

She didn't realize she was crying until he wiped the streaks from her face. Griffin whispered to her, soft, soothing words she barely heard or understood.

Even then, they didn't stop kissing.

They were the best kisses, the truest, she'd ever shared.

The most dangerous.

HIS SENSES WERE STILL buzzing when he left Sunny's apartment. Griffin took the cabana plans with him, but he didn't go home. Instead, he made repairs around the complex, unable to stop thinking about her. Who had turned her into this woman who shied away from a touch? Who ran? Griffin felt as if he were nuts, but he'd made up his mind. He couldn't let this go.

At his sister's house he knocked on the door, then let himself in. Bronwyn poked her head out from the kitchen and grinned.

"Supper's almost ready," she said. "I'll set another place."

Chris came out of the main floor master bedroom, flashing his trademark grin. He was wearing a smaller bandage on his forehead, and his color looked better than it had at the Seaside during the party.

"Hey, man. Just in time." He gave Griffin a one-armed bear hug. "Caught some grouper today. Bron's cooking them now. You don't want to miss this," he said.

"No, sorry. I left the kids with Miss Carrie for an hour, but I have to get home." He glanced at Bron. "Could we talk a minute, Chris?"

"Sure. The sunroom okay?"

Bron sent Griffin an arch look, then went back into the kitchen, obviously sensing this was guy stuff. She'd get any information from Chris later.

Griffin sank on to a floral-patterned rattan chair he didn't recognize—Bron's latest redecorating choice?—then stretched out his legs. Tried to look casual.

"About your sister," he said. "What do you know about her life before Nate?"

She'd said *we were fine*, which meant the problem started farther back.

Chris dropped onto the chair opposite Griffin. "Hey, I grew up with her. I know a lot. Grade point average 4.0. Phi Beta Kappa. Why?"

"No, I meant her personal life."

Chris shook his head. "She was never the social butterfly, if that's what you mean. Sunny had tons of friends—girlfriends—and she tends to keep them. Laura, for instance. They hadn't seen each other in years, but when Sunny came to Florida, they picked up where they left off. My sister inspires loyalty." He thought a moment, then continued. "If I remember right, she had one serious boyfriend in college. Didn't date much before that. Sunny was so much The Brain in high school that the boys kept away. Or she pushed them."

Griffin frowned. He was all too familiar with that. "And after college?"

"Top of the heap in law school," Chris said. "Clerked for an important justice afterward, then took the job in the DA's office. But I wasn't living in New York, and by then she was with Nate. I doubt she was ever a party animal. End of story."

"I don't think so."

Chris leaned forward. "What are you saying?"

He didn't quite know how to phrase this.

"That Sunny must have had some sort of traumatic experience. Something that makes her…jumpy around people sometimes." Me. He thought of the cabana and then of the day she'd moved into her apartment.

"I've never seen that, but then I'm her kid brother." Chris's gaze narrowed. "You give her some reason to jump? Because if you did—"

"Relax. I'm glad you'd defend Sunny—as I would Bron—but her problem must go way back. I wonder if her marriage was more a safe harbor than a love match."

Chris nodded. "Safe? I'm not sure about that, but the three of us—me and my parents—always thought *something* was missing there. At times Nate and Sunny seemed more like colleagues than husband and wife. Certainly she was focused on where she wants to go in her job." He added, "Nate, not as much. My dad says the atmosphere at their place was like a gathering storm. Low pressure with a heavy feeling in the air. But Sunny didn't see the clouds."

"And your mother?"

Chris frowned. "She used to say Sunny was driven toward becoming DA. Now she thinks she's running away from something instead."

"You don't know of any specific reason?"

"If there is, she hasn't said a word to me."

Griffin didn't think she would, but it had been worth a try. She'd certainly clammed up with him. That had been a change—normally he was the one who didn't spill his feelings. "Whatever happened, she's buried it deep inside."

Chris's gaze had sharpened.

"Any reason this has come up now? Why are you here?"

He half smiled to deflect Chris's suspicions. "I smelled grouper."

Chris sat back in his chair. "Okay, stonewall me. But if you want to know what makes Sunny tick—and I'm not opposed to that interest—you'll have to ask her."

"She won't tell. Even after we…" He didn't stop himself soon enough.

Chris pounced on his misstep. "You put the moves on my sister. Right?"

"Not 'the moves,'" he said. But what would he call it? Their kisses were still making his thoughts run wild. He'd loved that silken feel of her hair in his fingers and the way her mouth fit his so perfectly.

Chris wasn't fooled. His eyes lit up.

"No kidding. You serious?"

He shouldn't be. He admired Sunny's grit, her determination to succeed—as he hadn't done in Boston. He liked how she was with his children. He sure liked how she looked. But it was the wrong time for him. He had to think about his kids. He had to find Rachel.

This was the wrong place for Sunny, who would soon go back to New York. He knew that—and when she left, Josh and Amanda would suffer again. Everything about him and Sunny together was wrong. Yet, after he'd really kissed her, that no longer seemed to matter.

"Yeah," he finally said, surprising himself. "I am serious."

"You're sure? This is a serious offer?"

With her cell phone glued to her ear, Sunny couldn't suppress her excitement. The apartment had a buyer! That same couple had accepted the counteroffer, and for the first time since Griffin had kissed her, she stopped remembering the warmth of his mouth on hers. The dark secret she feared would make him think less of her.

Nate was just as enthusiastic. "It's not half

bad," he said. "The buyer is as motivated as I am—we are—to sell."

They discussed the details. Sunny had no objection to the furniture and artwork the buyers wanted to purchase with the unit. Most of what remained was Nate's anyway. Let him decide.

"Thanks, Sunny. I'll fax you the new forms to sign. We can get this done right away. It's an all-cash deal."

Sold. So fast. Now Sunny could begin to look for her new home in Manhattan. Nate and his fiancée would get their house in Connecticut, if not the same one they'd first wanted.

"You know what this means," Nate said.

"Yes." The official end of their relationship. Just as whatever she had with Griffin would probably be over soon. "But don't you feel a bit…torn?" she asked. "A lot of memories are there."

He tried to brush away the sentiment. "Time to let go."

Yet now that the sale was real, Sunny couldn't let go just like that. As with the nightmarish memories that swamped her at the most inopportune times, she had no control over her feelings about her marriage.

"Remember our first Christmas? We got the last tree on the lot somewhere on upper Madison. It was a spindly little thing with half its branches missing."

"All I remember is it was snowing like blazes."

Unlike Griffin, Nate had never been the most optimistic person. "Of course you remember. We dragged it home between us, leaving a trail on the sidewalk in all that snow. We popped corn and made cranberry garlands to decorate. Then half the tree lights went out as soon as we plugged them in." Her eyes began to fill with tears. "You tried to find which bulbs were dead, but they were out everywhere. We lit candles in the fireplace that didn't work anyway." And, wrapped in each other's arms, they had watched what was left of the glow and glitter.

"I don't remember any candles."

Sunny blinked. But he must. That memory was as much a part of her—and their years together—as the nightmare remembrance of the Seaside, the bus stop. Just as the comforting kisses she and Griffin had shared today were now a part of her.

"Don't you remember that other holiday when I burned the turkey to a cinder? And we ate it anyway because you said I shouldn't feel bad—"

"Sunny, what is this?" His tone had chilled. "Some weird trip down memory lane like in an old movie?"

"No," she said. *Yes*. When she'd left New York and come to Florida, she'd been hurt but angry, too. Now, she only felt sad. "The memories still make me cry."

She dabbed at her eyes. There was a long silence.

"You've always been the touchy-feely type," he said, "but after the papers are signed, the new owners will move in. So why cling to all those feelings?"

"They'll change the paint colors we chose," she said. "Maybe knock out the wall between the living/dining room and kitchen, as we had planned to do. Someday." She blinked again, then went on. "They'll grow tomatoes and peppers in pots like we did on the terrace—"

"Or nothing at all," Nate said. "Maybe they'll be too busy."

Was that a dig at her job again? "But even if they are, they might haul a scrawny tree down Madison Avenue some Christmas Eve, having forgotten to plan for the holiday."

"They might forgo a tree altogether." Nate

sighed. "What are you trying to say, Sunny? You wanted us to stay together? Work out everything that went wrong? I'm with Lisa now."

For a moment, she sat, stunned and miserable.

She had wanted to revisit the time when she'd been happy and her marriage was new, filled with promises that were later broken, a time when her worst memories had receded and she'd felt safe. For a while.

So this was it. The end before some new beginning she couldn't yet envision.

"I'm happy," Nate said. "I haven't been able to say that in a long time."

His voice brought her back to reality. She was being maudlin, overemotional as she'd been weeks ago in Judge Ramsay's courtroom. Yet his words had made her ache. *Were you ever happy with me?*

"Nate, I wasn't trying to make you feel guilty. I only wanted to touch our past once more—make it matter to both of us—before I move on, too..." To what, she didn't know. "I wish you both the best," she managed.

Nate waited a beat too long. Then, "Take care of yourself, Sunny."

It was over. Finally over. She hadn't expected to feel this bad. She thought again of Griffin, of his arms around her and of their kisses, but that made her feel even worse.

Her ex-husband had a new life, a new love. Soon, they would have a baby. For all the obvious reasons, Sunny doubted Griffin was in her future. But what if he could be? She already loved little Josh. She was doing better with Amanda. Over the past weeks she'd even learned to separate work from her personal life, to look around and see what had been missing.

Now she was free to go as far as she could. *I need you.* In New York, once the media storm ebbed over Wallace Day, the DA slot she wanted so badly—that she'd probably wrecked her marriage for—would be within her reach. That should have made her feel better. But it didn't.

In the silence after Nate rang off, she sat with the phone in her hand, as if she could see through it to New York and the apartment that was no longer theirs.

"I was only trying to say goodbye," she said to herself.

CHAPTER SEVENTEEN

LAURA SAT BACK in her chair and twisted her napkin with both hands. Sunny had agreed to meet her at the mall for lunch, despite the lousy weather report. The bright afternoon was about to cloud up and become a pretty bad storm. Somewhere in the Atlantic, another hurricane was also brewing. But Sunny had welcomed this chance to leave the apartment before it rained and escape her thoughts about Wallace Day.

"I can't believe you're sitting across from me looking perfectly fine," Laura said. "The man's a murderer. Aren't you scared?"

Yes. Yet Sunny tried to appear normal because that was what she did—what she'd done for years. But ever since Ralph's call yesterday, Sunny had felt she was being followed. Watched.

In line at the bank, from the corner of her eye, the man behind her had looked suspicious. He had the same hair as Wallace Day.

Her heart pounded until she saw his face. He was only a stranger with warm dark eyes. Wallace Day's gaze was soulless. Sunny would never forget that.

"I've long been convinced you can tell a killer by his eyes," she said. "Day killed poor Ana Ramirez without a thought. He's been asked why many times, and his answer is always the same. *Because I could*, he says. Then he smiles that falsely angelic smile."

Remembering his mug shot, Sunny felt a shiver run down her spine. Nobody smiled for a police camera except Wallace.

"I have goose bumps just hearing about him," Laura said.

"I can't let fear stop me. I'm working, I'm living, I'm having lunch with you. Normal," she said, trying to reassure herself at the same time.

"Did you tell your parents?"

"No, but I mentioned Ralph's call to Chris. Really," she said, "there's nothing to worry about."

Laura looked skeptical. "I think your mom and dad should know. Sunny, you have people who love you. You're not alone."

She knew that, but Sunny kept fiddling with the saltshaker, moving it from one side of the table to the other. She wouldn't mention Griffin. She would tell him later. After all, there was no rush. Wallace Day hadn't escaped. So far his threats were empty.

"Thanks, Laura. Can we talk about something more pleasant? Let me see those new pictures of your kids."

Sunny took the small album of prints she offered and thumbed through it. Three towheads with big smiles like Laura's and what must have been their father's eyes. Her husband was a good dad, she told Sunny. Her oldest must be in Amanda's class.

"We had no problem getting pregnant," Laura said, grinning. "Believe me. But we decided to stop at three."

Sunny's heart lightened. Back in the day Laura had always been the one to coax her from a mood—maybe as Dixie did for Amanda when one of them wasn't plotting some new experiment.

She handed the album to Laura. "Thanks for sharing your family with me."

Laura held her gaze. "Sunny, we're friends. My life is an open book with you." Laura paused. "How long have we known each other? We met in first grade, so we must have been six—my daughter's age now."

Sunny began to feel uncomfortable. Seeing pictures of Laura's kids was fine, but… "We used to run back and forth in our neighborhood all the time."

"Until we moved across town," Laura remembered, "and although we weren't living as close, we could have play dates and sleepovers." She brightened. "Oh, and don't forget dinners at the Seaside. I always remember you when I'm there."

Sunny's pulse quickened.

"That was a long time ago. Hard to believe," she said.

Now Laura had a beautiful family, a wholesome life without all the bad memories Sunny couldn't seem to overcome.

Laura laughed. "Remember that wonderful old baby carriage you had? Every time you came to play at my house, you wheeled all your dolls in it. I was so jealous."

"It was my grandmother's." She'd hoped the carriage would protect her. Who would pick up a little girl walking down the street with something that size? It hadn't been enough, though, and the woman at the bus stop hadn't intervened.

Sunny started to stand up. She couldn't bear to share any more memories. Or to envy

Laura what she had. "I have to go. Sorry to cut this short—" One more memory, and she'd fall apart as she had with Griffin.

But Laura wouldn't let her leave. She drew Sunny back down. "What's wrong?" she asked. "You used to get this same look sometimes at my house. I always wondered why. Is it because you're frightened now about Wallace Day?"

"No," she murmured.

"Is it because—oh, no. Oh, no," she said. Laura was the one who looked haunted now. "Oh, Sunny. The last time we had lunch when you asked about my mother—"

"I should visit her before I leave. I hope she got her roof replaced before Mom and Dad. They waited forever."

She wouldn't visit, though. She never wanted to step inside that house again.

Sunny pulled free of Laura's hand. "Please, tell your mother I asked about her."

But Laura's eyes met hers, and she seemed to see everything.

"I told you my parents had divorced, but you don't know why. It was after my mother learned about his…problem. But I never thought he—that you—" They exchanged a long look, and Sunny could see tears in Laura's eyes. "Was that really why you and I lost touch, Sunny?"

Abruptly she left the table. Not stopping when Laura called out for her to wait, she threw a quick goodbye over her shoulder. Blindly, she rushed through the restaurant and out into the mall, where people bustled into and out of stores on both levels. Protection, she thought, in a crowd.

She'd never asked Laura about her parents' divorce. She hadn't wanted to even say his name. The back of her neck prickled as she walked toward the parking garage. She was halfway there when Laura caught up with her. She grasped Sunny's arm.

"Sunny. Let's talk."

"I can't. Please, Laura." She tried to pull away, but Laura held on.

"I love you," she said with tears running down her cheeks. "I can't believe I didn't know... I should have known..."

"Sunny?" She turned to see Amanda standing there with Dixie, both of them frowning. It was clear from the girls' expressions that they'd been quarreling. Amanda was clutching a bag from Old Navy, her arms folded across her chest. "Are you *sick*?"

"I'm fine," she insisted. She forced herself to take a few slow breaths and introduced Laura to Dixie and Griffin's daughter. "Laura, don't worry. I'm going home now."

"You are home," Laura murmured. She hugged Sunny this time without any resistance.

Amanda cleared her throat. "Can I help?"

Even at thirteen, she could see that Sunny wasn't all right.

"No, you and Dixie enjoy your shopping. What's your favorite store? Hollister, American Eagle...or Forever 21?"

"None of those are cool," Dixie said. "And my...stepmother just called. She's worried about some storm. She thinks we should leave now."

Amanda glanced at Dixie, her eyes shooting sparks. "We can shop some other time." Dixie returned the glare. Whatever they'd argued about, their friendship was clearly on hold for now. Then Amanda looked away at someone.

Sunny turned around and saw two boys lounging against a storefront looking at the girls. Did Amanda know them? If she did, she didn't say so, but her cheeks turned pink. Sunny half smiled. Her admirers were really adding up.

Amanda turned back to Sunny. "Could I ride home with you? Dixie's stepmom would have to go out of her way to drop me off."

Sunny put an arm around her shoulders, as eager to leave the mall as Amanda seemed to be. "Of course. I'd be happy to drive you home."

BY THE TIME Amanda called to say she was on her way home, the wind was beginning to rattle the trees throughout the Palm Breeze complex, which today seemed aptly named.

Griffin eyed the yard through the front windows, trying to decide if he should put the storm shutters in place. If he didn't, he could have broken glass everywhere. He'd learned his lesson in the season's earlier hurricane, the one that had torn off part of the Cabots' roof. Mother Nature always won.

This wasn't going to be one of the area's usual afternoon thunderstorms but something closer to an approaching hurricane. He was glad Amanda would be here soon.

As soon as he saw Sunny's car pull up, he opened the front door. He was down the walk and leaning in the driver's side window before Amanda got out.

"I want to talk to you," he told Sunny. "Now."

Sensing that trouble was brewing, which it definitely was, Amanda cast him a glance, then hurried inside. Griffin wasn't sure, but he thought he heard her say "take care of her" as she swept past him.

"I should check my apartment," Sunny said, not meeting his eyes. "I might have left some windows open. The storm's about to break."

"You bet it is." Griffin reached inside, shut off the engine, and took her keys from the ignition. "Your windows can wait. Come on in."

When he and Sunny entered his apartment, Amanda was nowhere in sight. Josh was in his room. In the foyer Griffin stopped to face Sunny.

"Why didn't you tell me about Wallace Day planning to escape?"

"I meant to tell you when I got here. Who told you?"

"Chris. Then Bron weighed in, too." They told each other everything. He took a breath to steady himself. "If something happens, and that lunatic does come here, I live in the next building from yours. I'm your first line of defense."

She shook her head. "This is my problem to handle."

"Like hell it is," he said in the low tone he usually reserved for Amanda's transgressions. "You're not handling this by yourself, Counselor. Whether you trust me or not, whether you think it's any of my business or you don't, I don't care. I'm not going to turn my back and hope you're okay. Even Amanda could see you're not."

He was getting up a full head of steam now. Just when he'd decided he was serious about a relationship with Sunny, he'd had to find out about this threat from someone else? "If that madman breaks out with some crazy idea to hurt *you*—I'm not going to let that happen! Understand?"

"They're only threats, Griffin. I've heard them before." Her face was ashen. "They'd catch him before he got here."

"You think?" He drew another deep breath. "I'm something of an expert on people who disappear, who just walk away, like Day could from that upstate facility."

"You're wrong. He doesn't even know where I am."

"He could find out. And if you were that certain he couldn't, you wouldn't look like you do right now. You're plenty scared. And it shows."

Her mouth trembled. A sob broke from her throat. "Oh, but I don't want it to."

"Ah, baby," he said. "I'm here." Then he gently drew her to him. She didn't try to resist, to step away or run. She buried her face in the crook of his neck, her warm tears soaking his skin.

"This is getting to be a habit," she murmured.

"It's okay," he murmured in her ear. "I won't let him hurt you."

And to his utter surprise she said, "He already did."

For a moment Griffin didn't understand. There was no way Wallace Day had touched her. Even now he was still in confinement. In court he'd been in leg irons.

But her slim body shook in his arms. She must be breaking under the pressure. "You aren't talking about Wallace Day now, are you? Tell me," he said.

Who hurt you, Sunny? Who was he?

And at last, her voice muffled by the fabric of his shirt, his embrace, she began, her words halting. "From the age of eight or so until I was Amanda's age...my friend Laura's father, he...molested me."

Griffin shut his eyes as she spoke. And tightened his hold. Her story, even though she glossed over what he suspected must have been the worst of it, was an ugly one.

"I should have done something to stop him," she said in what passed for a controlled voice.

"How? You were only a child," he said. "You didn't tell Jack?"

She shook her head. "I've never told anyone. Not until today when Laura guessed what had happened. I love her so much," she said, her voice breaking, "yet I couldn't bear to even see her when I first came home. I didn't want to get anywhere near those memories."

"And yet they're always there," he said softly, rocking her in his arms. "What about your mother?"

"You know how she is. Mom's always like 'Is everybody happy?' I couldn't do that to her." She shuddered against him. "I couldn't hurt her."

"Even when he was hurting you," Griffin said.

"Chris doesn't know, either," she hastened to add. "He's my kid brother. How could I tell him something like that?"

"You can tell me. Anything."

She shivered. "He used to wait for me, track me. Halfway to Laura's house, wherever I was along the way, he'd suddenly be there. His car at the curb. His trunk open. He'd take my doll carriage, put it in, and slam the lid. He'd talk me into that car…and every time I went. I couldn't say no."

The slow roll of anger was almost more than he could control. What kind of man could do that? What sort of monster stole a child's innocence, robbed her of her girlhood? For once, he couldn't chide himself for watching Amanda so closely. And yet, was that close enough? Jack and Kate were great parents and still Sunny had been harmed. He was amazed that she was as put together, as strong a woman, as she was. With that history, she could easily have lost her mind, her way.

She sagged against him, and Griffin let her. He would hold her up forever. He would breathe for her if he had to. My God. The little girl inside her was still protecting everyone else. That was why she fought so hard for other girls. Like her.

"No more," he whispered in her hair.

Shaking too, Griffin put a light hand over the back of her neck and lifted her face, slowly bending toward her, angling his mouth for a better fit. He kissed her, oh, so gently, trying to let her know she would be safe with him. It stunned and surprised him that she let the kiss go on. Trusted him enough.

"Griffin," she murmured, but he didn't stop.

When she would have eased back, he folded her hand in his against his chest, then kissed her again. He could do this all night. Which only complicated matters, of course. He and Sunny had become way more than friends. *Yeah, I'm serious.* He'd been falling in love with her for a while, and she had just bared her soul. Whatever happened between them, with her life in New York and his endless search for Rachel, and with his kids, he would be there for her. Somehow.

They needed a serious discussion about that. Soon. After one more…

"Dad!" The strident tone was like a shock of cold water. He and Sunny jerked apart. Amanda stood in the hallway, hands on her hips. Her freckles dark and vivid on her skin. *"What are you doing?"*

Her words echoed through the apartment. They overcame the sounds of the palm fronds rustling in the breeze, the first clap of thunder overhead. Lightning flashed, but she didn't seem to notice.

"Amanda," he began. He could feel the flush creeping up his neck, as if his teenaged daughter was the parent and he was the kid caught smoking. Or, rather, necking.

She clapped her hands over her ears. "I don't want to hear it!" And glared at Sunny. "When I said to take care of her, I didn't mean like *this*. You lied to me. You said you wanted to find Mom—but you don't!" She plowed on, tears in her eyes. "You never did. Did you even care for her?"

"Of course I did."

"And this is how you show it? Gross," she muttered. "I don't think you love her at all. No wonder she left." She whirled to face Sunny. *"He* never cared about me! He probably doesn't love Josh, either! He won't love you!"

Then she was running past Sunny, past him, to the door. Amanda yanked it open, and the wind poured in. So did the first drops of rain. Before he could stop her, she had vanished. The door slammed shut behind her.

Sunny let out a long breath. And with that she seemed perfectly normal again. It amazed him how quickly she could come back to herself after what she'd told him. "Griffin. I tried to tell you she was there. I don't know for how long…"

His heart ached. Sunny had seen Amanda first. She'd been trying to push at his chest. She'd said his name in warning. "I really blew it, didn't I?"

"Yes. You did."

For a moment he didn't believe she had said that. Not that he'd expected her to pat him on the back. He was surprised Josh hadn't come out of his room after all the noise.

Her voice hardened. "I know she was shocked to see us. She had no idea that we are—we were—whatever we are."

His mouth tightened. "It wasn't as if she caught us in my room, Sunny. I had no intention of taking this to the next level, especially with my children in the house."

"I didn't say you did."

"Then what?"

"You should have worked things out first with Amanda."

"Well, obviously. But I haven't."

She shook her head. "Griffin, you're deluding yourself. You have been ever since we met. Can't you see? When Amanda tried to talk about her mother, you kept silent. You refused to share your own emotions with her, including your ambivalence about Rachel. And why didn't you show her the note? Years ago. That would have gone a long way toward avoiding this…debacle."

"Fancy word, Counselor," he said, crossing his arms over his chest.

"Maybe. But you're still hedging your bets—with Rachel, with your children. Now with me. Where did you think *we* were going? When you can't even be honest with your kids?"

He grabbed his jacket, then started for the door. He didn't need Sunny to tell him about his situation. "That's just it. They're kids, like you with that monster years ago. They're not adults. I'm responsible for them. Rachel's disappearance was mine to deal with, not theirs."

He'd done his best. He'd been responsible for others since he was ten years old. *Make Daddy proud.* He hadn't been much older than Sunny when her abuse began, the same woman who'd stripped her feelings bare just moments ago.

She followed him to the door. "Do you think—did you ever think for one minute—that you should level with them as much as possible?" she asked. "Tell them *something* of how *you* feel? I know you can't tell them everything. But all they see is their father being closed off as if nothing ever happened."

He opened the door. The wind blew in. "I'm protecting them."

"No, Griffin. You're hiding from them. Didn't you hear Amanda? If you want to know what I think—even if you don't—her rebellion has been her way of begging you to open up. Because of your refusal to share anything of yourself, she thinks you don't care at all."

Breathing hard, he stepped outside. "You don't hesitate to share what you think, or how you feel—except for one thing." He watched her face turn white again, yet he couldn't seem to stop. "Until now, no one knew about that man and what he did to you," he said and saw her flinch. "You've kept that secret, Sunny, even though it's been hurting you for years."

"And I shouldn't have told you!" she cried, but Griffin wasn't done.

"Just like my secret," he said, "about Rachel's note. Maybe you're the one who feels abandoned—not Amanda."

GRIFFIN WAS GONE before she could respond. Sunny closed the door, then leaned against it, fighting for breath, fighting not to cry. She couldn't leave. Josh was still in the apartment. Sunny would stay. As if she were really Josh's mother. As if she belonged here.

Until a few minutes ago, that had been her other secret. Her secret hope for the future.

After the hurtful words she and Griffin had exchanged, she supposed they were done. She could only pray he found Amanda before it was too late for him to make amends.

CHAPTER EIGHTEEN

GRIFFIN COULDN'T FIND Amanda anywhere. In the rising wind, he searched the entire complex.

Where could she have gone?

His van was still in its usual parking spot, and she didn't drive yet. That battle, which he might welcome just now, hadn't begun. Dixie couldn't pick her up, either; neither of them was old enough to have a license. Though her age hadn't stopped Amanda's friend from snatching her father's cigarettes...

Amanda must be somewhere in the Palm Breeze complex.

He forged on through the growing storm. He knocked on doors, even the Grump's, but Walter Lynx seemed more concerned about his faulty ceiling fan than a missing girl.

At Miss Carrie's apartment, Griffin peered through the screen and asked, "Have you seen Amanda?" She hadn't, but Amanda often spent time with the older woman, who loved to ply her with cookies and conversation. Amanda had become friends with her just as she'd warmed up to Sunny. That is, until she'd seen her with Griffin.

"She can't have gone far," Miss Carrie fretted. "Not in this weather."

He took a second to reassure her that he'd find Amanda, but she looked shaken. And Griffin had to plunge back into the storm.

"Amanda!" he shouted into the wind.

He'd left Sunny behind with Josh. He knew she wouldn't abandon his son, but after the bitter words they'd traded, he doubted she'd want anything more to do with him. That new phase of their relationship had been short-lived. She was probably embarrassed to have told him her secret, and after Amanda's outburst, she'd use this rift as an excuse to shut him out.

Griffin jogged through the rain and wind.

Eyes focused ahead, he stumbled over an exposed tree root, lost his balance—and fell. He landed hard in a puddle. Water was gushing down the street and beginning to overflow the storm drains. Rain pelted his already-wet jacket.

He didn't care.

All he wanted was to *find Amanda*.

Later, he would try to repair the damage with Sunny. If it could be fixed.

Getting to his feet, he ran through the gate into the pool area.

"Amanda!" He had shouted himself hoarse, but still she didn't answer.

Panic gripped him. The day Rachel left home, he hadn't known she was gone until his day, or rather night, at the studio ended. Griffin had come home to a house where two young children had huddled together.

Appalled that they'd been left on their own, he'd gathered them close. Amanda had been at school all day, but the parents' car pool had dropped Josh off from day care around the time she got home. After that they'd been alone.

"Amanda, why didn't you call me?" he'd asked.

And her gaze had strayed from his. "I know you're busy."

In those first days he'd nearly lost his mind. Had Rachel been abducted? Her car hijacked? Then it was found at the mall with the note he'd told Sunny—if not his children—about. But it was Sunny's words about Amanda that he remembered now.

*Because of your refusal to share yourself,
she thinks you don't care.*

Had that been true of Rachel, as well?

Griffin picked his way around the swimming pool to the cabana. In its present state
it wasn't the sort of place Amanda might take
shelter, but he had to look.

Where are you, baby?

The empty cabana smelled musty. He
couldn't wait to tear the thing apart, make
something better of it. Now, even the dark
corners of the bathroom appeared to be im-
penetrable. It was like trying to see through
ink. He remembered Sunny, and her fear,
here. The way she'd run from him.

He flipped the light switch, but nothing
happened.

He stepped back out, then closed the door.

His skin clammy in the wet jacket, he
slumped against a wall.

Where else to look?

As soon as Griffin opened the door to his
apartment, the wind slammed it shut again.

"I can't find her," he said, dripping in the
entryway. "What if she fell or a rotten branch
hit her and she's out there, unconscious or…"

Sunny hurried to him. She laid a hand

against his mouth. For the moment, their earlier quarrel—and what it meant—would have to be forgotten. All she knew was he loved his daughter. If only Amanda knew that.

"It was bad enough when Chris got stranded on his boat with Josh. But this storm could turn lethal," he said, sinking on to the nearest chair.

The sky outside was dark with heavy clouds. The power had gone out half an hour ago. Sunny ran to the linen closet in the hall and came back with a stack of fluffy towels.

"Here. Dry off. You're shivering."

She laid the towels beside him, but he ignored them to reach for her hand.

"Sunny. I want to say I'm sor—"

She was gone before their fingers touched. Not now, she thought. Amanda had to stay uppermost in her mind. And his. Once she was found, Sunny would try to make sense of what she'd done in telling him about Laura's father.

She was headed for the bedroom to find Griffin dry clothes when Josh appeared in the hall. He'd been in his room building something with Legos, and Sunny gave him what she hoped was a reassuring smile. So far, since the night on the boat, he hadn't seemed overly worried about this storm.

In the living room he launched himself at Griffin.

"Hey, buddy."

In his father's arms, Josh looked around. "Where's Mandi? Is she still mad?"

Sunny almost wished Griffin would lie. *Amanda's in her room.* But he didn't.

"She went out," he said instead. "Probably to see a friend."

Josh shook his head. "She and Dixie had a fight today."

"Well, then, one of her other friends."

"She doesn't have other friends."

That surprised Sunny and apparently Griffin, too.

"We'll find her."

"What if we don't? You didn't find Mommy," he said, then tucked himself into the crook of Griffin's arm like a small animal needing to hibernate.

"Not yet," Griffin agreed. Gently, he set Josh away. "I need to get back out there."

"We'll both go." Sunny wouldn't take no for an answer. She waited until Griffin had changed his clothes. "We can drop Josh at my parents' house. He can stay with them."

ON THE TRIP across town to the Cabots' house, what little traffic there was had snarled at every intersection, and Griffin chafed at the few miles that seemed to take hours. When they finally arrived, Kate met them at the door.

Her home was warm—too warm with the AC out—and cozy. The new roof seemed to be holding.

"Josh will be fine here," Kate said. "Just find her."

Jack poked his head out of the hall closet with several battery-powered lanterns in hand. "Chris and Bron are going out, too. His four-wheel drive can handle any conditions."

Leaving Josh in good hands, Griffin and Sunny headed for Dixie's house.

"When Rachel disappeared," he said, eyes fixed ahead on the wet street, "there was nothing I could do. I felt helpless, like the night Josh and Chris were lost. But now, with Amanda—how can she protect herself? That's my job," he insisted in a strangled tone.

Sunny didn't say anything, but Griffin almost missed her advice now.

The big house on the next corner, like the Cabots', was dark. Griffin said a quick prayer that Amanda had come to her friend, even after their quarrel. The same way Sunny was sitting next to him now, lending her support as if they hadn't taken each other apart earlier.

This time Dixie's father answered the door. He had the kind of polished good looks Griffin had seen every day in his TV career.

"Sorry," the man said. "We haven't seen Amanda since the girls went to the mall."

Disappointed, Griffin tried again. He didn't know where else to look.

"What about your daughter's other friends? My son says the girls had an argument, but Amanda's alone, so maybe she'd try one of them."

"I wouldn't know about that. Dixie doesn't tell me much." He paused. "In fact, my wife says Amanda is her only friend."

Recalling Josh's words, Griffin frowned. Why didn't Dixie have friends, either?

"Not that surprising," her father said. "My daughter has only lived with us for a little over a year. She stays for the school term, then spends summers with my ex and her new husband. Oh, and we have her every other holiday season."

"I see."

Both Amanda and Dixie had been up-rooted from environments where they had friends and extended family to support them. He had only himself to blame for Amanda's rebellion. And for her running away.

Dixie's father asked his daughter about Amanda, but she had no idea where her friend might be. Back in the van, Griffin and Sunny checked hospitals and clinics next. They looked in shelters and churches.

Then Bron and Chris called to say they'd turned up nothing, either.

Griffin's head ached. He felt bone-tired, and every TV news story about a missing girl replayed in his mind. He'd covered more than one. They rarely ended well. *Please, let us find her*, he thought, a growing emptiness inside him. He would never make another mistake. He would somehow convince Amanda of how much he loved her. Like Sunny, he'd bare his very soul.

Because she had been right. He didn't share his deepest feelings. His kids didn't know how much he cared.

But they would. If he got one more chance.

HEAD DOWN, AMANDA sloshed through the puddles on the sidewalk. When she'd dashed out of the apartment, she'd had no idea where to go. All she wanted was to get away. For hours she'd been walking with no notion of where she was. She'd passed the convenience store on the corner long ago. Then she'd plunged into another neighborhood where nothing looked familiar. And another after that. Somehow she'd gotten turned around. Now, with the rain falling harder, she was nowhere near the Palm Breeze Court. Was she?

Maybe she'd never go back...like her mother.

Amanda hugged her wet sweater around her. Her hair straggled in her face. She felt cold all over, even when the temperature must be seventy-something. The air had that thick, dense feel. If her father was in love with Sunny Donovan, as much as he could love, that meant he had given up on finding Mom. How could he just forget her?

She didn't care if she never saw him again.

She stumbled but didn't fall. To be fair, she'd said mean things. He might still like Josh after all, but little brothers were cute and cuddly. Just wait a few years until he grew a foot overnight and his legs got so long he looked like a stork. Amanda already had those big feet. Her nose kept growing, but nothing else did, except her freckles, and most of the time she hated herself. No wonder her dad didn't love her. Well, let him have Sunny, then. Amanda had been on the verge of really liking *her* when *he* had ruined everything.

She'd just keep walking. Even if the storm blew the whole state of Florida off the map, she wouldn't care. Amanda looked around the unfamiliar street, the houses she'd never seen before. They were all dark now. So were the streetlights that hadn't come on when the sky grew black and the wind began to howl. Her damp sweater made her shake inside.

Where could she go? Grandma Kate and Grandpa Jack would take her in—her Aunt Bron and Uncle Chris, too. But they lived… were they far away? Or had she walked halfway there already? Amanda fished her cell phone from the pocket of her jeans, but to her dismay its screen stayed blank. Had it gotten wet?

She shook it, but nothing happened. If her cell was dead, the GPS wouldn't work, either. Now she was alone out here in the rain, and she couldn't call Dixie, if she would even answer the phone after their fight. Amanda couldn't remember now what they'd argued about.

A car passed her on the empty street. Amanda gave it a second glance. She'd seen the same dark sedan before. Circling the block? Confused, like her? What should she do? She didn't like the way the sky looked, and the rain wasn't going to let up anytime soon. The wind whistled between the strange houses like someone calling a dog. On the next corner a signpost rattled. What if it tore from its base and struck her in the head? She was alone. She was lost.

If only she'd had some plan when she left home. She and Dixie always had plans. But, no, not home. She meant the apartment. She would never think of it as home, especially after seeing her dad kissing Sunny.

Gross. They were disgusting. They were...

"Need a ride?" The same car she'd seen before rolled up next to her. The window was halfway down, and a guy leaned toward her, but she couldn't quite see his face. "I'm going your way," he said, but how could he know? Amanda didn't know where she was going.

"That's okay," she said. "Thanks anyway."

The car stopped. "You live at the Palm Breeze Court, right?" And in that instant she recognized his car. The brown sedan looked darker when wet. She recognized the driver, too. "Get in," he said, his tone coaxing. "You don't want to walk in this rain. I'll drive you home."

She hesitated. He kept smiling. The car would be warm and dry. She could feel the heat from the open window. Amanda was soaked through by now, and her teeth had begun to chatter. When he flung open the passenger door, her hesitation vanished.

She didn't know him very well, but he wasn't a stranger. Tommy was the older of the two brothers who'd played Marco Polo at the pool until her dad sent them away. *Dixie calls him my stalker.* She'd seen him today at the mall, and as usual she'd felt torn between wanting his attention and worrying about what it meant.

She got in the car, then glanced at him. "Thanks. I bet we're only a mile or so from my house."

"I bet," he said, his smile broader.

Amanda's pulse leaped. Up close she didn't like his smile. There was something weird about it and the way he always watched her like a cat stalking a mouse.

But it was too late. Amanda heard the click of the automatic door locks.

She wasn't going anywhere.

She was trapped.

GRIFFIN DROVE BACK toward the Palm Breeze complex, his thoughts spinning. He and Dixie's father were alike.

"If only I hadn't pulled my children away from Boston, or even before from Philly and Uncle Theo," Griffin said, half to himself. "If Rachel hadn't left. Or if I found her before too much damage was done."

At least the cops were on the lookout for Amanda now. That had been another of their stops—filing a missing persons report. For his daughter, a minor, he didn't need to wait as he'd had to when Rachel vanished.

"The first year after my wife disappeared," he told Sunny, "I pulled out all the stops. Hired that PI. Plastered flyers everywhere. Jumped on Facebook every fifteen minutes to post another be-on-the-alert. All for nothing," he said. "What if the same thing happens now?"

"Griffin, don't beat yourself up." Sunny glanced at him. "You're doing all you can. Right now."

Without answering, he swung the van in at the front gate of the Palm Breeze Court. If he were doing all he could, he'd have found Amanda by now.

Griffin would start yet another circuit of the streets that wound through the complex. But his first stop was home. She might have come back while they were gone. Amanda's temper flared, but just as quickly her anger tended to die. To his dismay, the apartment was still empty.

As he and Sunny cruised the dark, silent streets, they didn't talk, and Griffin's spirits sank even further. He had no idea where to go next. All he knew was, he couldn't give up. As he neared the swimming pool area, Sunny touched his arm.

"Griffin. I just thought of something. Amanda does have one other friend, sort of. Remember those boys at the pool?"

He frowned. "Amanda knows I don't want her to see them again. That guy is way too old for her."

"But she has seen him," Sunny said. "The one named Tommy-something picks up his youngest brother at her school. Amanda said he seems to like her."

His mouth set. "Why didn't you tell me this before?"

Her hand dropped away from his arm. "I didn't think of it, really. She's at the age when there's a lot of drama and intrigue about boys, most of it theoretical. But earlier today at the mall, I think he might have been there. I'm sorry," she said.

He reached for his cell phone. His cop friend could get Tommy's full name and address from the guys in motor vehicles.

At the corner he turned—and saw Miss Carrie standing in the street. Wearing a yellow rain slicker, she looked distressed. Walter Lynx stood beside her, brandishing a baseball bat. Their attention was fixed on the gate across the street that led to the swimming pool, and they'd clearly been arguing. Walter had one foot poised to move when Miss Carrie saw the van and stopped him.

Griffin pulled up next to them. "What's going on?"

Walter's scowl deepened. "Just saw someone," he began.

"Dragging a girl, Griffin—she looked like Amanda," Miss Carrie said. She wrung her hands. "I'm sure it was her. They went toward the pool."

Griffin's heart almost stopped. Even at her age Miss Carrie had keen eyes.

He got out of the van, heart already pounding. How, in a few hours, had Amanda gotten involved with a guy who obviously wanted to hurt her?

Sunny was right behind him. "Stay here," he said, "all of you," then tossed her his cell phone. "Call 911."

"Griffin, wait. Let the police handle this—"

"They won't get here in time." Without a backward glance, he left Sunny in the middle of the street with Miss Carrie and Walter Lynx.

Sunny stood frozen, watching Griffin run across the street, then stop at the gate. He eased it open, moving slowly to avoid making a sound.

All at once Sunny was back in Judge Ramsay's courtroom, giving her so-called brilliant summation. She heard the jury's disappointing verdict. *Not guilty by reason of insanity.* Then the shouted threats as the prisoner was led away. *Keep looking over your shoulder, Donovan. One day I'll be there.*

She'd had the feeling of being followed, watched, all day. Even Amanda had noticed at the mall.

"Sunny." Miss Carrie took Griffin's cell phone from her. She punched in the emergency number, then spoke to someone. Still holding the cell, she said, "The dispatcher is sending help. I wasn't quite sure what to tell her about the 'nature of the emergency,'" she said, "but I'm to stay on the line."

"Thank you, Miss Carrie." And still, Sunny hadn't moved.

In the next instant she heard a high-pitched cry that chilled her blood. Amanda? Footsteps pounded around the darkened pool— toward the cabana.

Stupid, she thought, and willed herself to move. Wallace Day was in upper New York State. He couldn't be here now. He wouldn't think to harm Amanda. He didn't know her at all. But he hadn't known Ana Ramirez, either.

"He isn't here," she said aloud. Wallace Day wasn't here. Laura's father wasn't here, and he couldn't hurt her anymore. She whirled to face Walter Lynx. Sunny caught a glimpse of Miss Carrie's worried face, but once she moved—and blocked Wallace Day from her mind—she didn't think to stop.

Sunny grabbed the baseball bat from Walter's hand.

Then she was running across the street, through the gate, and toward the cabana.

CHAPTER NINETEEN

HEART RACING, CLUTCHING the baseball bat, Sunny stopped just outside the old cabana. What could she possibly do to help? For a too-long moment, she peered into the darkness, seeing Griffin's broad-shouldered form in front of her. His legs were planted wide in a fighting stance, and he appeared taller.

Sunny tried to look past him at the man who had Amanda in his grip, one arm around her neck. And her pulse sped even faster. *No, she told herself again, this isn't Wallace Day.* But in that moment Sunny was a girl once more, trapped in the dark.

She fought the urge to turn and run, as she'd run from Griffin. But that escape hadn't saved her from herself. Now it was time for Sunny to face the rest of her fears and save Amanda if she could.

Yet there was no way, even with the baseball bat, that she could overpower Amanda's captor. If she tried, even with Griffin's help, they might simply endanger Amanda.

She stiffened her spine. Edging closer to Griffin, she was finally able to see the guy—a boy, really—who held Amanda. It was Tommy. Sunny wasn't happy that her hunch had been proven right.

"Give up, Tommy," she said. "Law enforcement is already on the way."

He hauled Amanda even closer. There was nothing she could do.

What if Tommy panicked and, cornered, killed Amanda?

Sunny squared her shoulders. *No.* He would not. If there was one thing she believed in, it was the justice system. The law was her passion even if, in Wallace Day's case, justice hadn't been served.

If she didn't find a way to defeat Tommy and turn him over to the authorities, he would win. She wasn't about to let that happen. Not again. Not like Wallace Day. Not like Laura's father.

"LET HER GO." Griffin's voice was flat. He'd walked into a nightmare. And behind him, Sunny had stepped into the cabana.

"Or what?" The guy holding Amanda

didn't budge. He wore dark pants, a T-shirt of some indeterminate color and scuffed sneakers with the laces untied. Several days' growth of scruffy beard shadowed his jaw, but all Griffin could focus on were his eyes.

Sunny had been right. This was one of the two he'd caught playing Marco Polo with Amanda and Dixie. The older one. *Tommy-something*, Sunny had said, but he didn't need to know his full name now. Tommy had Griffin's daughter and wasn't letting go. Her blouse was torn, the first two buttons gone. Rage boiled up inside him. It didn't take any imagination to guess what had been about to happen here. If Miss Carrie and Walter Lynx hadn't seen them, if Griffin hadn't come back to the Palm Breeze Court…yet he didn't know what to do without jeopardizing Amanda.

Tommy was solidly built for his age. It wouldn't be easy to overpower him.

Sunny tried to reason with him, and Griffin could have groaned. Why endanger herself? In one hand she gripped a baseball bat, but her words were more of a weapon.

"If you don't let Amanda go, now," she said, "you'll be charged with kidnapping." With each word her voice gained strength.

She was in her element now, and if Griffin hadn't been so worried about Amanda, he might have cheered. This couldn't be easy for Sunny, either. "The FBI will be called in. You'll be facing a federal prosecutor then— life without parole."

Griffin knew that was more than Wallace Day had gotten, but he kept his expression neutral.

Tommy only seemed amused. "Wow. I like a good story."

Amanda wriggled in his grip, trying to get away, but he barely noticed.

"That is the story," Sunny said, taking a few steps until she stood beside Griffin. "What do you possibly have to gain by hurting this girl?"

Griffin knew right away that Sunny shouldn't have asked the question.

Tommy laughed, his hold on Amanda getting tighter. She managed a strangled cry.

Griffin tried to send her a message with his eyes. *Stay strong. We'll get you out of this.* But Tommy hadn't budged. Only his eyes shifted, looking wild and desperate.

His arm pressed harder on Amanda's windpipe. She couldn't even cry out now. "I could choke *her*—" he pushed Amanda forward, then jerked her back, his arm still at her throat "—right in front of you."

To her credit—Amanda was a gutsy kid— she tried to pull away, but he easily won their tug of war. His biceps bulged under the faded T-shirt, and the tendons stood out on his neck.

Griffin growled, low in his throat. Determined not to fail Amanda, he gritted his teeth. Rachel was gone. He would not lose his daughter, too.

Griffin's mind raced. If only those cop cars would come streaming in, lights strobing the sky and sirens blaring. By now the rain had begun to move on. The wind was dying down. Or was this the lull before the next part of the storm? Too bad he couldn't use its fury to overcome Amanda's abductor. And did the guy have a weapon? If only he had some distraction…

But the street outside remained silent.

"I don't see help on the way," Tommy said. "Do you?"

Amanda's eyes stayed on Griffin. Begging. It was up to him.

He tensed every muscle, but did he dare take the risk? It would take only a second for Tommy to pull out a gun, a knife—or snap

Amanda's neck. As if she knew he meant to lunge at Tommy, Sunny touched his shoulder. "Griffin, don't. He'll do it."

But while he had breath in his body, he would not fail his daughter. He loved her more than his own life. This would be his only chance.

Griffin launched himself at the guy. Obviously startled, Tommy let go of Amanda's throat. Just for a second. It had to be enough.

Griffin hit him like a battering ram, and they both crashed into the wall.

"Amanda, run!" he shouted.

But Tommy wasn't done yet. He shook his head to clear it, then lurched toward Griffin, slamming him in the stomach. If he took him down, it would be over.

Tommy hadn't counted on Sunny, though.

She pushed Amanda out of the way and brought the baseball bat down on his head. With a groan he crumpled to the floor.

Gasping for breath, Griffin tried to straighten. He'd had the wind knocked out of him, but that didn't matter. As he fought to drag in air, he and Sunny exchanged a quick look. And from outside, at last, he heard sirens.

Then Amanda ran into his arms, and Griffin clutched her to him. She couldn't speak, but her tears began to flow.

"It's all right," he said. And, even with Rachel still missing, it really was.

He looked down at Amanda, clinging to him. It was the best feeling ever.

Still breathing heavily, he smiled.

GRIFFIN CLOSED THE door to his room, then went across the hall. He had stalled long enough. For two years, in fact.

Tommy-something was now in police custody, and not for the first time. He had a rap sheet of similar incidents, including statutory rape.

Sunny was at her apartment, and Griffin had brought Josh home from the Cabots' house. He needed both his children with him tonight.

So why couldn't he stop shaking?

He knocked softly at Amanda's door, then went in. She was in her usual spot—thank goodness—on her bed with her arms wrapped around her legs, her chin resting on her bent knees. She looked just as she always did in blue-and-white pajama shorts and top.

Except for one thing.

She smiled, obviously happy to see him.

"You okay?" he asked.

She nodded at the mattress beneath her. "I can't sleep," she said.

"No wonder. Neither could I."

Griffin walked past her dresser and sat next to Amanda, taking care not to crowd her, not to expect too much. The danger was over, in part thanks to Sunny, but Amanda was still Amanda.

Still, it was past time for him to be honest. No more sugarcoating the truth or trying to hide it. As Sunny had said, he didn't share his feelings—and in not sharing them, he had almost lost his daughter.

He cleared his throat. "Today was something, huh?"

"I was so scared." She was still shaking. Amanda's hair trailed over her cheek. When he dared to smooth the strands from her face, his hand trembled.

"You were afraid, too," she said.

Time to man up. Or rather, to confess.

"I was terrified," he said. "Amanda, I haven't been quite straight with you. I want to be now. And I want to tell you why." He paused, looking for the right words to begin. "When I was only ten, my dad died, and I had to be an adult in some ways—before my time. I loved my mother, and I tried to help her, just as I thought my dad would have done. I cared for Uncle Theo—when he wasn't caring for me like a substitute father. When I actually grew up, I cared—so much—for your mother." He stroked Amanda's hair again, his throat tight. "And, please, believe me when I say I've always loved my kids."

But enough, he wondered? Or had he been holding back, had he pushed them away to keep that little boy inside him safe? To be a man who could withstand anything without relying on others? Like Sunny with her secret.

"Tonight, I was scared to death. I wasn't the grown-up. I was that ten-year-old kid who couldn't cope with what was happening."

"But you did. You and Sunny saved me." As if to comfort him, Amanda nestled closer. "You kept me from freaking out. Too much," she added with a half smile. "I kind of like it—in a weird way—that we were both afraid."

"Your old man's human after all?"

She nodded. "For now, at least."

Griffin laughed. "Take no prisoners. That your motto?"

Then he sobered. No more teasing to lighten what had happened. When he pulled Amanda even closer, she didn't resist. For the first time in a long time she cuddled against his shoulder. Her hair slid over his arm, and she rested her full weight on him. Trusting him.

He couldn't blow this as he'd blown it earlier with Sunny.

"Mandi, from now on I'm going to say what I feel. And first, I need to tell you about your mother."

Her head came up. "Did you find her? Is she coming home?"

The hope in her eyes nearly undid him. "No, I haven't found her. As far as I know— and I don't know much more than you do— she isn't coming back."

She let out a sob. "Are you sure? Maybe if you—"

"I won't stop looking for her. I promise you that."

"How do you know she won't? She might—"

"Anything's possible, Amanda, but don't spend the rest of your life watching the door. Waiting for the mail. Searching online yourself." He knew she did. Like any teenager, she had better computer skills than he did.

"You haven't found anything either, have you?"

"No."

"Then maybe what we need to do is... just go on. However we can. Be a family together, you and me and Josh." He wanted to add Sunny to that mix, but the memory of Amanda seeing them kiss might be too fresh. And he had things to say to Sunny later. Now was for Amanda. "You said I don't care for you. I want you to know how untrue that is. Because I do love you—with all my heart." He could barely get the words out. "I'll never forget how close I came to losing you tonight."

"You didn't, though."

Like Josh, she was being literal. "Thank God. And I'll never forget how grateful I am to Sunny for having that baseball bat. What you saw earlier, what is obviously a relationship between us—"

She rolled her eyes. "Duh. You think I couldn't see that?" she said, then paused. "She's not so bad, I guess."

He couldn't help but smile. "Don't be too generous with your praise."

"I like her. I wouldn't be a very good kid if I wasn't thankful that she helped you save me. And at the pool that day when I…well, she's okay."

Setting that aside for now, Griffin took a deep breath. It wasn't right for Amanda to keep hoping, when he knew Rachel wasn't coming back. Amanda was old enough to handle the truth.

He had to tell her about Rachel's note.

Amanda suddenly leaned past him to reach for the album she always kept on her nightstand, and the words he was groping for weren't said.

"You want to see our pictures with me?"

"Sure, baby." He blinked. "Sure I do."

The note, like Sunny, could wait a little longer. As the night sky turned from gray to pearly white and then a haze of pale blue, they hunched over the pages together.

There was Griffin with Rachel on their wedding day. And him holding Amanda in the hospital minutes after she was born. She couldn't fail to see the love, the wonder, in his eyes. He smiled at Josh, in similar photos with him, with Rachel. Their once-intact family in snapshot after snapshot. Camping in Pennsylvania. At the Philadelphia zoo, where Amanda at nine had proudly pushed Josh in his stroller. There were birthday cakes and Christmas trees and the houses where they had lived. Uncle Theo grinning on his porch. Waving goodbye the day they left for Boston. If you looked closely, you could see the sorrow in his eyes. Griffin wanted to do something about that, too. And there, the album ended.

Why hadn't he taken more pictures in the past two years?

It was as if his life, and the existence of their family, had stopped the day Rachel disappeared. The only photos now were the selfies Dixie and Amanda had taken on Amanda's cell phone.

He swallowed. Rachel wasn't the only one who'd left. In his heart, so had Griffin.

At the last page Amanda closed the album. Her hand lingered on the cover. "Sometimes, when I can't sleep, I look at this. I see Mom— and I remember just how she looked. How her voice sounded."

"How she laughed," Griffin murmured. "And that look she used to give me—remember?—before she laid into me about something."

Being late for dinner again. Forgetting to pick up the dry cleaning. Missing Amanda's parents' night at school because breaking news had kept him at work. Hearing Josh's first words.

"Or me." Amanda's soft smile died. "The last thing she said to me was 'pick up your room. Or else.'" She had almost whispered the words. "I've always thought that meant she was coming back."

Griffin flinched. He had meant to tell her—and later on Josh when he was old enough—about Rachel's note.

For another moment he thought he couldn't do it. Surely Amanda had a right to some illusions.

But, no, he knew in the next moment.

Hadn't he learned today that holding his emotions close, keeping secrets from his kids only hurt them more? Amanda, already on her way to becoming a woman, deserved to know that her mother had wanted to leave.

With a sigh Griffin went across the hall to his room. He came back with the note. He held her while she cried. And cried himself a little.

After a while, he kissed the top of her head and felt his heart ache.

Much later, after she'd quieted, he dried her tears. Then Griffin rose from the bed. For a long moment he looked down at Amanda and smiled at that spray of freckles across the bridge of her nose. "All right now, baby?"

"I'm not your baby," Amanda said but with a still-watery smile.

"You'll always be my baby," Griffin told her. And, as she picked up her stuffed giraffe, she didn't seem to mind.

CHAPTER TWENTY

THE NEXT DAY the Cabot/Donovan/Lattimer clan met again at the Seaside. With Tommy-something in custody, there had to be another celebration. Griffin was all for it.

Amanda was the heroine of the day. She sat beside Dixie, whose parents, across from Sunny's friend Laura and her family, had also been invited.

Sunny leaned in to Griffin. "Those girls can't stop giggling," she said.

"Apparently their quarrel has been resolved. As soon as the word on Tommy went out, Dixie arrived at our apartment. She and Amanda fell into each other's arms weeping with joy." Griffin had changed his view about their friendship. They weren't a bad pair after all, just typical teenage girls who had gone through a lot. "From now on, Dixie will be spending as much time at the Palm Breeze Court as Amanda will at Dixie's home. There'll be moody, sullen, difficult days ahead, but the parents are now on the case," he said. "Maybe, united, we even have a chance."

This being a celebration, a toast was needed. Griffin raised his glass. "To Amanda—and her best friend forever."

Bronwyn lifted her soda. Snuggled in Chris's arms, she looked smug every time their eyes met. Griffin's big-brother radar went on alert. What was going on there?

He wasn't the only one who wanted to know. "What are you two hiding?" Kate asked.

"Nothing," Bron said, batting her eyes.

"Something," Kate murmured. "When you're ready to tell us, I hope your news starts with the letter P." She beamed, the storm obviously far from her mind. That is, until Chris brought it up again.

"Good thing that rain moved out to sea. The hurricane behind it has weakened, but I don't envy the people in Bermuda. It's headed their way."

"Those few hours were more than enough for me," Griffin said.

"Par for the course," Jack agreed, "if you live in Florida." He glanced at Kate, who was twisting her napkin into a tight spiral. Griffin felt sure Jack was giving his wife a cue to speak her mind.

"I've gone through more than one hurricane in my lifetime," she said. "I guess I can make it through another if I have to. You were right," she told Jack. "It comes with the territory."

Sunny's face brightened. "You're not going to sell the house?"

"As you said, it's our family home." Kate smiled. "Your father and I talked things through, and I realized that I overreacted after this season's first, and last, I hope, hurricane. I felt so badly for our friends who lost their homes then—and about the damage to our house. I'm over that now. Everyone's fine." She patted Jack's arm. "Besides, we just got a new roof." She turned to Sunny. "And your father has promised I can buy a better sofa for his den."

Griffin smiled. He was glad Kate and Jack meant to stay here. Their presence might help his plan about Sunny, because he wasn't going anywhere, either.

"One good thing about yesterday's storm," he said. "After the police and everyone finally left, the last gusts of wind half tore down the old cabana. Now I can work on the new structure." He couldn't wait. "But first," he went on, "I have to make repairs on Miss Carrie's apartment and the others, including Mrs. Moriarty and the Grump." But Griffin was going to have to stop calling him that. "Would you believe? As soon as the rain and wind let up, Walter Lynx banged on my door offering to help."

"With luck, keeping busy will improve his mood," Sunny said.

"I think I'll have Lynx start at Miss Carrie's place. If anyone can crack him, she can." He felt a tug at his elbow. Josh stood there, holding his blue Stitch doll. "You need the bathroom?" Josh shook his head. "What, then?" he asked.

"Is it going to rain again?"

"Not for the rest of the week," Griffin said. "Sunshine every day." In fact, today was gorgeous, just like Sunny. "You worried, Josh?"

"A little."

Griffin noticed Sunny watching them. She sent him a faint smile. "You don't need to be afraid of the rain or wind…" he began.

"Is Mommy afraid?"

His heart sank. With that, the celebration seemed to fade into the shadows. Amanda was doing much better, but he hadn't talked to Josh.

"I hope not," Griffin said.

"But she doesn't have us."

"I know." He cradled his little boy and Stitch close, ran a hand over Josh's silky hair. "You'll always have her, though," he said around the lump in his throat. "She's right here, Josh." He touched his boy's heart. "She'll always be here."

I hope you're in her heart, too.

He would never understand Rachel's reasons for leaving them. Last night he and Amanda had shared their memories, but his children would never stop needing their mother.

Griffin didn't include himself.

He rose from his seat. He'd given Rachel enough time. He'd given everything he had to find her.

Now he couldn't wait any longer to settle things with Sunny.

SUNNY GLANCED ACROSS the room. All day, ever since last night in fact, she'd felt…out of sorts. What were Griffin and Chris talking about in the corner of the restaurant? Their conversation probably didn't involve her, but there appeared to be some negotiation going on. Sunny took another sip of her soda, then looked away.

Laura and her husband were helping their three kids into their sweaters, preparing to go home. But when Laura looked over and met her eyes, she said a word to her husband and walked toward Sunny.

Laura hugged her. "*Wow*, that was some experience yesterday." She paused. "Not the first bad one you've had with a…man like that."

Sunny's pulse jumped. "Laura." Today especially, she didn't want to revisit the past. *Is that why we lost touch?*

"No, please. I need to say this. I've been waiting for the opportunity. I told you when we first reconnected that my parents had divorced. I hinted later at why. Then yesterday I realized I didn't need to tell *you*." She held Sunny's gaze. "My own father hurt my best friend in the world—there were other girls, victims, as you could probably guess—and I despise him for that. I always will." She hesitated once more. "Our mothers were friends once, Sunny. How could they help it when you and I spent so many hours together? Then, when we weren't friends anymore, they drifted apart, too." Laura glanced at the table where Sunny's parents were chatting with Dixie's father and stepmom. "So I'm guessing you never heard what happened."

She couldn't ask. She didn't have to.

"Sunny, he's dead. He'll never hurt you again." Laura's words were so similar to Griffin's, and at last Sunny could believe them.

Dead. She wouldn't wish that on anyone, even him. But now, at long last, there would be no reason why she couldn't drive by that bus stop or visit Laura's mother or walk past the bathroom here without panic clawing at her.

"Thank you, Laura."

"No, I should have known." She blinked. "Best friends?"

"Yes," Sunny said, glancing toward Amanda and Dixie. "I love you, too."

After they hugged again, Laura said goodbye for now and rejoined her family. And Sunny saw her mother bearing down on her. Without a word she drew Sunny into her arms.

"I saw you with Laura. I'm so glad you've mended your fences. I hate it when my girl is hurting."

"I'm okay, Mom."

"No," she said. And for once she didn't try to make nice. "Not yet. But you will be."

She was about to say more when Griffin returned. "I'm stealing your daughter, Kate. Jack says you two will watch the kids. Thanks. This is too beautiful a day to not get out on the water and enjoy the sunset up close and personal." He emphasized the last word. "You okay with that?" he asked Sunny.

She didn't jump at the idea of a boat ride. The harsh words she and Griffin had exchanged were too much on her mind. Alone time with him now might not be the best choice.

And Sunny was still reeling from her talk with Laura.

He's dead.

She was truly free now. She should be thinking—once Wallace Day was no longer a threat—of going back to New York. Finding a new place to live. But she didn't just feel out of sorts today. She felt terrible, and Griffin was looking at her with an expression that said they really needed to talk. Did he intend to say a polite goodbye? If so, there was no avoiding it.

"Let's go," she said at last.

With a hand at her lower back—like that

night in her parents' garden—he guided her from the restaurant along the dock to her brother's newest boat.

"You take guys fishing on this?" she asked Chris as Griffin helped her climb aboard.

The sleek white boat had a living room—a saloon, Chris called it—a tidy kitchenette, and even a stateroom with an adjoining bath, or head, as he informed her.

He grinned with pride. "This is my sunset cruise/honeymoon getaway business. Not active yet, but Bron and I are working on a marketing campaign. Next season we hope to be booked every week."

Sunny hesitated. "This is the boat on which you and Josh got stranded at sea?"

"All fixed," he said.

Bron poked her head out of the stateroom. "My husband is a genius."

"Hey, I have a wife and future child to think about." Chris flushed.

"Did I hear right?" Sunny asked, remembering their sly looks before. "You two are pregnant?"

He grinned. So did Bron.

"I'm going to be an aunt," Sunny said. "That's great news!"

Griffin agreed. Then Chris sobered. "Sunny

Cabot's younger brother has finally grown up." He paused. "Maybe I didn't make superior grades like you, sis. I mean, every September I got another of your former teachers who praised you to the skies. But every year I made more friends," he said. "My popularity has paid off. Many of my clients are old classmates who are still friends. Like you and Laura."

The steady look he gave her made Sunny wonder. Had Chris, and even their mother, guessed her secret? If that was true, it seemed she had nothing left to hide. Her family loved her anyway.

"Griffin is my first customer for this type of cruise," Chris went on. "He asked Bron to come along, too."

"I thought Sunny would feel more comfortable as a foursome—your own suggestion more than once, Captain." Griffin touched her shoulder. "Let's go on deck while Chris gets us under way."

The fresh air, even tinged with marine fuel, smelled like heaven. Bron and Chris were keeping each other company on the bridge as she and Griffin, in companionable silence, watched the sky turn from blue to rose. Sunny let the warm sun soak into her bones. The breeze felt soft on her arms, her face, but she couldn't quite relax. Her family was one thing. Why had she told Griffin about Laura's father?

Finally, he said, "Ah, that Florida sunset."

Sunny wasn't going to ruin that. "All we need are some hibiscus blossoms."

Griffin shifted, looking as if he had something to say but didn't know how to begin. When he did, the words sounded rehearsed, which almost made her smile.

"Thanks for what you did yesterday. I bet Tommy's ears are still ringing."

She shrugged. "He'll survive."

Griffin's shoulder brushed hers. "I finally had that heart-to-heart with Amanda." He recapped their conversation. "I showed her Rachel's note, too. No more hiding the truth. I am learning," he said.

"I think you did the right thing," she said. "I'm glad you told her how much you love her." But for Sunny and Griffin, what else was there to say?

In the silence that followed he moved behind her to brace both arms on the rail, as if to shield Sunny, his chin resting against the top of her head. She didn't think to move away. This might well be the last time they were close like this. Even if she wanted things to work between them, probably they couldn't. Soon she'd be gone.

"You still mad because we argued?" he asked.

Suddenly she couldn't seem to breathe right. "It's not a matter of being 'mad.' It's a matter of not being able to take back what was said." He tensed behind her, and she held up a hand. "No, there's no need for you to rebut."

"Fancy word, Counselor. You may need that in court but not with me."

Sunny sighed. "Obviously, I do." She didn't want to rehash their quarrel. Griffin was still married. Sharing a few kisses—forbidden, really, on his part—didn't change that. Neither did wishing for a future with him. Especially after her bitter words. *I shouldn't have told you.*

"Look," he said, "I'm not good at this yet. But I said some lousy things yesterday and I'm sorry. So did you. And they were all true. For both of us. You're probably sorry, too."

"I am," she admitted. *In not sharing, you push your children away.* At least Griffin's relationship with Amanda would be better now.

"What am I missing, then?" he asked, but she had no answer.

"Okay, fine. Me first." Griffin turned her until her back was against the rail. "I've promised my kids I'll keep looking for Rachel, and I will." He held her gaze. "It's not because I hold out any hope that we could make it after all. Or because I still love Rachel—because I really don't." He waited for the words to sink in. "I want to find her for the kids, sure. Then, if they want her in their lives, they can have that. But for myself?" His tone thickened. "I want to ask her just one question—*why* did you hurt my kids?" His tone held no anger, only sadness. "Because, you know what, they aren't hers any longer. They're not ours." The last was whispered. "They're mine."

"Oh, Griffin." When he opened up, he really did.

"I don't know why I didn't tell you sooner. I should have—but maybe I wasn't ready until I finally talked with Amanda." Before Sunny could react, he framed her face in his hands. "Sunny, I need to tell you about what happened when I lost my dad. I loved my mother and she loved me, and I sure miss her—" he hesitated "—but, as I said before, she placed a burden on me that I wasn't prepared to shoulder at the age of ten."

"I'm sure she didn't mean to," Sunny murmured.

"No, but she always said 'make Daddy proud' when I think she really meant herself. I went into broadcast journalism in part to honor his memory, but my father would have been fine with anything I chose to do." He paused. "Turns out, my Uncle Theo was right. I'm happiest working with my hands."

"And now you can start the new cabana." Though she wouldn't be around to see it finished.

"I could use some help," he said. "One of these days I'm going to call Theo again. Maybe I'll even convince him to move south after all, start our own construction business." For a moment he watched her expression. "Now you," he said. "What's the rest of your story?"

Sunny couldn't look away. Griffin had finally faced his demons. He deserved to know the truth about her, too. Yesterday she had faced some of her fears—if not all of them. All right. She would tell him the rest and then…there'd be nothing left to tell.

Sunny swallowed. "Laura's father told me

it was our secret, and no one would believe me anyway. If my father knew, he always said, he would be angry."

"Sure he would." Griffin's voice was tight. "So would Chris. So am I."

Now that she'd begun, she had to keep going. He would know everything and then… "I told myself that nothing really happened," she murmured. "I wasn't hurt. There was no real harm done. If I didn't feel quite 'normal,' I was able to push that aside, bury it, make something of my life. To protect myself." She swallowed again. "But afterward I used to wash my hands until the skin was raw. I couldn't get clean." She hesitated. "I know. Classic victim stuff," she said, "using my strength against myself. Keeping *his* secret for him."

"It was *his* fault, Sunny—his alone." Griffin's tone held the anger she had rarely seen in him. "Just as Wallace Day's crimes were his and no one else's. Laura's father was an authority figure who was supposed to protect *you*. Instead, he violated your parents' trust—and yours. He used your friendship with Laura to gain access. He placed a burden on *you* that no little girl should have to bear."

"As an adult I know that's true. But there's always that girl inside me who thinks she's to blame. And the primal emotional response—something I can't control no matter how I try."

"Fight or flight response," he said, probably thinking of Sunny's panicked run from the cabana.

He drew her to him and simply held her. "I admire you," he said, "for trying to help girls like Amanda. I hope you continue to help them. But not because you feel ashamed or guilty, when you're not."

Sunny closed her eyes for a moment and took a deep breath. "I didn't have the power to stop him then," she said. "I do now, though."

"Yeah," he said. "You do."

The sun had slipped below the horizon, leaving behind a display of red and almost navy blue. Feeling chilled, Sunny relished his warmth as he swayed with her in time to the gently rolling motion of the boat.

"I do wish—no, I'd love the chance to prosecute Tommy, since I didn't get a conviction for Wallace Day. Wouldn't that be satisfying?" She paused. "But if only Ana Ramirez had gotten justice…"

He shook his head. "You can't win them

all, Sunny. I should know." He stayed silent for a long moment before he said, "So. We've talked about me, about you. What about us?"

She eased away. The question made her spirit sing—but only for a moment. She had never felt closer to anyone than she did to him, yet…

"Griffin, I have so much to do—not in New York but with myself. I've read a lot of self-help books, but I should probably see a counselor. And right now you need to be with your children." She paused. "Then there's Rachel—"

He ignored that. "I also need to spend more time with you. I was hoping you'd want to spend lots of time with me." Griffin squared his shoulders. "That's it in a nutshell," he said, "except for one thing." He paused before he went on, as if he were gathering his courage. "I need a good lawyer."

Her mouth dropped open. It was the last thing she'd expected to hear except for what he said next.

"Sunny, my marriage to Rachel is over. It has been for a while."

"I know we talked about that in theory. But it's not over, Griffin, until—"

"—you walk me through that legal process for divorce."

For a few seconds she didn't comprehend. Her head was spinning. Then her lawyer side kicked in. There was no better way to safeguard her heart.

"A divorce will take time," she said at last.

"I can be patient," he replied. "Just don't knock on my door someday to tell me you're breaking your lease…going back to New York. I don't think you'll find what you're looking for there."

Sunny's gaze shifted to the water as a gull swooped down to catch a fish. Was New York the right place for her now? Or was it possible—

No one was standing in her way. Except Sunny. If she went back, she would hurt his children, hurt Griffin, too. But most of all, she'd be hurting herself. Leaving would be too hard. She couldn't do it. She took a deep breath.

"Griffin, I moved to Manhattan in part so I would never have to see that man again. As Mom guessed more recently, I was running away." She watched the gull fly off with the fish. "And I've missed out on some things, but I've come to see what they are.

That's your fault, I think. You and Amanda and Josh." She smiled a little. "I did—I still do—have a passion for the law."

Griffin held her gaze until she continued.

"I love being home, too. I love the weather here, when it's not storming, and the people and the Palm Breeze complex…especially the apartment you painted for me. I want to set my own hours, take off early when I want to, and swim laps at the pool."

"You mean it? I can't see you sitting on your hands for long," he said.

Sunny raised an eyebrow. For the wrong reasons she and Griffin had once been driven by their careers. Now, other things seemed far more important.

"What if I opened a private practice right here? In family law," she said. She'd have time for a personal life, a relationship. With Griffin, and his children. "That way I can continue to help girls like Ana Ramirez. Before it's too late. As you once told me, that's helping, too—in a different way."

For Sunny, the past would always be with her, a part of the woman she had become— but it was time to let the worst memories go. She and Griffin knew each other's darkest secrets. She was no longer alone with hers. Neither was he.

"Of course I'd need to extend my lease," she said with a coy look.

He grinned. "I insist upon it."

And everything fell into place. Sunny held out a hand, feeling lighter than she had in years. Her beaded watch sparkled on her wrist. "Then we have a deal?"

Griffin didn't shake on it. "Not without the rest. You know this is a package deal," he said. "Me, Amanda, Josh..."

"Perfect," Sunny murmured.

"And we'll need to take things slow, but I more than care for you, Sunny," he said. Griffin wrapped his arms around her and looked into her eyes while she tried to take in what this meant. "I really should warn you, though."

"Full discovery?" She was smiling again, too.

"And in the interest of fairness." He nuzzled the side of her neck, then kissed the corner of her mouth. "Did I ever tell you? This place right here makes me crazy. I love you, Sunny. And one of these days—just so you know—I'm going to show up with a ring in my pocket. At least three carats."

"That's evidence of intent," she murmured.

"Always the lawyer," he said, shaking his head a little.

"Well. While we're being fair, I have another summation to make. Don't worry," she said, "it's short. And with this, I rest my case." Sunny looked deep into his eyes. "I love you, too, Griffin."

"Works for me," he murmured.

They kissed to seal the deal, and Sunny wound her arms around his neck. Her heart lightened again until she was soaring like that gull, flying free. Letting the bad memories go at long last. When Griffin angled his head and took the kiss deeper, her senses swam.

Sunny held him close. She knew he would spend the rest of his life letting her know exactly how he felt. But then, so would she.

Her future with Griffin and his children—their children—looked as bright as the sun.

* * * * *

LARGER-PRINT BOOKS!

GET 2 FREE LARGER-PRINT NOVELS PLUS 2 FREE MYSTERY GIFTS

Love Inspired®

Larger-print novels are now available...

LILP15

LARGER-PRINT BOOKS!

**GET 2 FREE
LARGER-PRINT NOVELS
PLUS 2 FREE
MYSTERY GIFTS**

Love Inspired®

SUSPENSE
RIVETING INSPIRATIONAL ROMANCE

Larger-print novels are now available...

LISLP15

YES! Please send me **The Montana Mavericks Collection** in Larger Print. This collection begins with 3 FREE books and 2 FREE gifts (gifts valued at approx. $20.00 retail) in the first shipment, along with the other first 4 books from the collection! If I do not cancel, I will receive 8 monthly shipments until I have the entire 51-book Montana Mavericks collection. I will receive 2 or 3 FREE books in each shipment and I will pay just $4.99 US/ $5.89 CDN for each of the other four books in each shipment, plus $2.99 for shipping and handling per shipment.*If I decide to keep the entire collection, I'll have paid for only 32 books, because 19 books are FREE! I understand that accepting the 3 free books and gifts places me under no obligation to buy anything. I can always return a shipment and cancel at any time. My free books and gifts are mine to keep no matter what I decide.

263 HCN 2404   463 HCN 2404

Name	(PLEASE PRINT)	
Address		Apt. #
City	State/Prov.	Zip/Postal Code

Signature (if under 18, a parent or guardian must sign)

Mail to the **Reader Service:**

IN U.S.A.: P.O. Box 1867, Buffalo, NY 14240-1867
IN CANADA: P.O. Box 609, Fort Erie, Ontario L2A 5X3

* Terms and prices subject to change without notice. Prices do not include applicable taxes. Sales tax applicable in N.Y. Canadian residents will be charged applicable taxes. This offer is limited to one order per household. All orders subject to approval. Credit or debit balances in a customer's account(s) may be offset by any other outstanding balance owed by or to the customer. Please allow 4 to 6 weeks for delivery. Offer available while quantities last. Offer not available to Quebec residents.

MMLPBPA15